Gerber nodded. "Let's check it out."

They spread out so that there were about three yards between each of them, then the four men walked into the village, weapons ready, but held in a nonthreatening posture. Updike and the others covered them from the tree line.

Everywhere it was the same. The walls of the houses had either been blown out, probably by some kind of satchel charge, or burned, leaving only blackened ash grown over with weeds. There were no animals in evidence.

In the center of the main street was the skeleton of a dog. Like the skulls that had lined the trail into the village, it was bleached white by the sun, indicating that it had been there for some time. At the center they found the village well. It, too, had been blasted with explosives and was filled in with dirt.

As they stood there surveying the destruction, Fetterman spoke softly. "Captain, I don't think we're alone."

VIETNAM: GROUND ZERO.

WARLORD

ERIC HELM

A GOLD EAGLE BOOK FROM
WORLDWIDE.

TORONTO · NEW YORK · LONDON · PARIS
AMSTERDAM · STOCKHOLM · HAMBURG
ATHENS · MILAN · TOKYO · SYDNEY

First edition December 1990

ISBN 0-373-62725-4

VIETNAM: GROUND ZERO®

WARLORD

This book owes much to a great many people and is, therefore, dedicated to all of them:

The staff of Midwest Ambulance, Grinnell, Iowa Division, who endured my moods the many weeks I labored to finish the book, particularly Bob Paulson, the director, who kindly loaned me a corner of a very drafty garage where I could work during my on-call hours, and later gave up his apartment for the cause, a much better writing environment, even if it wasn't furnished; Judy Belz, who helped type the glossary while I was out cheating death, driving fast and pushing drugs; Yody Neely, who covered my shifts when I needed time to research or compose my thoughts; and that special paramedic who promised to kill me if I put her name in a book, but convinced me the story needed telling and that I had it in me to do so. All in all, they are some of the finest, most caring people I've ever known.

Mr. Doug Tracy, my good friend and a true computer genius, who solved all the problems created by the staff of a computer store in Iowa City that sold me a laptop they couldn't get to talk to my PC and printer, and a word processor I didn't need, ensuring the book would be late. Thanks, Doug, I owe you a big one.

Finally, and most of all, the 300,000 Hmong soldiers who fought for America in the Secret War in Laos and the nearly 30,000 of them who died there.

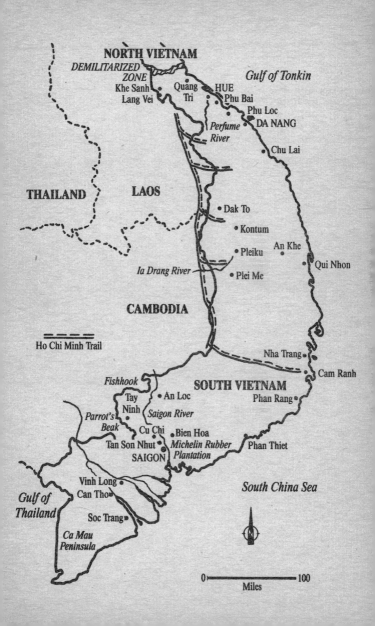

1

**SKUNK RIVER LODGE
SAIGON, REPUBLIC OF
VIETNAM**

Special Forces Captain MacKenzie K. Gerber stood just inside the doorway of the smoke-filled bar a block off Tu Do Street and peered through the heavy veil of acrid smoke while trying to tune out the blaring country-rock music assaulting his eardrums. It was almost as noisy inside the bar as any two firefights he'd been in recently.

The swirling blue-white atmosphere pulsated with red and green neon from the bar signs, and Gerber was dimly aware of a deeper blue pool of light intermittently broken by the brilliant white flashes of a strobe centered over the stage. Here, a dancer wearing a white cowboy hat, white boots and little else gyrated more or less in time with the music. A two-holstered belt of cheap white leather set with rhinestone, a pair of white gauntlets and a white neckerchief completed her costume. She had a large chrome cap pistol in each hand and occasionally fired at the club's patrons when she wasn't busy holstering one of the pistols in the fuzzy black triangle between her thighs. The reports of the caps were completely lost in the sound blaring out of the overpowering, six-foot-high speakers on either side of the stage.

Under other circumstances Gerber might have taken a few minutes to watch the act, despite the fact that the dancer's Oriental features clashed with her costume. The young lady did a mean six-gun belly dance. But Gerber hadn't come here to be entertained. He was here on business.

Gerber had just passed his thirtieth birthday, stood six feet tall and was deeply tanned. His brown hair had become a shade lighter under the tropical sun. He had fond memories of the bar's namesake, a quiet little place built on pilings on the bank of the Skunk River near Brighton, Iowa. He had often stopped there during his college days in Iowa City when he would take a weekend off from his GI Bill-financed studies at the University of Iowa and drive down to Lake Darling just west of the town. He used to make the trip twice a month, winter or summer, in the battered old Sunbeam Alpine he had purchased third-hand from a political science graduate student in need of rent and marijuana money. It was a nice little lake, without the crowds of college students that infested Lake McBride, the principal warm-weather hangout for the university crowd.

But the place he was in now retained little of the charm of the old Skunk River Lodge except for the name and the weathered barn-board siding on the walls. Gerber had found the bar by accident one night while cruising the watering holes of the Paris of the East with his team sergeant, Master Sergeant Anthony B. Fetterman. Now he scanned the crowded room carefully, looking for Fetterman, but it was impossible to see more than a few yards through the crowd, and the master sergeant, with his short, wiry build, black, receding hair and unassuming appearance, was easy to overlook in a packed room. Looks were deceiving, though. Fetterman was one of the most dangerous men Gerber had ever encountered; after all, the man had served in three wars.

Reluctantly Gerber gave up his position near the exit and shouldered his way through the press of people, checking for Fetterman on either side. Slowly he worked his way through the crowd, covering about half the room and ending up at the bar. He wedged himself into the throng in front of the counter and waited for an opportunity to signal one of the bartenders.

Behind the bar was a broad shelf with the standard assortment of glasses, mugs and bottles of imported hard liquor, as well as the tape deck and control panel for the massive stereo system that made conversation all but impossible. Two fairly attractive young Vietnamese girls, dressed in short skirts and sandals, served as topless bartenders, and Gerber watched with appreciation as they poured drinks, drew beers or opened bottles, all the while shifting glasses and mugs about and collecting piasters, MPC and American greenbacks from customers. A third girl was kept busy just rinsing the bar glasses in a big metal sink.

Hollering for a bartender would have been useless with all the noise blaring out of the sound system. Gerber simply waited until one of the bar girls looked in his direction, then waved some money at her. Eventually it worked and he got his bottle of beer.

Bottle in hand, he made a slow circuit through the half of the room he hadn't covered yet, still looking for a familiar face in the crowd, but found none. He had known the bar was a long shot, but he had already checked out all the other bars and restaurants where Fetterman was likely to be, as well as leaving messages for the master sergeant at their hotel and the MACV/SOG in-transit safehouse where Fetterman sometimes went to drink beer and swap war stories with other SOG Green Berets. By the time Gerber worked his way back to the door, he was fairly certain Fetterman wasn't in the bar.

Finally giving up, he drained his beer, put the bottle on an already crowded table and headed out the door. As he was leaving, he glanced back just in time to see the dancing cowgirl dazzle the raucous crowd with a few bizarre rope tricks.

Forcing his way through the crush of people, Gerber finally made it outside.

After the smoke-filled environment of the bar, his eyes smarted, and the sudden decrease in population density and air pollution was almost too much for him to handle. He walked to the curb and stood there for several minutes, gulping in lungfuls of relatively cleaner air while he watched the late-evening traffic whiz by. Then, checking his watch, he saw that it was nearly 2200 and decided to go back to the hotel for some sleep. There was nothing else to do; he had looked for Fetterman everywhere. The man had simply vanished.

After trying to hail a cab unsuccessfully for several minutes, he gave up and decided to walk back to the hotel. He'd gone only half a block when he nearly bumped into Fetterman coming in the opposite direction down the crowded street.

"Captain Gerber," Fetterman greeted him. "Didn't expect to run into you down here tonight, sir. Are you slumming, or did you lose your lady friend?"

"Robin left Saigon this afternoon on a photo assignment up north," answered Gerber. "I came down here looking for you."

"Ah," said Fetterman. "You *are* slumming, then. I hope you and Robin had the opportunity to spend some time together before she had to leave. I'm sorry to have missed her."

"I've spent most of the afternoon and evening looking for you, Tony. Where've you been hiding yourself."

"Haven't been hiding at all, Captain," Fetterman assured him. "Did you think of trying Madame Vu's?"

"I admit I didn't think of that," said Gerber, "although I should have, I suppose. I take it the poker game you were preparing to get involved in when I saw you last night went well?"

"I've had better, but I think you'd have to say that it went fairly well for me. Not so well for the other players. It's kind of funny you know. You'd think those Air Force flyboys would have a better grasp of the fundamental principles of Five Card Draw. After all, it was their idea to play it. I was quite happy with Seven Card Stud.

"How much did you fleece them for?"

"The flock was shorn for just over sixteen hundred," Fetterman said, grinning.

"You won sixteen hundred dollars playing poker last night?" asked Gerber. "I'm sorry I missed the show. I bet those men will remember you for a long time. Tell me, Tony, just how does Madame Vu feel about your bankrolling her orphanage on the ill-gotten gains of poker?"

"Madame Vu's a very pragmatic woman, Captain. She couldn't have brought five hundred orphans down from North Vietnam back in the fifties and founded a new home for them here in Saigon without being pragmatic. She's clever enough to know that the Good Lord works in mysterious ways, and that sometimes it's better not to be too curious about exactly what those ways are."

"Yeah," said Gerber. "I suppose every little miracle helps."

"Exactly," said Fetterman. "You said you'd been looking for me. Was it anything important, or were you just hunting for a drinking buddy after Robin had to leave? If so, you're headed in the wrong direction. The bar's back that way. I understand from a usually reliable source that they've got a new dancer who does an amazing routine with a cowboy hat and a couple of six-shooters."

"I think you could call it amazing, all right. I caught her act and it's all of that. You'd be surprised how handy she is with a rope, let alone the six-guns."

"I can harldy wait."

"Anyway, according to Sergeant Major Taylor, Colonel Bates is looking for us. It seems we have work to do. We're manifested on a flight out of Tan Son Nhut at 1300 hours tomorrow."

Fetterman's interest suddenly perked up. "Where to?"

"Nha Trang."

"That doesn't tell us anything. Any idea what it's all about?"

"Not a clue. All I know is that the colonel expects to see us in Nha Trang tomorrow afternoon, and I think it's safe to assume he isn't summoning us all the way to Nha Trang just for a social chat."

"Well, then, in that case I suppose we'd better go see what he wants."

Fetterman consulted his watch. "The flight is at 1300 hours you say? Well, then, it seems to me that we still have plenty of time to catch the late show. Maybe even a couple of performances. Care to join me in a drink, sir?"

Gerber considered for a moment. He had no desire to go back into the smoke-filled bar and fight his way through the mass of people to drink an overpriced beer while slowly choking to death on the fumes of other people's cigarettes. He ought to go back to the hotel, pack a bag for tomorrow's flight and get some sleep. Then again maybe he should take the opportunity to have a good time. Colonel Bates certainly wouldn't be sending him on a picnic. The next while could be pretty grim. "What the hell. I suppose a captain ought to look after his team sergeant. There's no telling what kind of trouble you might get into without someone along to chaperon."

"In that case, sir, the first round's on me. Let's go see if we can't fight our way up to the bar. Shall I take point?"

"I'll take the point," said Gerber. "You might get distracted by the dancer and forget the purpose of the mission. I've already had a peek, so I'm immunized."

"I'd never do that, sir. Forget the purpose of the mission, I mean." He really sounded offended.

"I know that, Tony," said Gerber. "Just wanted to make sure nothing interfered with your initial reconnaissance of the young lady. And, Tony, you could call me Mack when it's just the two of us around?"

"Yes, sir," said Fetterman with a smile. "I could do that, sir."

Gerber clapped the shorter man on the shoulder. "All right, Master Sergeant. Eyes open and alert. Forward, march."

2

FIFTH SPECIAL FORCES GROUP, SFOB NHA TRANG, RVN

Gerber should have gone back to the hotel and caught some sleep. The previous night was only a blur. With a hangover big enough to build a shopping center on, Gerber staggered into the bathroom. He turned on the shower and let the cool water beat him in the face for ten minutes before he woke up enough to realize he was still wearing his uniform. Stripping off his clothes, he left them in a sodden mass on the floor of the shower, turned on the hot water and finished showering. By the time he stepped out, he was awake, but dozens of miniature VC were fighting an artillery duel inside his head. He stumbled over to his shaving kit on the sink, dug inside it for the aspirin bottle and swallowed four tablets, washing them down with water he held cupped in his hands from the sink. Then he went back into the bedroom, where he was blinded by sunlight.

Closing one eye against the inhuman glare, he bravely approached the window long enough to close the blinds. Then he checked his watch. It was only a little after 0800. He called the desk and told them to ring him at eleven, then went back to bed and prayed the aspirin would work. It didn't, and when the ringing of the telephone awakened him, he felt even worse. He snarled a thank-you into the mouthpiece, took another shower and wolfed down four more aspirin. Then he gathered up his nonessential gear, including the wet uniform, and stuffed it all into his stay-behind bag. Having cleaned out his room, he went out to find Fetterman.

The master sergeant had already checked out. Gerber found him in the restaurant, eating an obscenely huge breakfast, the mere thought of which nauseated the captain. To Gerber's considerable disgust, Fetterman appeared positively chipper. If he hadn't been such a good friend, Gerber would have seriously considered strangling the man.

At Tan Son Nhut their flight was delayed, naturally, and they had to spend more than two hours in the noisy, crowded air terminal, which did nothing to improve Gerber's outlook on the past evening's activities, his opinion of airports and air travel or his attitude toward life in general. While they waited he went to the men's room and took some more aspirin, but cut it down to two tablets this time, since he wasn't sure how many it would take to make him really sick.

Finally their flight was called and they collected their gear and marched onto the sweltering tarmac to the plane. The aircraft turned out to be an aging Fairchild C-119 Flying Boxcar, a Korean War-vintage twin-engined transport. It had been used for paradropping supplies to remote Special Forces camps, which meant it had no rear doors. Nor were there any troop seats. The two men, the only passengers, sat directly on the metal floor, and the cargo master pulled a three-inch-wide nylon strap across their legs to keep them from sliding around during takeoff and landing.

Gerber did his best to sleep during the flight but had no luck. The wind rushed through the cargo compartment of the aircraft with a roar only slightly less than that of the big R-4360 radial engines, and when he tried to lie down, the metal deck transmitted every rattle and creak of the aircraft directly to the bones in his skull until he was sure the plane would fall out of the sky at any minute. It was with a feeling of intense relief that he finally stepped out of the aircraft in Nha Trang.

With Sergeant Major Taylor, Bates's administrative aide, still holding down the colonel's other office in Saigon, there was no one to greet them at the airstrip, and they had to make their own way over to Bates's office at the FOB. By the time they did so, both men were soaked with sweat as if they had just come in from a rainstorm. The only good thing Gerber could say for the walk was that at least it sweated some of the alcohol out of his blood. But the miniature VC still waged war in his head.

The colonel had moved his office since their last visit, or what was more likely, some general had moved him.

Gerber and Fetterman signed in and walked along the corridor until they found Bates's former office, noted the freshly painted logo on the door proclaiming Deputy Director of Operations, Second Field Force, and prudently didn't enter. They continued down the corridor until they spotted a door marked Special Operations Chief, knocked, got no answer and tried the knob. The door was unlocked, so Gerber opened it and they went inside.

It was a small, dark office crowded with beat-up olive drab filing cabinets, several of which featured formidable hasps and padlocks or large combination dials. There was a battered battleship-gray desk with a telephone and an intercom on it, along with a couple of mail trays, while a splintered secretary's chair squatted behind the desk. The concrete floor was painted a shade of gray and the walls were a sickly yellow mixed with green that reminded Fetterman of something he had seen in a toilet bowl once. A couple of dark green folding metal chairs placed along two walls completed the decor, if you could call it that.

The whole place was, however, as neat and well organized as any office Gerber or Fetterman had ever been in on an Army post. The only decorations were a framed picture of the late President John F. Kennedy greeting General Yarborough at

Smoke Bomb Hill, Fort Bragg, North Carolina, autographed by both men, and a portrait of Colonel Aaron Bank, first commander of the Tenth Special Forces Group (Airborne), also autographed. The one nonmilitary item in the room was a small gold-framed blowup of a snapshot showing Sergeant Major Taylor's wife and children. It occupied a prominent location on the desk.

Reasoning that Bates wouldn't have left the office unlocked if he had gone out, Gerber and Fetterman crossed to the inner door that bore Bates's name neatly hand-stenciled in black paint on a small piece of light green wood. Fetterman knocked and stood aside for Gerber to enter first.

There was a muffled but resonant "Come in" from the other side, and Gerber turned the knob and pushed the door open. The inner office was almost but not quite a carbon copy of the outer one. The walls here had been completely overpainted in dark green and the chairs were wooden with padded seat cushions. A ceiling fan that looked as though it might have come over on the ark with Noah turned slowly overhead, creaking noisily as it struggled valiantly to stir the sultry air seeping through an open window.

Colonel Alan Bates, Director of Special Operations for MACV/SOG, sat behind his desk dressed in rumpled jungle fatigues and looking, as usual, as though he hadn't slept for a couple of nights, which was probably the case. Unlike most of his ticket-punching brethren in the U.S. Army's officer corps who changed into freshly pressed khakis several times a day in order to look sharp for visiting dignitaries and be able to display their fruit salad campaign ribbons, Bates was content to wear the working man's kit of the grunt. His fatigues bore only his jump wings and the combat infantryman's badge with two stars, both of which meant more to him than the fairly impressive boxful of medals he had been awarded in three wars.

A man in his mid-forties, Bates had close-cropped graying blond hair and startling blue eyes. He had the blocky build of someone who had played college football, as indeed he had, and his love of Special Forces, like Gerber's, had slowed his career in the regular Army, despite an outstanding record.

Bates's desk was littered with papers, maps and personnel files that barely left room for his favorite ashtray made from a 75 mm shell casing. He was chewing on the butt of an unlighted cigar, a sign that he had been contemplating something important when Gerber and Fetterman entered.

The Special Forces captain and master sergeant both stopped in front of the desk, came to a position of attention and saluted as Gerber said, "Captain Gerber and Master Sergeant Fetterman reporting as ordered, sir."

Bates returned the salute. "Now that the crap's taken care of, come on in, shut the door and pull up a chair. Master Sergeant, close that window for a minute, will you? There's no point in making things easy for Charlie."

Both Gerber and Fetterman did as they were told, then sat down.

"Good to see the two of you again," began Bates. "Hope your in-country R and R was a good one and that you're feeling rested up. I've got a little job for the two of you, if you're interested. Something you might want to finish out your tours with."

Fetterman arched an eyebrow but said nothing.

"Colonel, Master Sergeant Fetterman and I each have over six months time remaining on our tours of duty," Gerber reminded Bates.

"I'm well aware of that, Mack," replied the colonel.

"I take it then we aren't talking about another short-term recon, prisoner snatch or assassination," said Gerber.

Bates smiled. "I'm taking the two of you off the real cloak-and-dagger spook stuff for a while. How would you like to get back to running an A-Detachment?"

Gerber and Fetterman looked at each other and quickly offered the opinion that they would, in fact, be very interested.

Working with an A-team advising indigenous troops was what they did best. It was what Special Forces was all about.

"Good," said Bates. "I was hoping you'd feel that way. I've been given a set of requirements calling for the activation of a number of special A-Detachments, working outside of normal U.S. Army channels. For a number of reasons I feel you two would be uniquely qualified to head up one of those teams."

"Does 'outside normal channels' mean we're going to be loaned to the CIA again, sir?" asked Gerber. "If it does, the master sergeant and I might want to reconsider our enthusiasm for the assignment."

Bates smiled again. "What's the matter, Mack? Don't you like working for Jerry Maxwell and his Langley East cronies? We're all on the same team, you know."

"Sometimes I wonder if the Agency knows that, sir," answered Gerber. "It isn't that we're unwilling to help them out. It's just that lately every time we wind up working with Maxwell, my team winds up getting the shit shot out of it. It's getting so it's kind of hard to find volunteers. Sort of makes a fellow cautious, if you know what I mean, sir."

Bates chuckled. "I can well imagine that it might. Just to put your mind at ease, I suppose I can tell you that it's a MACV/SOG show. The Agency first proposed the idea, I'll admit, and it'll be involved to a limited extent in the support role, but this is a straightforward GW mission we're talking about. No oddball spooks tagging along. No triple-cross sacrifices or straw men. This time it's just going to be doing what you were trained for—going into an area and recruiting and training the locals to find, fix and finish off the enemy."

"In that case, sir, I'm just a little bit puzzled," said Gerber. "Why come to SOG for the personnel? Why not just use regular Army SF units?"

"For various political considerations the mission is of a covert nature. Since SOG has considerable experience with that sort of op, and since the target area is one in which we also have considerable experience, the big boys upstairs at the Puzzle Palace have decided to turn things over to the experts. That's about all I can tell you at this point. You'll get your mission particulars and area studies information once you enter isolation," Bates told them. "It's not an assignment. I'm looking for volunteers. The job is yours if you want it."

Gerber looked at Fetterman, who shrugged. "Nothing like buying a pig in a poke. We might as well have a go at it."

"The master sergeant likes the idea, so we accept," said Gerber. "Count us in, sir. Do I get to pick my own team?"

"Afraid not. You'll have to make do with what I give you. However, you'll be relieved to know that they're all experienced men. No first-timers. Each of them has at least one tour under his belt. You'll meet the rest of your team in Kontum. I've had the two of you manifested on a flight for there tomorrow afternoon."

"You seem to have been awfully sure we'd say yes, Colonel," remarked Gerber.

"I was sure you'd find the idea intriguing, that's all," said Bates. "Besides, as I said, your records lead me to believe you and Master Sergeant Fetterman are uniquely qualified for the job. I wanted my best men for it. I was hoping you'd take it. If you'd said no, I'd have had to find another team leader and team sergeant. The time frame I've been given to put this thing into operation is rather brief, so I went ahead and planned for that. Now why don't you two mavericks get out of here and let me get some work done. Go to the beach and bag some rays. Go into town if you like. Whatever. I'll meet you later at the PCOD Lounge and buy you guys a drink, say around 1900. Then we can go get a bite to eat and you can get some rest. Tomorrow it's back to the salt mines."

Gerber and Fetterman stood, saluted and left, reopening the window as they went out.

"Well, Tony, what do you think?" asked Gerber when they were in the outer office and had closed Bates's door behind them.

Fetterman shrugged. "If we're staging out of Kontum, it stands to reason we're talking an exterior operation, Captain. It could be either Laos or Cambodia. Maybe we're finally going to get a chance to make some of those untouchable sanctuary areas a little less safe for Charlie."

"It would be nice to finally take the war into the enemy's own backyard for a change," agreed Gerber. "The question is, which backyard? I guess we'll see soon enough."

"Yes, sir," said Fetterman. "We'll see."

The two Special Forces soldiers signed out of the headquarters building and made their way to the transient personnel barracks, a white clapboard structure that might have been any barracks on any military base anywhere in the world. As an officer, Gerber could have opted to stay in the VOQ, which offered fairly comfortable private rooms, but he preferred the company of his friend and comrade. Special Forces wasn't an organization that was long on formality, especially not the regular Army policy of nonfraternization between officers and enlisted personnel, and most especially not between men who had served on an A-team together. In the SF the officers and men lived together, fought together and got drunk and partied together. It was a camaraderie quite different from anything found in the regular Army and promoted a spirit of teamwork unique in modern warfare.

Gerber and Fetterman signed the registry that the duty NCO passed across the counter to them, then went along the corridor past the rec room and latrine and into the big, open platoon bay of the barracks. They found a couple of unoccupied double bunks and threw their gear onto the top beds to give themselves a little added protection from shrapnel in case Charlie decided to mortar the camp, as he sometimes did. Next, by mutual agreement, they stretched out on the lower bunks to catch up on a little sleep, something they had sacrificed the night before in the name of artistic dance and liquid refreshment.

A couple of hours later, when it got too warm to sleep comfortably, they donned their swimming trunks, promoted an ice chest and some beer with the assistance of the duty sergeant at the desk, pulled on their leather-and-canvas jungle boots, topped off their beach costumes with floppy boonie hats and olive drab Army towels, and clomped off to the beach. They found a spot far enough away from the watchtowers and concertina wire so that they could forget the war for a while, erected a poncho on a couple of bamboo poles stuck into the sand and settled down to the two things the American soldier does best besides fighting: drink beer and watch girls.

There were only a few females on the beach, off-duty nurses from the military hospital, but the sight of several pale-skinned, round-eyed beauties with blond or red hair was a welcome change from the dusky, dark-eyed young Vietnamese opportunists of Tu Do Street. Their brightly colored bathing suits and bikinis made it almost possible to leave the war behind for a while.

Fetterman was even successful in getting a couple of the women to join them for a few hours by the simple expedient of refusing to give back their volleyball until they had agreed to have a beer with Gerber and him. The two girls, both in their early twenties, one a tall redhead covered with freckles and the owner of a substantial chest, and the other a compact dark-haired woman slightly less endowed, took their ball and the offered beers and stayed to talk.

The redhead, Cindy, was the older of the two. She was an operating-room nurse on her second tour in Vietnam. Though friendly enough, she was a bit cool, as if she'd rather be someplace else or had other things on her mind, or perhaps had simply seen too much of man's inhumanity toward his fellow man in two tours.

There was nothing at all reserved about the speed with which she guzzled Gerber and Fetterman's beer supply, however. Fetterman had known a number of top sergeants with impressive abilities for dissipation, yet he doubted seriously that any of them could have matched the lady on a beer-for-beer facedown. She drank the stuff as if it were water and she had just come in from six days in the desert and had two hollow legs. Fetterman decided that it would be interesting to spend an evening with her, cruising the night spots off Tu Do Street. It would probably cost him a month's pay to keep her in beer, but he figured he could more than double his expenses by placing a few side bets on her capacity for consumption.

The other nurse was named Patty. She had heart-melting cocker spaniel eyes, sipped her beer and chain-smoked Marlboros. She'd gone to college on the Army nursing program, had been out of school for a little more than a year and had volunteered for Vietnam because she had a brother serving there.

There was something about her general build and the shape of her nose that reminded Gerber vaguely of a younger version of Karen Morrow, a nurse he had once been in love with, and the sister of his current girlfriend. The memory Patty's appearance triggered old feelings he had thought were buried, and he found himself wishing she would just go away, despite the fact that he had nothing personal against her. The situation wasn't helped any by the fact that she seemed attracted to him.

Eventually the ladies made their exits accompanied by the excuse that Patty had to work the night shift and needed to get some sleep, and that Cindy had "some things she needed to do." There had been no talk of getting together later or of seeing each other again sometime. It had simply been two men and two women spending a pleasant afternoon at the beach in the shadow of M-60 machine-gun towers. Gerber and Fetterman went for a short swim and then went back to the transient barracks to dress for their cocktail date with Colonel Bates.

THE PERSONNEL COMING OFF DUTY LOUNGE, as it was officially known, was, like the transient personnel barracks, a peculiarity of the Special Forces. The regular Army might have its officer and NCO clubs, but the men who wore the green beret had no time for such artificial social situations. Behind the white rabbit-head logo painted on the black door of the Playboy Club, as the lounge was unofficially known, the officers and NCOs drank whiskey and beer together and sat down to an occasional friendly little game of poker, ignoring bars, oak leaves and stripes.

When Bates arrived, a little late, he found Gerber and Fetterman indulging in Toronto Boilermakers, a shot of Canadian rye chased by a short draw of beer. "Christ! I don't know how you guys can stand to drink that stuff," said Bates. "Let me order you something decent. Bartender, we'll have three Beam's Choice. Make 'em doubles."

Bates pulled a fresh cigar out of the inner pocket he'd had custom-tailored into his jungle fatigues, stripped off the wrapper, then seemed surprised to find that he still had the stub of a cigar in his mouth, apparently the same one he had been chewing on when Gerber and Fetterman had come to his office. The colonel examined the stub for a moment, decided it wasn't worth lighting or saving and crushed it into the ashtray on the bar counter. The mysterious cigar quickly forgotten, he twisted the fresh one in to the side of his mouth, but didn't light it.

"Did you boys just get here, or have I got a lot of catching up to do?" asked Bates.

"Yes and yes," said Gerber.

"Meaning?"

"Yes, we just got here, but you have a lot of catching up to do. Tony and I started several hours ago with a cooler full of beer at the beach."

"Actually, Colonel, a couple of nurses drank most of our beer. That is, at least one of them did. Which accounts for the fact that we're still sober, despite our best efforts to the contrary.''

''Hmm,'' said Bates. ''Well, damn it, we'll have to remedy that.'' He downed his bourbon in one giant gulp and called out, ''Bartender, bring us another round of the same.''

Bates turned back to Gerber and Fetterman. ''Before we get too drunk, though, I think we'd better do something about getting something to eat. Club Nautique okay with you guys? My Jeep's outside.''

Gerber and Fetterman nodded, and after polishing off their drinks, they went out to Bates's Jeep and drove the short distance south along the coastal road to the Club Nautique.

Founded by a French restaurateur, the Club Nautique was one of the finest restaurants in all of South Vietnam. Seafood was, of course, the primary component of the menu, the specialty being freshly steamed or boiled lobster, but it was also possible to get a decent steak from a real steer, and there was a good selection of French vintages on the wine list. If you were a purest, you could even order your steak without all the usual fancy sauces the French love to disguise their food with, and the chef would grill it to your specifications; but if you ordered it plain and well-done, you would get an argument before he finally threw up his hands and said, ''*D'accord*. I will not be responsible for its edibility.'' The steak would, of course, be wonderfully edible, although it would have probably broken his heart if anyone said so.

Knowing that it might be some time before either of them enjoyed such a feast again, both Gerber and Fetterman ordered the surf and turf while Bates settled for just lobster. By mutual agreement they washed everything down with a bottle of Pouilly-Fuissé 1963 and topped off their meal with cherry cheesecake.

During dinner the three men swapped war stories of a nonclassified nature, mostly incidents where something funny had happened, although it might not have seemed particularly funny at the time, and they caught up on what had happened

to various other Special Forces personnel of common ac-
quaintance. They carefully avoided any mention of the new
mission, or any of the still-secret aspects of previous ones.
Gerber thought that Fetterman seemed a bit preoccupied and
that he checked his watch more frequently than was normal,
but finally put it down to a case of premission jitters. Everyone in Special Forces had their own way of dealing with the
tension. Some paced, some checked and rechecked their gear,
some wrote letters home and some just seemed a bit more
keyed up than usual. Gerber had learned a long time ago that
the best way for him to deal with butterflies in his stomach was
to sleep on them, but he was usually too keyed up before a
mission to sleep unless he'd had several drinks.

The road back to Nha Trang, Route 1, paralleled the often-
sabotaged coastal railroad and was, despite the large American military presence in the area, officially listed on DA maps
as "Not Secure After 2200 Hours." They negotiated the road
on the return trip in Bates's Jeep in about half the time it had
taken them to drive down, on the theory that a rapidly moving target was harder for enemy snipers to hit. Fetterman
wasn't at all sure the theory made much sense when you were
driving with blackout lights, especially since the VC and NVA
snipers suffered from a chronic shortage of decent night sights.
He was much more concerned about hitting a farmer's water
buffalo on the dark road as Bates sought to push the little
Jeep's imaginary airspeed indicators up past Mach 1, a veloc-
ity the Army's design engineers had never intended the low-
geared transmission to perform. Fetterman figured that at that
speed they would dash through an ambush before they could
trigger it and would probably sail right over any land mines
the enemy might have planted in the roadway. But if they
contacted any domesticated Vietnamese livestock, the buffalo, two-wheeled farmer's cart, Jeep and all the occupants
would make one hell of a mess.

It was while they were negotiating a particularly tortuous
stretch of the road lined with a bamboo thicket abutting a

canebrake that Bates made the only reference to the forth-
coming mission that was to pass between the three men that
evening.

"We're planning to put in more than one team. The exact
number will depend on whether we determine each team to
be a go or a no-go for their specific mission during the briefback. Each team will go in, establish contact with the locals
and set up their specific operational objectives. The teams will
then split and expand their AOs. One team won't split. Instead, it'll become B-team for the overall operation. The determination of the B-Detachment will be made in part on their
geographic location, but the principal determination will be
the speed with which they can establish a secure base of operations. It'll be a fairly classic GW operation. When everyone's in place, we'll begin conducting operations against the
enemy.

"You're to have no contact with the other teams until the
mission actually begins," he continued. "Each team will be
housed in a separate area inside the SOG compound at the
FOB in Kontum. When you get there, go directly to area
twelve. Part of your team will already be there. Don't attempt
to communicate with any of the other teams. The remainder
of your team will join you in a few days, and I'll be coming
along with the briefing team. Take your shaving kits only. All
other items will be provided. You can leave your gear at my
office and I'll have Sergeant Major Taylor look after it for you
when he returns from Saigon. You two clear on all that?"

"Yes, Colonel," both men answered.

"Good. I want to tell you boys that—Jesus Christ!"

Fetterman was nearly thrown from the back of the Jeep as
Bates locked the brakes and slid the tiny four-wheel-drive vehicle sideways in the road to avoid smashing into half a dozen
pigs. The animals scattered in six separate directions, squeal-
ing and grunting.

One of the hogs had the misfortune to charge straight down
the road and detonate a land mine some VC sapper had left

behind. The charge had been buried in the wheel track of the roadway less than a hundred yards ahead of the Jeep, and the explosion blew bits of steaming, smoldering pork all over the road, showering the front of the Jeep with entrails.

Gerber and Fetterman immediately dove over the sides of the Jeep, Gerber drawing a Model 1917A1 .45-caliber pistol from the shoulder holster under his fatigue jacket, while Fetterman produced a customized .44 Magnum revolver and an M-26 hand grenade from his pockets.

Bates was late in joining them, and the other two Green Berets were beginning to be concerned that he might have been hit. But the Colonel, who had been lying on his side in the back of the Jeep, fighting the padlock on a long metal toolbox, finally succeeded in opening the case and came tumbling over the side of the Jeep with three M-2 carbines in his arms and an engineer's shoulder bag filled with 30-round magazines.

"I keep these locked up in the Jeep in case I get stupid and get caught without my M-16," Bates explained, handing each man a carbine and a handful of magazines. "Like this evening." All three men had left their issued rifles in Nha Trang.

"It pays to be prepared," observed Fetterman.

Bates nodded. "I was a Boy Scout in my youth."

"I don't suppose you were prepared enough to bring a radio along so that we could call for some help to get our asses out of this?" asked Gerber.

"Truth of the matter is, I only made Star Scout, not Eagle," said Bates.

"I take it we can't expect to radio for assistance, then," said Fetterman.

The three men crouched behind the scant cover of the Jeep, half expecting at any moment to hear the whoosh of a B-40 rocket or RPG and have the flimsy protection of the vehicle ripped away from them, but nothing further happened.

"You don't suppose it was a single mine, do you?" asked Gerber after several minutes passed.

"Captain," Fetterman suggested, "why don't you slide over to the left side of the road and I'll take the right-hand ditch? We'll work out way up the road a couple of hundred yards and see what gives. Colonel Bates can cover us from the Jeep."

The others agreed, and Gerber and Fetterman sprinted for the roadsides, slid down out of sight into the ditches and then slowly edged their way forward. Twenty minutes later they were back, and Bates, straining his eyes in an effort to see in the darkness, heard his two friends whistle from either side of the road. He answered, and Gerber and Fetterman returned to the Jeep.

"Left-hand side's clear," said Gerber. "No wires and no sign of anybody."

"Right-hand's clear, too," Fetterman reported. "Looks like some lonesome Charlie planted a mine and then bugged out. Guess he didn't want to hang around to see the show if he got lucky and hit point on a convoy. Too much firepower for one Charlie to deal with."

The danger apparently past, they checked out the Jeep, determined that it hadn't been damaged and cleaned the roast pork off the front end. Climbing aboard, they resumed their high-speed run up the road to Nha Trang, but kept the carbines handy.

When they arrived back at Nha Trang, Bates checked his watch and announced that he would buy everyone a nightcap since the Playboy Club was still open. Gerber accepted, but Fetterman begged off, saying he had some things to take care of. It was the last Gerber saw of his team sergeant before morning.

3

**MACV/SOG COMPOUND
SPECIAL FORCES
OPERATING BASE
KONTUM, RVN**

The next morning all Fetterman would say about his mysterious mission was that the company had been soft and lovely and named Cindy. He left the rest to Gerber's imagination.

That afternoon there were five other Special Forces troopers, two officers and three NCOs, manifested aboard the Air Force C-7A Caribou transport that carried Gerber and Fetterman out of Nha Trang. It was obvious they were all going to the same place, and presumably for the same reason, but they didn't speculate about it among themselves. Each man simply nodded cordially to the others and then kept his own counsel during the hour-long flight to Kontum. If the silly-assed rules of the game said they couldn't discuss their new assignments, so be it. They were all professionals and they would damn well all just sit there and pretend nobody knew anything and that it was all one great big surprise when they all got off the airplane together at the same location.

The Caribou came in hot at Kontum, holding altitude until the last possible moment. Then it sideslipped rapidly to lose height and banked sharply at final approach to avoid ground fire from a 12.7 mm machine gun that Charlie had managed to sneak up somewhere close to the end of the runway during the night. It almost worked, but not quite, and the pilot lost oil pressure in the starboard engine just as the wheels clattered down on the PSP runway. The sudden loss of power meant he couldn't use the thrust reversers on the props to slow the plane down without risking a ground loop, and he burned out the brakes just before the wheels dropped off into the soft dirt past the end of the runway.

The passengers and crew exited the aircraft in a hurry, then stood around joking and examining the bullet holes in the wing and engine nacelle while a couple of helicopter gunships took off looking for the 12.7, and the local mortar crews plopped a bunch of 81 mm shells in the general vicinity of the DShK to give the enemy gunners something to think about besides the new targets the helicopters presented them with.

Eventually a deuce-and-a-half with a canvas cover over the back and driven by an SF staff sergeant lumbered up, and the seven Special Forces soldiers climbed into the bed. The driver dropped down the back cover, making it both hot and dark in the rear of the truck, but didn't tie it down. Then he got back behind the wheel and drove everybody to the MACV/SOG compound, leaving the aircrew to wait for their own transportation.

They passed through a seemingly endless number of checkpoints, first at the airstrip, then at the SF compound and finally at the MACV/SOG isolation compound itself, the latter being staffed by steely-eyed Nung Tai security guards who somehow managed to make each of the Special Forces soldiers feel a little bit like a shoplifter who had been caught red-handed by the store detective. When all their bona fides had been evaluated and passed on, they were finally admitted through the double gate and into the compound.

Gerber and Fetterman found a small, arrow-shaped white wooden signpost neatly lettered in black directing them to area twelve, and followed it and a series of others until they wound up at a small white wooden barracks with a corrugated tin roof. Rubberized green sandbags were stacked window-high around the outside of the building. The windows themselves covered nearly the upper half of the walls and were screened over. A series of wooden shutters made out of full-size sheets of Marine-grade plywood were now hooked up out of the way, but could be quickly lowered for protection against the rain, although not from inside the building. A small sign next to the screen door said simply 12. There was a barbed wire enclosure and gate separating it from the rest of the compound, but its construction suggested that it was there more as a reminder to the men not to go wandering around the compound and mixing with the other teams than as any real security measure. It did have a guard, though, who checked their names against the sheet on his clipboard before admitting them.

Inside they found a small break room with a couple of card tables and an assortment of folding metal chairs. A pair of two-burner Coleman stoves and an assortment of canned goods and boxed foodstuffs, along with a bizarre assortment of pots, pans and kitchen utensils, sat on a broad shelf lining one wall. And an apartment-size electric refrigerator occupied a spot on the adjoining wall near the end of the shelf, humming merrily.

"Looks like we do our own cooking this time," observed Fetterman.

"It could be worse," said Gerber. "Last time we were out here it was C-rations for breakfast, lunch and dinner and we lived in a bunker."

"You call that worse?" said Fetterman. "Obviously you haven't eaten any of my cooking in a while."

Gerber smiled. He knew that Fetterman was, in fact, an excellent cook, although only a Green Beret gourmet could probably really appreciate what the master sergeant could do with a few condiments and a couple of snakes.

"We can always send out for pizza," joked Gerber. "Come on. Let's see who else is here."

They went through the doorway and into the barracks proper, where they found half a dozen other men playing pitch and cleaning weapons. Gerber introduced himself and Fetterman, and the others followed suit.

A tall blond fellow with the build of a college basketball player stepped forward and held out his hand. "I guess I must be the XO for this herd. I was sort of hoping I'd be running the team, but you must have eight or nine years date of rank on me. Captain John Updike. Honest to God, it's John Updike. No relation to the writer. I'm new to SOG and this is my first tour, but I've got five months in-country. I've worked in the Highlands around here with the Rhade mostly."

Gerber and Fetterman each shook hands with Updike.

A second blond giant introduced himself. "Sergeant First Class Christopher Paulsen, Intelligence. One tour up in I Corps. I'm just back to start another one." Paulsen spoke with a faint but noticeable Scandinavian accent.

"Klaus Breneke," said a third. "Sergeant first class. I'm the light-weapons specialist. Two tours." Breneke was a typical, stocky, blond, blue-eyed German American.

"Otto Gunn," said another, who could have been Breneke's twin brother. "This is my third tour."

"I've heard of you," said Gerber. "Heavy weapons, isn't it?"

"Not if I can find a light one, sir," said Gunn. "At least not if I have to carry it."

"Felix Portland, although don't let the name fool you, sir. I'm actually from Seattle. Medical staff sergeant. This is my first tour, but I've been in-country six months. Just got back from R and R."

Like the others, he was tall and blond, but more bookish than athletic in appearance. He wore black plastic-framed Army-issue glasses.

There was one more left to go, and Fetterman was just beginning to think that Bates had put together an entirely Nordic A-team for them, out of some bizarre sense of humor, when a seventh man, previously unnoticed because of his size and the fact that he had been lying on a bottom bunk with the cover pulled up over his head despite the heat, thoroughly dispelled any such notion.

"Staff Sergeant Bernard Chavez, Captain Gerber. Combat engineering and demolitions specialist. I did a tour in the Delta, and then extended for six months. When I came back, I volunteered for SOG and they sent me here. The boys in the Delta, they used to call me Blasting Bernie because I like to blow things up so much."

"Glad to have you aboard, Bernie," said Gerber. Then he turned to the remaining man. "What about you?"

"Sergeant Gordon Rawlings. I blow things up, too. You might say that I live by the maxim that a pinch of plastique is worth a pound of powder. I'm new to SOG. Five months in-country on my first tour." Rawlings looked every bit as Nordic as his blond teammates, but his accent was pure Oxford English.

"You're British?" Gerber asked, somewhat surprised.

"Canadian, actually," said Rawlings. "My parents emigrated from London when I was in my second form and I've never really thought of myself as British. Please don't look so surprised to find me in an American uniform, Captain. Traffic across the Canadian border moves in both directions, you know, and not all of my brethren are busy giving aid and shelter to your draft dodgers. Some small handfuls of us actually think it might be a good idea to give you Yanks a hand in this war. I did an enlistment with the Canadian Combined Arms Force before I decided to try my luck in the Lower Forty-eight. Unfortunately the only thing I'm really good at is, like Bernie here, making things go boom."

"Welcome to the war, Canada," said Gerber sincerely. He and Fetterman each shook Rawlings's hand with feeling.

The last member of the team to arrive that day turned out to be one of the Green Berets who had ridden out from Nha Trang on the same airplane as Gerber and Fetterman. He had the same height and athletic build as the other Nordic giants on the team, but that's where any resemblance ended. He was a sergeant first class, the team's senior medical specialist, and this was his third tour in Vietnam, his second with SOG. His name was Jim White, and he was as black as midnight.

The remaining two members of the team, a pair of communications specialists, arrived early the next morning from Da Nang and put an end to the Viking flavor of the team once and for all.

Sergeant Bryon Wysoski was perhaps the tallest man on the team but probably also the skinniest. He had a thick shock of reddish-brown hair and a nose and cheekbones that could only be described as Slavic. He was entirely new to Special Forces but had served a tour in Vietnam with the Eleventh Pathfinder Company (Provisional) of the Eleventh Aviation Group of the First Cavalry Division (Airmobile).

The final member of the team was Staff Sergeant David Dollar from West Baton Rouge, Louisiana. He had receding brown hair, a clipped mustache and a bit of a paunch for a Special Forces soldier. He also had a Louisiana drawl that was all but impossible to decipher until one got used to it. He had spent his first tour in Vietnam as a B-Detachment radio operator and had limited field experience, but if his scores on the Army aptitude exams were any indication, he could probably build a working radio from a Coke bottle, a coat hanger and a set of Tinkertoys. Before their mission was over, Gerber was to decide that he had only known one finer commo man, the almost legendary Galvin Bocker.

For two days the men did little but sit around and play cards and take restless walks around the small compound that was area twelve. A captain, presumably from the FOB—he didn't identify himself and wore no name tape on his fatigues—came in and made sure each man had made out a will and power of attorney, that medical and shot records were current and that pay and personnel files were up-to-date, all of which took about half a day. Then it was back to the pitch and poker and an occasional beer from the refrigerator.

The men spent a lot of time just sleeping. Sack time was a precious commodity to men fighting a war, and all of them knew that once they were in the field, they would be operating on long hours and short sleep for an extended period of time. No one really believed you could build up a reserve of zees in the sleep bank, of course, but that didn't stop anyone from trying.

On the third day the nameless captain returned with a stack of sealed folders and handed one out to each team member. "I haven't been told what's in those," said Captain No Name, "but I assume your target folders, mission statements and general area study guides are inside. Frankly I don't want to know. Other personnel will be arriving tomorrow to brief you. I'm supposed to tell you to study the material carefully. Since each of those things weighs about two pounds, and the briefing team will be here around 0900, you've got your work cut out for you. All I can really say is, good luck, and wherever it is you're going, give 'em hell."

As soon as the FOB captain had left, the men broke open the seals on their folders and dug out the papers inside. There were dozens of typewritten reports, aerial photographs and small- and large-scale maps. All would have to be studied in careful detail, but for the moment none of that held any interest. The answer to the question they had all been dying to know was printed on the cover sheet of the target area folder. It said simply: "The Kingdom of Laos: A Country Study."

Gerber knew what most of the folder would contain: a political analysis of the country; geographic information; population studies, including density and ethnic or religious breakdown; an analysis of the national economy that would include manufacturing and agricultural production figures as well as communications and transportation facilities; and a national security survey covering political and military command and control as well as paramilitary and internal security forces along with their strengths and order of battle. Then there would be an analysis of the terrain and climate along with major geographical subdivisions; an analysis of the people, including their standards of living, culture, ethnolinguistic groups, religions, customs, traditions and taboos, political interests and leanings; and an evaluation of their suitability or effectiveness as guerrillas. Finally there would be an analysis of the enemy forces in the area, an overall mission objective statement and a list of potential targets.

And that was just the tip of the iceberg. Once all the information in the folders had been absorbed, the detailed Intelligence and mission briefings would begin. The data in the folders covered Laos in the broadest sense. It was information about the target country, but not about their specific target area. That wouldn't come until tomorrow morning when they received their operational area briefing and additional packets of specific information.

For now, Gerber knew enough. Whatever the mission specifics turned out to be, whether a reconnaissance, a raid or raising an army of indigenous troops, ultimately it would be aimed at one goal. The only thing in Laos worth worrying about militarily was the Ho Chi Minh Trail. Whatever the mission specifics, it would all come down to one thing in the end—disrupting enemy traffic along the Trail. If the flow of supplies and men through Laos could be stemmed, it would shorten the war in South Vietnam and allow the South Vietnamese to get on with the business of running their own country. It would also save a lot of American lives.

Gerber and the others spent the rest of the day and long hours into the night poring over the material in the packets. For most of the men it was new material, but for Gerber and Fetterman, who had both been to Laos before, much of it was review. Nevertheless, they studied the material as if they had never seen any of it before, and as though their lives depended on a thorough knowledge of the information.

Finally, after he thought his eyes would drop out of his head, Gerber pushed back his briefing materials, looked at his watch and was surprised to see that it was nearly a quarter to five in the morning. He glanced around the break room and saw that he was alone; the other team members had already called it quits and gone to bed.

Gerber gathered up his papers and tucked them away in the folder, shook his beer can and found that it was still nearly half-full, although it had long since grown warm. He considered getting another from the refrigerator, but for some reason a beer no longer appealed to him. He thought about making a cup of coffee on one of the Coleman stoves but was afraid the caffeine might keep him awake, and he knew he ought to try to get some sleep before the briefing team arrived in a few hours. Yet he knew he was still a little too wound up from all the information floating around in his head. Instead he went over and rummaged around on the shelf until he found some cocoa powder. He boiled some water on the Coleman and mixed himself a cup, adding enough syrup from a can of Hershey's to produce a thick, rich cup of hot chocolate. Then he took the heavy china mug and went outside for a breath of air and a chance to spend a few moments in private, quietly drinking his chocolate before going to bed.

As he eased the screen door shut behind him and stood on the wooden steps for a few moments, waiting for his eyes to adjust to the darkness, Gerber became aware of the aroma of pipe tobacco. It smelled good, and as he tried to penetrate the darkness and find the source, he found himself wishing he hadn't given up smoking, because he suddenly craved a cigarette. Even when he had smoked regularly the only time he really missed a cigarette was late at night or early in the morning when they were out on an ambush or patrol and he couldn't allow himself the luxury of one. But tonight, well, there was just something in the air. Maybe it was the upcoming mission, maybe it was the team of new men and maybe it was just all the secrecy that seemed attached to this particular mission, but something seemed amiss, and he yearned for the comfort of his old friend, nicotine. At last his eyes grew accustomed to the night and he spotted a familiar silhouette seated a short distance away atop the rows of sandbags surrounding the lower half of the barracks.

"Good evening, Master Sergeant," said Gerber. "Didn't expect to find you out here this time of night. Also didn't expect you, of all people, to let me sneak up on you unnoticed."

"Good morning, Captain," Fetterman corrected politely. "I can't see my watch, but I think it must be nearly five, judging from the sounds outside the wire."

Gerber was instantly alarmed. "Somebody sneaking around out there, Tony?"

"No, sir. I just meant the animals and birds. Night sounds are starting to give way to the early risers as the nocturnal critters pack it in. Usually happens about an hour before sunrise. The differences are subtle, but you can learn to pick them out with practice. And just for the record, sir, you didn't sneak up on me. If my hearing hasn't gone sour, and I don't believe I'm deaf yet, you're still standing on the steps and holding what smells like a cup of hot chocolate in your right hand." Fetterman turned to confirm his analysis.

Gerber chuckled. "All right, Sherlock, I concede the acuity of your hearing and sense of smell despite that Latakia you're burning, but how did you know the cocoa was in my right hand?"

"Elementary, Captain," Fetterman replied. "I know you're right-handed, so you wouldn't be carrying the cup in your left unless you had something else in your right. And this time of night you wouldn't be carrying anything else, unless it was a weapon, in which case you wouldn't be carrying hot chocolate. In other words, I guessed."

Gerber laughed again and moved closer. As he did so, a second aroma reached his nostrils—the pungent smell of whiskey. "You been drinking, Tony?" Gerber asked.

"Yes, sir," Fetterman answered truthfully. "I finished up with the briefing materials about an hour ago and I've been out here ever since, so there's not a lot left, but I'd be honored if you'd take a touch with me. It's Beam's."

"Beam's, is it?" said Gerber. "Can't very well say no to that. Pass it over."

Gerber put his cocoa down on the sandbags and took the proffered bottle. He uncorked it and put it to his lips, took a pull and passed it over to Fetterman. The master sergeant drank and passed it back. Gerber then took a second drink, fulfilling the prerequisite, and made the toast to complete the ritual.

"To the mission," he said. "May it go down smooth."

"Thank you, sir. I feel better now," said Fetterman, meaning it. For as long as he had known Gerber, they had always toasted the success of a mission before departing, and while the missions hadn't always gone smoothly, he and Gerber had always returned alive. The superstitions of men about to go into combat have been founded on less.

"Want to talk about it?" asked Gerber.

"What makes you think there's anything I want to talk about, Captain?"

"Come on, Tony. Cut the bullshit, will you? It's me, Mack, your friend, talking now. Not Captain Gerber. You and I have been through the meat grinder together. When I find Master Sergeant Anthony B. Fetterman drinking alone in the dark, I know something has got to be bugging the hell out of him. Besides, you gave up smoking your pipe some time back, as I recall, and here you are polluting the atmosphere again."

"I see I'm not the only Holmes around here tonight," replied Fetterman. "I always kind of thought you liked the smell of my pipe tobacco, though."

"It smells as good as ever," said Gerber. "That's just the problem. It's making me wish I had a cigarette."

Fetterman fished in the pocket of his jungle fatigues and handed something across that crinkled with the sound of cellophane. In the dim light Gerber could just make out the Camel filters logo.

"My old brand. When did you start sucking on these coffin nails?"

"Hell, Captain, we're all sucking wind out here, every time we hang our asses out by going back into the bush. Besides, I never did acquire the habit. Oh, I'll smoke a Kazbek when I can find one, or one of the other Russian Brands, but cigarettes have never been a major part of my diet. I always carry a pack or two around with me, though, in case one of my smokeless friends needs to bum one. Help yourself."

"Why the hell not? Just one, though. I'm getting to where I'm so old and feeble that my lungs probably wouldn't stand the shock of two."

He stripped back the cellophane-and-foil wrapper of the fresh pack, shook a cigarette out and bent forward, cupping his hand around the flare of light as Fetterman applied his Zippo to the end. He drew in a lungful of the acrid smoke, felt it tickle his nose and couldn't decide whether to cough or sneeze. Then he took a second puff and decided it still didn't taste bad, although it definitely wasn't as good as he remembered it being. He figured he was safe from reacquiring the habit as long as he didn't ask for a second cigarette. If he smoked two or three, he might actually start enjoying it again.

"All right," said Gerber. "We've had our little drink and our little smoke. Now don't you think it's about time you tell me what's on your mind?"

"It's no big deal, Captain. Really. It's just that I got kind of a funny feeling about this one."

"You mean funny like we're not going to come back from this one?"

Fetterman chuckled. "Always the team player, aren't you, sir? What you really meant to ask was, 'funny like I'm not going to come back from this one.'"

"Well," said Gerber, "is that the kind of funny we're talking about?"

Fetterman chuckled again. "Hell, no, Captain. I always get *that* little funny feeling before a mission, and it's always wrong. So I learned to ignore it a long time ago. This is different. I don't know what it is exactly. Sort of a sense of déjà vu."

"We have been here before," said Gerber. "This isn't the first time we've staged a mission out of Kontum, and it isn't the first time we've gone to Laos together."

"That's not what I mean, sir. It's the whole setup. We're going in with a whole A-Detachment, not just some special-action team. We already know from what Bates told us that it's going to be a GW mission. That means arming and training the locals. And we know we're going to be there for a while. That's why we're getting the full treatment with the country study first and a full briefing team coming in to give us the particulars on the target area. It's pretty obvious we aren't the only ones they're planning to send, either. They've got a full twelve teams in isolation here, and God only knows how many other teams elsewhere. I think we can pretty safely infer that at least the other eleven A-Detachments in the compound are briefing for more or less the same thing we are."

"So?"

"There's more, sir. Nearly all the men are experienced."

"Which is exactly what you'd want on a covert operation into Laos. Besides, Tony, by this stage of the war, practically everybody in the SF is highly experienced."

"That's not true and you know it, sir. The way the Army's been expanding the Special Forces, half the goddamn guys on Tu Do Street are wearing the hat and calling themselves Green Berets. Which, fortunately for us, makes it easy to distinguish them from real SF troopers. Next thing you know, they'll be letting them wear the tab, too. I tell you, Captain, the RA's palming off a lot of dopers, drunks and deadbeats on us."

"Relax, Tony. The nubies still can't serve in an A-Detachment, not unless they're Q course-qualified."

"But they're sure as hell filling up the B-Detachments and C-Detachments, sir, and we have to depend on those mothers for our intel, supplies and support when we're out there in the elephant grass with the bullets whistling between our legs. Really experienced men who are still in one piece are in such short supply that I'm surprised they could find so many, presuming the other teams are as well stocked with old hands as we are."

"All right. Maybe you're right," said Gerber. "I still don't see where that gives us anything to be worried about."

"It's not just worry, sir. It's hard to define, really, but like I said, it just sort of feels like it's all happened before. I was in Laos before, you know. I mean, before you and I linked up with the old Triple Nickel. I was on one of the White Star Mobile Training Teams."

"That does help to explain how you speak Lowland Lao and Hmong," said Gerber. "I suspected, of course, but it wasn't in your 201 File."

"Of course not. Our mission was considered highly classified and we were under cover orders. Anyway, I went through the same sort of thing back then. Lots of teams getting prepped at the same time for missions all over Laos. Lots of secrecy. Lots of experienced old hands being pulled in for the job.

"And the makeup of the team, sir. Christ, it's like a carbon copy. Only the names have changed. One of the new guys, that senior commo man, Dave Dollar, he's practically a dead ringer for the commo guy on my White Star team. The guy was named Phil Reed. He was a whiz with radios and damn near as hard to understand as Dollar. He came from Mississippi. Our senior medic was a Southern boy, too. His name was Calvin Lockheed, and he was every bit as black as White. And the light-weapons guy was a German. His name was Smelzer, but everybody called him Schmeisser. He was absolutely convinced that a better machine pistol than the MP-38/40 had never been invented. We've got two Teutonic types on this team—Breneke and Gunn. It used to be Gunther, you know. His family shortened it when they emigrated, then later added the extra *N*. I've never worked with him, but I understand he's a good man.''

"Okay," said Gerber. "I can see where you could get the feeling that this is a syndicated rerun, but that's not the whole story, is it? You're holding something back. What was it, Tony? Did the team get zapped?''

Fetterman puffed on his pipe for a moment. "No worse than usual. We went in, set up a camp, trained a bunch of the in-dig, then split the team. I went with the group to set up the new camp. Captain Crawford, the CO, got shot up pretty bad. We were able to get an Air America flight in to Medevac him out. I never did hear what happened to him. Anyway, with the team split like it was, I wound up running the second camp for several months.''

"And then?" asked Gerber, knowing there had to be more.

"And then some dumb-ass numb nuts State Department types decided they could negotiate an end to the war in Laos. They convinced enough people with enough muscle that making peace with the VC and Pathet Lao would be better for everybody, not understanding that the only peace that can be negotiated from the Communists is a bullet in the brain. Somebody very high up, I presume in the White House, told the Agency to cool its heels, and our operation was shut down. Just like that. They pulled us out and left the villagers we'd been advising to fend for themselves after we'd got the bad guys good and mad at them. I've no way of knowing for sure what kind of bloodbath followed, but it had to be a massacre. Those Hmong were good fighters, Captain, but we took away their weapons and left them to the mercy of the wolves. And you know as well as I do what kind of mercy they could expect from Charlie.

"They were my people, Captain. My Hmong. And I handed them over to Charlie just as sure as if I'd chopped off their heads and passed them over on a silver platter. All because some bureaucratic knuckleheads who'd never even been to Laos and probably couldn't even find it on the map thought they could negotiate with the VC and Pathet Lao. I did it because I had my orders, and a good soldier follows his orders, even if they suck."

"Seems to me there wasn't much else you could do," said Gerber.

"I could have done something, damn it. I should have. I shouldn't have left them. I should have said screw the orders and stayed behind."

"And done what? Get yourself killed? Throw your career in the toilet? Buy yourself a ticket to Leavenworth for gross insubordination?"

"Hell, Captain, you're talking about one man's career. I'm talking about the lives of a whole village. Leaving those people like that, knowing what was sure to happen to them, it was just about the hardest thing I've ever had to do."

"Sound like you got pretty close to the villagers, Tony. Maybe a little too close. We're supposed to keep our objectivity, you know."

"With respect, sir, you weren't there. You don't know what it was like, what those people were like. The village chief—his name was Tou Bee Cha—made me his son, sir. And then one day I had to go tell him that the Pathet Lao had killed his oldest boy and his son's sons. That was the day we got our recall notice. We left on the day of the funeral."

They were silent for a long time. Neither man spoke for several minutes.

"I appreciate you telling me this, Tony," Gerber said at last. "I can understand how you must feel and I sympathize with you, but I don't know what I can do about it."

Fetterman said nothing for a moment, then let out a long, slow breath. "Nothing anybody can do about it, I suppose. I just want to know that it's not going to happen again, that we won't turn our backs on our friends and let them die."

"I wish I could give you that guarantee, Tony. I really do. But I can't. It's not my decision to make. Politics change with the direction of the wind. All we can do is do the best job we can while we're there," said Gerber.

"Yes, sir. I know that," said Fetterman. "Guess I just needed to blow off some steam. Thanks for listening."

"Hey," said Gerber, "no problem. That's what friends are for, right? Now what say we finish that bourbon and get some shut-eye. The horizon's starting to look pink over there to the east. Bates and the briefing team will be showing up pretty soon."

"Right, sir."

Fetterman drank first this time. Gerber took a swallow and passed it back, leaving him to make the toast.

"To the Hmong," said Fetterman, "and to old friends. May we never turn our backs on them."

"To old friends," agreed Gerber.

4

MACV/SOG ISOLATION COMPOUND SPECIAL FORCES OPERATING BASE KONTUM, RVN

The briefing team arrived at ten o'clock. In addition to Colonel Bates, the MACV/SOG operations, logistics, Intelligence, signals and senior medical officers were present, along with representatives of the area specialist team and the assistant S2 and S3 for plans. Each of the A-Detachments preparing to launch their respective missions were briefed separately over the next several days and remained in ignorance of the precise nature of the other A-teams' missions. All briefings were conducted in the new, air-conditioned briefing center, the various teams being let out of their area compounds one at a time to walk to the center.

The briefing center was a white concrete single-story building without windows. Such was the sophistication of satellite reconnaissance that having a window was like providing an open invitation to Soviet Intelligence, and hence, ultimately, to the North Vietnamese, Vietcong and their Pathet Lao allies. In order to keep the more mundane human eavesdroppers at a safe distance, the briefing center was located within the maximum-security isolation compound and had armed guards stationed outside the doors. The actual briefings were conducted in an inner room, also guarded. During the briefings both inner and outer doors were locked.

The briefings began with Bates outlining the specific mission for the A-Detachment in question as perceived by higher command authority. They then went on to cover the involvement of each of the separate staff positions in formulating the mission and in their support activities, followed with detailed briefings by the area specialist team, the communications and medical officers and the S2 Intelligence estimate. In the case of Gerber's team, it began with some bad news.

"By now you're all aware that the United States has been conducting both ground and air operations in Laos for some time," said Bates. "Some of you have been involved in them. I'm not just talking about crossborder operations conducted under Prairie Fire, but also about the White Star Mobile Training Teams and other operations conducted for the most part by contract employees or Army personnel that have been, shall we say, loaned to the CIA.

"If you read the newspapers, you know about the bombings. We can't seem to keep that sort of thing out of the press, no matter how much good it may be doing the enemy. You may be less aware of the role of Butterfly and Raven Forward Air Controllers, who have served to direct artillery fire and air strikes flown both by the Royal Lao Air Force, and by Meo, or as they're sometimes known, Hmong, pilots trained by U.S. Air Force air commandos. If you've done a proper job of studying your briefing packets, you'll at least have some idea what I'm talking about and you'll learn more before the briefing team gets through with you. One of the things you probably don't know about is the highly secret electronic and aerial navigation facility known as the Rock. I'm going to tell you a little bit about it now. Why I'm doing so will, I think, become apparent as we go along.

"The Rock is a razorback ridge some fifty-six hundred feet high, located on Phou Pha Thi Mountain. I'm told the Meo consider it a sacred place. The Rock itself doesn't appear on any maps except as a ridge on the mountain. In the valley below it there's a dirt landing strip only about seven hundred feet long, designed for use by short-takeoff-and-landing aircraft. The airstrip appears on aerial charts as Lima Site 85. The Rock is a sort of natural fortress, sheer on one side of the ridge and heavily fortified and protected by mine fields on the other. It was guarded by a force of about three hundred Tai and Meo mercenaries. I say it *was* guarded, for good reason.

"The Rock is situated only about 160 miles west of Hanoi on terrain higher than any surrounding it. It is also only about twenty-five miles from the Pathet Lao's self-proclaimed capital of Sam Neua, smack in the middle of Indian country. Despite the unfriendly neighborhood, the Rock was, until recently, considered to be invulnerable to anything but a mass heliborne assault, which was felt to be beyond the capabilities of the enemy.

"About two years ago the Air Force installed a highly sophisticated tactical air navigation system atop the rock, staffed by USAF and Lockheed Aircraft Systems personnel. The facility was used to help guide our bombers over northern Laos and to direct them to downtown Hanoi itself. Last year the Air Force upgraded the facility with a more elaborate system using the latest radar. The new electronics allowed our planes to bomb their targets successfully at night and under all weather conditions. I believe that the upgrade involved something like a 150 tons of equipment, which had to be flown in by special heavy-lift helicopters. All this activity didn't escape the enemy's attention.

"On January 12 of this year the North Vietnamese launched an air strike against the Rock. Three Antonov An-2 Colt biplanes buzzed the facility while their crews dropped mortar shells and fired machine guns out of the windows of the aircraft. This infuriated an Air America helicopter crew who happened to be in the area, and they took on the Colts. One of the North Vietnamese aircraft was brought down by gunfire from an Uzi fired by the crew chief of the Air America chopper. The second was forced down some eighteen miles north of the Rock, following a chase by the helicopter pilot. The third biplane crashed into the mountains. At this time it isn't clear if the crash was the result of pilot error, or if the aircraft was hit by gunfire from the chopper.

"The story was leaked to the press back in the States, which reported it as having occurred near Luang Prabang. It shouldn't have been leaked at all, but we can all be thankful that those who couldn't keep their mouths closed over such a story at least managed to keep the actual location a secret. For your information, the pilot of the Air America chopper figured no one would believe him without proof, so he landed and claimed a swatch of fabric, bearing the tail number, from one of the airplanes. It's number 665, if anyone's interested.

"Now, before you all start getting hysterical over this comic opera air battle, I'd like to point out that the North Vietnamese considered the Rock to be a threat, serious enough to risk such a fantastic assault. Yes, the bombing raid failed, but not the enemy's resolve to do something about our TACAN facility atop Phou Pha Thi Mountain.

"Almost as soon as the air assault failed the enemy began building a road from Sam Neua right up to the base of the mountain. The construction was first spotted by a Raven who tracked its progress over the next three months. Ground reconnaissance teams inserted into the area reported that a work force of several thousand coolies was being employed to push the road ahead at the rate of about a kilometer a night. The enemy intent was apparently to seize Lima Site 85, or at least put it out of action, and then bring up artillery to bombard the Rock preparatory to a mass ground assault.

"The Air Force, of course, attempted to protect its own by bombing the hell out of the road, but the effort was ineffective. Utilizing their vast resource of human labor, the enemy simply filled in the bomb craters at night and pressed forward with the construction. Marching right along behind the construction gangs were three regular battalions of the 766th NVA regiment. At 1815 hours on March 10 they launched an attack against the airstrip at Lima Site 85, spearheaded by sappers, while NVA artillery pounded the southwest side of the Rock.

"The Meo and Tai troops defending the Air Force facility atop the rock were well entrenched and prepared to wait out the night's shelling until U.S. and Royal Lao air strikes could be directed against the attacking enemy in the morning. It didn't work out that way, though. The enemy launched an almost immediate human-wave assault and succeeded in fighting their way up the heavily defended slope in bloody hand-to-hand combat, while a team of North Vietnamese commandos succeeded in doing the impossible—climbing the sheer cliff of the razorback and swarming the peak.

"At daylight Ravens, operating out of Na Khang, began directing air strikes against the enemy while Air America choppers went in to pull our people out. I'm told that only four Air Force personnel were rescued and that twelve are unaccounted for. The exact number of CIA and Lockheed contract personnel dead or missing is unknown at this time. By 2000 hours, the night of March 11, the battle was pretty much over. The Air Force has, however, been forced to bomb their own facility in order to keep the equipment from falling into enemy hands. This means the irretrievable loss of the equipment that directed nearly one-quarter of all bombing missions over North Vietnam. I'm told President Johnson is considering ordering a bombing halt as a negotiating gesture to the NVA. Frankly, he might as well, since we've lost the means to direct further air strikes."

Bates looked at the men. No one was laughing now, as they had at the news of the great biplane raid. "Gentlemen I don't exaggerate when I say that we've suffered a major setback in the war effort. The loss of the Rock has seriously crippled our ability to effectively bomb targets throughout Laos and North Vietnam. At this time it's considered impractical to reestablish the installation. It's evident that to retake the Rock and secure it from further assault would require a U.S. commitment of air and ground assets that's simply not politically feasible to make at this time. It would also require a considerable engineering effort to rebuild the facility. The damage, both from the Pathet Lao assault and the air counterstrikes, has been extensive. For the moment I want to leave you with that thought. We'll come back to it in a moment. May I have the first slide, please?''

Somewhere a switch clicked and the lights went down. A projector came on and a map of Southeast Asia, showing a generalized depiction of the Ho Chi Minh Trail running down from North Vietnam through Laos and Cambodia and branching off at intervals toward South Vietnam, appeared on a screen above Bates's left shoulder.

''For some time now,'' Bates said, ''a major obstacle to our resolving the war in Vietnam has been the Ho Chi Minh Trail. As you know, the Trail's actually a loose network of footpaths and roads over which the enemy has been able to move sufficient quantities of men and supplies into Vietnam to protract the war. From very early on in our involvement in the conflict here, it's been known that the Vietcong insurgency would soon wither and die without the massive influx of aid arriving via the Trail from North Vietnam. Just exactly how to go about preventing this flow of supplies has been something of a delicate question, complicated in no small measure by the fact that the Trail runs through Laos and Cambodia, two countries which are viewed as officially neutral in the war and which haven't always been overly cordial toward the United States. At various times over the past several years it has been U.S. policy to bomb or not bomb the Trail as the political climate shifted. The use of U.S. ground combat troops to clear and hold the Trail areas has been considered, but ruled out as politically unacceptable and requiring at least four U.S. divisions. We have had to content ourselves with limited bombing and with other, less dramatic measures.

"Our Prairie Fire teams have been conducting missions into Laos for some time now, chiefly to obtain Intelligence estimates of the traffic along the Ho Chi Minh Trail. They have, on occasion, also mounted limited ambushes and mined the Trail. For the most part, however, our actions against the flow of supplies down the Trail has been restricted to interdictory air strikes. Despite some spectacular individual successes, the effort to choke off the flow of enemy supplies moving down the Trail hasn't produced the desired results. Each year the enemy has actually managed to increase the tonnage shipped down the Trail. Occasionally we're able to disrupt the traffic on the Trail by heavy local bombardment, but the effect has always been short-term in nature.

"Slightly more effective, but also limited in scope, have been the actions of the Meo guerrilla army of Laotian General Vang Pao. General Pao's forces, headquartered at Long Tieng, have been conducting direct operations against the Pathet Lao and the Vietcong and North Vietnamese in Laos since early 1961. While some of these operations have taken the form of raids or ambushes against the Trail, the majority of them have been directed toward repulsing enemy incursions into the Plain of Jars region, which threatens the Royal Lao capital of Luang Prabang."

Bates paused to clear his throat and poured himself a drink from a pitcher of ice water on a small table near the podium. "Recently a decision was reached at the highest levels of our government to intensify efforts to stop traffic on the Ho Chi Minh Trail. In order to implement this decision effectively, it will be necessary to maximize our air strikes against selected portions of the Trail. This option was chosen because, at this time, political considerations make it difficult if not impossible to take large-scale direct ground action against the Trail with either U.S. or South Vietnamese troops. Although the insertion of from one to four allied divisions into Laos and Cambodia is seen by the Joint Chiefs of Staff as the only sure means of neutralizing the enemy supply routes, this choice has been ruled out because of the reaction a major widening of the land war into the sanctuary areas might provoke from Communist China. Such a move would also generate a fair amount of activity in the Western press and might generate adverse world opinion and domestic unrest, which the Johnson Administration is unwilling to risk in an election year.

"For us to be able to carry out this plan, we'll have to have precise, detailed intelligence of road conditions, traffic, antiaircraft defenses and local weather conditions along the Trail. This is especially important now that the rainy season is approaching in Laos. For this purpose a clandestine, secret, Special Forces company is being independently raised from within MACV/SOG for deployment inside Laos. C-Detachment company headquarters and administration detachment will remain inside Vietnam and will be located here at Kontum, rather than in Da Nang, for security reasons. Should some newshound discover that something big is going on, a cover story will be leaked that the C-Detachment is running covert trail-watching operations into Cambodia after appropriate initial covers have been exhausted. Since the press is already at least vaguely aware that trail-watch missions are conducted into both Laos and Cambodia from Kontum, the press should find the cover story believable.

"The twelve operational A-Detachments of the company will be deployed in various locations inside Laos, which will, for the most part, cover the length of the Trail. Three of those teams have been augmented in manpower and will establish B-Detachment headquarters to control the subordinate detachments once they've been able to establish secure command posts.

"An exception to this policy will be your detachment, which we've code-named Thunderhead. Your task will be not so much to provide information on targets along the Trail, but to raise from among the indigenous population of your operational area a Mobile Guerrilla Force to harass and stop any enemy forces attempting to move southward to take direct action against our teams monitoring the Trail. As such, you'll be the most northerly deployed team. You'll also conduct disruption-and-annoyance missions in what the enemy considers to be his private sanctuary. The purpose of such operations will be twofold: first, to deprive the enemy of the notion that he can feel safe anywhere, even in his own backyard, and second, to force the enemy to expend the maximum number of his troop assets to secure the area, thereby reducing the number of troops he has available to deploy against our other operational detachments monitoring the Trail.

"In light of recent events, you'll also have an additional mission," said Bates. "It'll be your task to find a suitable site for a new Air Force radar and TACAN facility that can be used to guide our aircraft on their strikes against the Trail and against North Vietnam. The site will have to be located well away from any direct operations you may conduct against the Pathet Lao in order to ensure that your raids have the effect of drawing enemy attention away from the site and not the reverse. Once you've found a suitable site and raised sufficient numbers of troops to defend it adequately, the electronics and Air Force personnel to operate the gear will be helicoptered in under cover of general air strikes. When the equipment is set up and operating, the real, concentrated bombing of selected portions of the Trail will begin. We've named that part of the overall plan Hard Rain. The code name for the entire operation will be Falling Rain," Bates concluded. "I'll now turn you over to the rest of the briefing team, who will give you their particular inputs into Operation Falling Rain."

For the next several hours Gerber, Fetterman and the rest of Special Forces operational team Thunderhead were briefed by each member of the briefing team at length. Essentially it was an overview of the specific target area, what needed to be done and the resources available to do it. The briefing covered climate and terrain in the target area; ethnic, cultural and religious background of the local populace; weather conditions to be expected; air assets available for insertion, extraction and resupply; logistics, airfields and helicopter landing zones in the area; enemy troop strengths, equipment and movements; weapons; communication gear, call schedules and radio codes; and special equipment items.

The team also learned that they wouldn't have artillery support available to them, but that light artillery, in the form of mortars, bazookas and recoilless rifles, could be provided for their use. They would have to train the indigenous personnel to operate them.

They were advised that, for the most part, close air support would also be unavailable. It was possible that some could be arranged for, either through the Royal Lao government or the Fifty-sixth Air Commando Wing, but in either event, the delay in its arriving would be considerable. Unlike Vietnam, which was rife with super-sophisticated jet fighter-bombers, helicopter gunships and flare ships that could light up the night like a football game, combat air assets in Laos consisted of a mix of armed T-28 trainer aircraft, aging A-1 Skyraiders and twin-prop A-26 Invaders, all of which were roughly of World War II vintage.

Nor could they expect to ride into combat aboard helicopters. The limited air assets of Air America, the CIA-owned airline created to serve the Agency's needs and as a cover for their air operations in Indochina, were busy with other duties. In an extreme emergency, it might be possible to get a chopper or one of the Agency's Helio Courier or Pilatus Porter STOL aircraft in to Medevac a seriously wounded team member, but as a means of riding into battle they were out. The team members of Thunderhead would get to the fight the old-fashioned infantryman's way. They would walk.

Resupply for the team, and additional arms and equipment required by the local guerrilla force would be handled by parachute drop, Air America helicopter or STOL aircraft. All supplies would be filtered through the CIA's secret city of Long Tieng, shown on aerial maps simply by the airstrip designator of Lima Site 20 Alternate. The supplies were being passed through the Agency because it was easier to "lose" several tons of arms and equipment in the Agency's secret operating funds, and because the Johnson Administration preferred avoiding the necessity of having to explain the situation to the Western press if some Army or Air Force aircraft carrying a lot of unusual weapons got shot down over northern Laos.

Fetterman was relieved to find out that the weapons available to them would, at least, be first-class hardware and not a bunch of worn-out old retreads left over from the Second World War and Korea. The CIA had been providing Vang Pao's Hmong guerrilla army with M-16s for some time now, and Thunderhead could expect to receive CAR-15s, a sort of carbine version of the M-16 with a shorter barrel and telescoping buttstock even more suited to the small-statured Hmong they would be working with than the lightweight M-16.

More esoteric weapons would be available, too: Browning 9 mm parabellum pistols instead of Colt .45s; Swedish-made Karl Gustav Model 45 submachine guns, known as Swedish Ks, fitted with silencers; and Israeli Uzi submachine guns. If a particular mission required a sniper rifle, an M-21, the most accurate sniping weapon in the world, would be made available. For close-range ambushes there were Remington semiautomatic shotguns fitted with twenty-inch barrels and eight-round extended magazines.

The communications gear was a mixture of the exotic and the mundane. For short-range communications they would have the familiar AN/PRC-25, a relatively light, portable successor to the PRC-10, which had been around since World War II, and which was beginning to replace the older model as the standard, platoon-level communications radio. For long-range traffic there were James Bond-like devices that could compress a message and squirt it out in a few seconds while automatically checking with the receiver up to five hundred miles away and confirming that the message was received exactly as sent.

The rest of the day was spent with members of the Area Specialist Team, which briefed them on the situation in Laos in general, northern Laos in particular and Houa Phan Province in particular.

The information they were showered with was exhausting, both in depth and amount. The presentations were frequently interrupted as team members asked questions or wanted to discuss or have additional information on some specific aspect of the briefing. Only in the Special Forces was a team so thoroughly briefed before being inserted into an operational area.

At last the briefings were over and the team retired to their barracks to formulate their operational plan. Bates and the briefing team had told them what must be done, had provided all the information they could think of that would help them accomplish the task, then had given Gerber and his men four days to come up with how they would do it. On the morning of the fifth day Gerber presented the plan to Bates and the briefing team in the briefback.

For five hours Gerber and his team members talked to the briefing team while Bates and the others tried to pick the plan apart. Every detail of the plan had to be considered in-depth. Every contingency had to be planned for. Every action had to have four, five or six alternatives in case the enemy didn't respond as anticipated, the weather didn't cooperate, the Hmong in the AO proved unfriendly, an important piece of equipment was lost or a member of the team became ill or was killed.

When it was over, Bates sat quietly for a moment, mulling over all that he had heard. "I have just one more question," he said at last. "What made you select this particular part of your AO to establish your base camp and attempt to contact the indigenous population? You've given us three alternates. Why did you pick this one as the primary?"

"We picked it because Master Sergeant Fetterman has been there and knows the area and the people," said Gerber.

Bates arched an eyebrow. "Indeed?"

"Yes, sir," replied Fetterman. "Six years ago with White Star. There's a spot on a mountain there that overlooks the Song Chu Valley as it runs into North Vietnam. On a clear day you can see Phou Mountain to the west-northwest and Phu Xai Lai Leng to the southwest. More importantly, you can see Route 6 all the way from the Song Ca to Sam Neua, and Route 7 from the pass at Nong Het to Khang Khai on the west side and clear down to Khe Bo on the North Vietnamese side. It's not the highest mountain in the neighborhood, but there aren't any higher ones between it and Hanoi, and to the southeast you've got to go all the way to Rao Co and Phou Co Pi mountains, almost to the Mu Gia Pass, before anything gets in your way. It's the best place I can think of for your Air Force transmitter, sir."

"What was your relationship with the Hmong in the area while you were there?" asked Bates.

"The village chief, who was also chief of the clan, made me his son," said Fetterman bluntly.

For a moment Bates was amused, although he gave no sign of it. It was hard to imagine Master Sergeant Fetterman as anyone's son. "And what was your relationship with the villagers when you left?"

"Well, sir," said Fetterman, "we were ordered to pull out because of efforts to negotiate a coalition government with the Communists. We had to disarm the villagers before we left. It was on the day of the funeral of the chief's son. He'd been killed in a firefight with Pathet Lao. I'm afraid the timing didn't make us very popular, sir."

"Supposing you get there and find the locals to be hostile toward you because of this previous event?"

"In that case, sir," said Fetterman, "we're prepared to escape and evade to one of the three alternate tactical AOs."

Bates drummed his fingers on the foldaway armrest of his chair, his chin cupped in one hand. At last he turned and looked at each member of the briefing team, who nodded in turn. "Okay," he said finally, "your plan is approved. You're a go."

5

HOUA PHAN PROVINCE
NORTHEASTERN LAOS

Fifteen olive drab parachutes cracked open in the pale blue early-morning sky. It was only a few minutes past sunup as the air filled the umbrellas of the rip-stop nylon canopies and lowered their cargos of twelve men and three equipment containers to the ground with relative gentleness.

It wasn't an altogether soft landing for the two officers and ten enlisted men of Special Forces team Thunderhead and their gear, however. The ground below them was rocky and uneven, and each of the men carried a heavy pack and load of ammunition clipped in front of his legs and below his reserve parachute. Furthermore, they had exited their aircraft at an altitude of only a thousand feet above ground level, about five hundred feet lower than the standard altitude for a military parachute jump, leaving them little time to correct any emergencies or prepare for the impact of landing. They had, in fact, calculated that there was an almost even chance of one of their number breaking a leg or at least spraining an ankle upon landing. It was a testimony both to their physical conditioning and skill, and to the quality of their equipment, that none did.

When Gerber hit the ground, he executed a forward roll, not the easiest of PLFs to do with your pack hanging in front of your legs, and immediately pulled the ring on the canopy release catch at his right shoulder to shear away one side of the canopy, spilling the air from it so that he wouldn't be dragged across the ground. He then popped out the safety clip, punched the circular plate of the quick-release assembly to disengage the strap lugs and shook his way out of the harness. Pulling his CAR-15 clear and lengthening the buttstock, he looped the straps of his pack over one shoulder and glanced around. The others were all down or coming down onto the DZ as planned. He left his chute where it lay and headed straight for the rally point at the edge of the DZ.

When he got there, Breneke and Fetterman were already waiting for him, along with Jim White. Both Breneke and Fetterman were armed with Swedish Ks equipped with sound suppressors, while White carried a CAR-15, specially modified with a 40 mm grenade launcher mounted beneath the short barrel. As soon as he arrived, Gerber pointed at Breneke and Fetterman, and the two men moved off in opposite directions to scout out the area and make sure no one had witnessed the arrival of the team.

When all the team members had reported in, Gerber and five of the others deployed in a defensive circle as the remaining four went back out to gather up the chutes, drag in the equipment containers and generally tidy up the drop zone. Gerber was always amazed at all the litter one could find scattered over a DZ after a drop. You would think that things would be relatively neat, but the cleanup team invariably found something. It might be a piece of equipment that had spilled out of someone's pack on impact, a loose round that had tumbled out of someone's ammunition pouch or bandolier, a flashlight or a first aid pouch that had somehow gotten unclipped from someone's webgear, somebody's beret or boonie hat that had fallen out of their pocket—almost anything. Gum wrappers and cigarette butts were popular items, even when none of the

jumpers had been smoking or chewing gum. They fell out of
pockets or were sucked out of the aircraft when the crew chief
opened the door to toss out the streamer. Once Gerber had
even found an aircraft manual and a fire extinguisher.

Once the cleanup team had policed the drop zone, they assumed guard duties in the defensive circle while four of the
previous guards broke out their entrenching tools and started
digging a hole to bury the chutes. When they were nearly done,
the equipment containers were opened and the items of additional gear, which had been broken down into portable loads
and tied into bundles or packed into stuff sacks and shoulder
bags, were taken out and distributed among the men. The
chutes were then stuffed into the empty containers, which were
pushed into the hole and covered with earth. By the time the
job had been completed, Fetterman and Breneke had returned.

"It looks quiet," Breneke reported. "No sign of anyone
around. Of course, that doesn't mean there couldn't have been
somebody sitting half a mile away up in those hills, watching
the whole show through a pair of field glasses."

"Not much we can do about that if there was except not
waste any more time getting out of here," said Gerber.

Fetterman's sweep wasn't quite as clean.

"There's been visitors through here," he reported. "Say
half a dozen people. Their tracks are two or three days old,
though. Nothing more recent. They were indigenous, probably Hmong."

"How do you know that?" asked Wysoski.

"Easy," said Fetterman. "They weren't wearing any shoes,
Pathet Lao or VC would have had sandals. NVA would have
been wearing boots or tennis shoes. These people were bare-
foot. Besides, some of the tracks are smaller than the others.
One set is real small. Looks like a mother and child. There are
some Man and mountain Mon-Khmer in this area, as well as
tribal Tai, most notably the Phong. The odds favor it being

Hmong, though. This was their mountain. Even the Lao Theung rarely come here."

"The last time you were here was six years ago, Master Sergeant," said Updike. "A lot can change in six years."

"That's true enough, Captain," Fetterman replied. "But the Hmong have been the only permanent dwellers on this particular mountain for over a hundred years. I doubt very much that that's changed."

"Right," said Updike. "So how do we go about finding these Hmong of yours?"

"We start," interrupted Gerber, "by finding the village of Muang Xam Teu. *If* we can. Master Sergeant, you've got the point."

"Yes, sir," said Fetterman. He picked up his share of the extra gear and moved off into the brush.

The others followed, with Chavez, who carried the third suppressed Swedish K, taking the slack position, Breneke bringing up the rear and the rest of the team strung out between them.

Fetterman had walked the point for Gerber many times during their two tours together in Vietnam. He was the best scout Gerber had ever known, with the possible exception of a Nung Tai scout they had worked with named Krung, and Gerber wasn't entirely sure of that.

Krung was a passionate, at times even hotheaded little tribesman with a deep-seated hatred of all Communists that sometimes clouded his better judgment. His family had been butchered by the Vietcong, and he wore a tattoo on his chest saying, Sat Cong, Death to Communists, as a permanent and visible reminder of his sacred pledge not to rest until he had killed ten of the enemy for each member of his family.

Fetterman, on the other hand, was coolly professional, the epitome of the career combat soldier. He liked to work alone because he trusted his own judgment, and he lived by the axiom that the only way to get killed in combat was to make a mistake.

Gerber normally liked to have him out several hundred yards in front of the patrol where he could spot trouble without being distracted by the movement or noise of the rest of the team and had time to give the rest of them plenty of advance warning when he found it. It was a system that worked well for them when they were following a compass course or more or less clearly defined route of march, but here it just wasn't practical. The maps they'd been provided with at Kontum were the best available, and that was all. They were based on aerial mapping surveys and the best guesses of Japanese and French cartographers who had attempted to plot out the area twenty or more years ago.

The region simply hadn't been that well mapped, and the aerial surveys told nothing of the lay of the land beneath the canopy of pine trees covering the uneven, rocky ground. A good deal of their navigating would have to be done by what Fetterman remembered from his visit six years ago. Their route of travel would be determined by that and by what they found.

You couldn't just follow a compass in the mountains. The terrain was cut by deep gorges and valleys. Paths could suddenly block up against a sheer wall of rock hundreds of feet high, or simply meander through the wilderness for hours and then suddenly end in the middle of nowhere. Trails could be blocked at passes by unmovable twenty-ton boulders from a rock slide or halt at the edge of a precipice, giving the unwary the opportunity to fall off the side of the mountain. Ravines and gullies that had been bone-dry moments before could be abruptly swollen by floodwater from the runoff of a sudden shower, sweeping men down the mountainside. And it was far easier to become lost in a branching maze of box canyons than a flatlander could ever imagine.

For just such reasons the team moved with a short point, the line strung out with enough distance between each man that he could just barely keep the one in front of him in sight, the distances lengthening or shortening as the terrain and trees required. Even so, it was difficult to keep track of everyone. The men struggled beneath heavy loads, and with greatly varying physiques among them; those with shorter legs had a hard time keeping up with the giants. They were forced to take frequent stops to allow everyone to remain caught up and not get separated.

They pushed steadily onward throughout the morning, but it was slow, agonizing progress. Besides his weapon and normal equipment for an extended patrol, each man carried extra food, ammunition and hand grenades; signaling and illumination flares; a firefly strobe; a small two-channel emergency radio and spare batteries that could be used to contact an aircraft, flying overhead; and at least two 100-round belts of 7.6 mm ammunition for the M-60 machine gun that Sergeant Gunn was packing.

Then there was the communications gear: two AN/PRC-25s and two high-frequency-burst transmitters, along with a couple of rolls of antenna wire. The satellite link had been left behind in Kontum. It would be sent out in a later supply drop once the team had successfully established an operating base. In the meantime there was only so much equipment the team could carry.

The combat demolitions and engineering specialists each carried a haversack containing eight two-and-a-half-pound blocks of C-4 plastique, a roll of detonating cord, electric and nonelectric blasting caps, priming adapters, a roll of M-700 safety fuse, M-2 weatherproof fuse lighters and a ten-cap blasting machine with five hundred feet of firing wire and a galvanometer, as well as wire cutters, cap crimpers, electrical tape and so forth, including two single-bit axes and two bow saws.

The two medical specialists had their first aid kits, as well as a supply of albumen and lactated ringers, suturing kits and emergency surgery kits, complete with ether inhalers. They also carried blood pressure cuffs in adult and pediatric sizes, stethoscopes and an array of antibiotics, antihistamines and snake- and insect-bite antivenins.

Paulsen, the intel sergeant, had nearly a million kip, both Royal Lao and Communist, on him, as well as salt, sugar, tobacco, ginger and other seasonings to be used for barter.

Several hundred feet of green nylon climbing rope with carabiners and pitons, four M-72 LAW rockets, a dozen claymore mines and twelve extra CAR-15s, enough to equip the first squad of Hmong guerrillas the team would train, were distributed throughout the team.

The men tired quickly under such heavy loads, and although they walked the first two hours without a stop, except for the brief pauses every ten to fifteen minutes to make sure everyone was staying together, after that they took a ten-minute break every hour.

As the day dragged on, the breaks gradually stretched to fifteen minutes and then finally twenty until about two in the afternoon when Gerber finally called a half-hour halt so that the men could rest and eat lunch. They then marched on until almost dark, when they set up a night laager in a thicket and rested until dawn, half the team always remaining on alert while the other half slept.

At daybreak they rolled up the firing wires of the claymores they had set out as a defensive perimeter during the night and pressed on, eating a cold breakfast on the trail. It was late afternoon before Fetterman finally pushed out of the tree line at a familiar spot and saw the rocky outcropping with the narrow cleft on the other side of a deep gorge that six years earlier had been guarded by a hidden machine-gun bunker and marked the entrance to the Hmong guerrilla base the White Star Mobile Training Team had called the Rookery.

There was no sign of any guard, but then, if they were there, they had always been taught to keep well hidden.

Fetterman cautiously approached the gorge while the other team members kept him covered from the tree line. He was appalled by the state of the footbridge, never a very sturdy structure. The planks were nearly all missing or rotted away, and only two strands of the nylon support ropes remained. He stood openly at the edge of the gorge for perhaps ten minutes, but no one either came forward to greet him or took a shot at him. Finally he sighed deeply and walked back to the forest to make his report to Gerber.

"It looks like they've pulled out," Fetterman told him. "Nobody challenged me and I didn't see anyone. The footbridge doesn't look like it's been used in a while, either. I'll have to go across, though, to make sure."

Gerber nodded. "All right. Get ready then. We've got to know for sure."

"Yes, sir."

Fetterman shrugged off all his gear and, taking his submachine gun, on which he had taped a second magazine, and two hand grenades, he prepared for the traverse. Tying a Swiss seat around his legs with a short piece of rope, he clipped a carabiner to it and tied a safety line around his waist. With Breneke and Gerber acting as belay on the safety line, Fetterman slung his weapon, clipped himself onto one of the decaying suspension lines and, holding his combat knife between his teeth like a Hollywood movie pirate, hitched his legs over the bridge rope and slowly pulled himself hand over hand across the dizzying depths of the ravine.

The suspension rope creaked noisily as Fetterman inched his way along. It sagged badly, and he knew he would have to pull himself uphill when he reached the center. As he crawled along the rope, he noticed many frayed spots. He tried to ignore them and pressed onward, glad that he had checked the anchoring stake to make sure it was still firmly in the ground before starting across. There was little he could do about the stake on the opposite side, except hope that it was as firmly planted in the rocky soil.

Fetterman had reached the center of the ravine and was just starting up the other side when the rope unraveled and parted under his weight, the end snaking out of the carabiner holding it to the Swiss seat. Fortunately he had a good, solid hold with both hands. Breneke immediately locked up on the safety line, and the opportunity to complete the crossing would have been lost if Gerber hadn't yelled. "Give him some slack!"

Breneke immediately let the rope run through his gloves, and Fetterman swung across the ravine, smashing into the far wall like a sack of potatoes. His steel helmet, which he had prudently worn, rang resoundingly as it struck against a rock. Gerber and the light-weapons specialist could clearly hear the even louder grunt that followed the impact.

For a moment Fetterman hung there against the face of the ravine, holding on to the rope with both hands despite the stunning blow he had suffered, while Breneke and Gerber held their breath. Then, slowly, the diminutive master sergeant began to pull himself up the rope. He had almost reached the top when the rope gave way again and he dropped like a stone.

Fetterman managed to find a handhold in the rock wall and stop himself before Gerber and Breneke got excited enough to start hauling on the safety line and swing him back across the ravine, where he could smash up against the other side. They nearly pulled him off the wall before they realized he wasn't going to fall, and let out a bit more line so that he could maneuver.

Fetterman had burned the palms of his hands on the rope before arresting his fall when it first broke and had silently cursed himself for not having the good sense to wear his gloves, a decision he had made because he found them awkward and was afraid he might not be able to get his finger in the trigger guard of the Swedish K if he suddenly needed to open fire halfway across the chasm. Now he was thankful for the omission. Had he worn the gloves he wouldn't have been able to fit his fingers into the tiny crevices in the rock wall he now found for handholds.

He dug around with the toes of his boots until he found a purchase for one foot that seemed solid enough to hold him, then pulled himself up until he could find another finger-hold. Gradually he free-climbed the last fifteen feet up the rocky wall, wedging the blade of his knife in a tiny crack in the rock to give himself enough purchase to make the final few feet to the top.

Once he had made the safety of the rocky shelf, Fetterman lay there for a few moments, breathing heavily, then reached back over the rim of the gorge and retrieved his knife. He signaled to Gerber and Breneke that he was okay.

The captain returned the signal with a look that said, "Too close for comfort."

Fetterman couldn't have agreed more. For a man who enjoyed jumping out of airplanes, he had a dislike of heights that no amount of argument or experience had ever been able to conquer. He had always claimed that parachuting was a different experience from climbing. In climbing, he had once said, the object wasn't to fall, while in parachuting it was exactly the opposite.

Having made the crossing safely, Fetterman untied the safety line and retied it around a large boulder, not wishing to risk his neck on the rotting anchor stake. Gerber and Breneke stretched the nylon line tight and secured it carefully at the other end. With his means of rapid escape provided for, Fetterman unslung his submachine gun, checked the safety and eased through the cleft in the rocks. When he was out of sight, Gerber and Breneke retired to the less-exposed position of the tree line.

Fetterman was ill prepared for the sight that greeted him, although he had more than half expected it. The barbed wire barricades were still in place, strung with tin cans filled with pebbles. Both wire and cans were heavily rusted, and there was still no sign of anyone.

Fetterman backed up and checked the machine-gun bunker where the Eagle-eye team had once kept watch over the entrance to the Rookery. It was empty and overgrown with weeds, with the roof timbers sagging badly. It told him what he needed to know, but not how or why. If he wanted answers, he would have to look for them, and he wouldn't find them outside the wire. He slipped back through the crevice.

For a moment Fetterman just stood there, studying the situation, trying to remember the safe route through the mines, flares and booby traps. There hadn't been time to remove them all before the White Star Team had pulled out, and now, with a secondary growth of low scrub and saw grass covering the once-clear killing field, the previously well-worn pathway was obscured and indistinct. Recalling the arrangement of the deadly explosives as best he could, he took the sensible precaution of getting down on his knees and probing carefully ahead of himself with the knife. It took him nearly an hour to reach the fort in this fashion.

The plank bridges over the moat filled with punji stakes were long gone. The ditch was filled with weeds, but the punji stakes were still there among the vegetation. The sharpened bamboo was old and brittle now, but still dangerous, and it took him some time to work through it.

Inside the fort little remained. The walls had begun to collapse, the bunkers had fallen in and the walls of the mortar pits sagged. It was obvious that there had once been a military installation there, but it might have been six years ago or sixty.

Beyond the fort the Hmong village was a ghost town, its once-crowded main street and square now empty. The big stone cisterns the Green Berets of Black Rook had once so painstakingly helped the Hmong construct to hold rainwater in this well-less spot were crumbled, broken and covered in dust, although water still stood in stagnant, stinking pools in a few of them. Many of the houses the Hmong had built remained standing, but in very poor condition. Some had partially fallen in and a few appeared to have been burned. Fetterman wasn't absolutely positive, but he could have sworn that a few of them were simply missing, as though their owners had disassembled them on the spot and carted them away to be used elsewhere.

After a while Fetterman came to the hut of Tou Bee Cha. There was nothing in particular to mark it as the village chief's—it was nearly indistinguishable from the other ruins around it—but Fetterman knew it as well as he knew how to fieldstrip a Garand M-1 blindfolded. It gave him a eerie feeling, standing before it, almost as though he were trespassing on sacred ground. Perhaps in a way he was. The Hmong believed that everything possessed a *phi*, a spirit, and the feeling of spirits was strong in this place. He debated with himself for some time whether or not to go inside, although he fully expected to find nothing, yet something seemed to draw him toward the doorway, and finally he entered the house of the only father he had ever known.

There was little to see except for the dilapidated walls and the floor of packed earth. The thatch roof that had once kept out the rain was filled with holes, although the shafts of late-afternoon sunlight filtering through it did little to dispel the gloom of the interior. An entire Hmong family had lived here once. Now there was nothing.

With a curious sense of loss and regret, he turned to leave. He was about to step through the doorway when something on the dirt floor caught his eyes. It wasn't much, just the faint glint of something shiny. Slowly he stooped and brushed away the dirt that mostly covered it with his fingers, got a grip on it and pried it out of the soil.

It was a pair of silver paratrooper's wings, badly tarnished now. Carefully he turned them over in his hand and rubbed at the grime on the back with his thumb, uncovering the engraved numbers he knew he would find there, written military style with the day first. 21-02-44. The date he had graduated from jump school. He had given the wings to his Hmong father as a gift, the only silver Fetterman had possessed. He balled his fist tightly around them, and stared at the ground for a while.

Sometime later Fetterman broke out of his reverie. He was annoyed with himself. It wasn't like him to let his mind wander whle he was in a combat situation. That kind of day-dreaming was a mistake that could easily get one killed. Yet the flood of memories triggered by finding the jump wings had been so overwhelming that for nearly half an hour he had found himself in another time.

For a while it was 1962, and the Hmong village of Muang Xam Teu, relocated to this natural fortress for protection from the Vietcong and Pathet Lao, teemed with life. Old men and young men, women and children, pretty teenage Hmong girls once more lived in its houses and walked its main street, if only in Fetterman's mind. They filled the air with the smell of ginger and citronella, with boiled pig, roasted gaur and water buffalo, and everywhere the smoke of pine fires drifted on the breeze. They danced in brightly colored costumes and were sedately resplendent in black cloth bedecked with enough silver jewelry to give a Hollywood starlet a stiff neck.

They engaged in the traditional courtship ritual of *pov pob* with visitors from another Hmong village, and they performed *zij poj niam*, marriage by capture, a mating tradition that would have brought a charge of rape against the Hmong male in most Western societies.

They grew maize and rice and the opium poppy on burned-off forest land as their fathers and their fathers' fathers had done before them. They fished the mountain streams with lines of vine and wooden fish hooks. They hunted the tiger, armed only with spears or crossbows. And they learned to use machine guns and mortars to hunt down and kill the Pathet Lao and Vietcong who called them barbarians and tried to make them slaves.

And when the enemy or illness was stronger, they covered their dead with *pa ndau* cloths, like brightly colored handkerchiefs, to ensure their spiritual wealth in the afterlife, and tucked them away in the ground in wooden coffins put together with pegs so that there would be no metal around them to attract evil *phi*. The funeral would often take four days to complete and involved the ritual of *tso plig*, the ceremonial sacrifice of a cow or buffalo to free the spirits of the deceased for the journey onward.

Looking out the doorway of the hut, Fetterman could see the distant shape of a mountain, as Hmong tradition demanded. He didn't know its name. It would be Phou something or other, as all mountains were known. Perhaps it was a mountain sacred to the Hmong, as Phou Pha Thi was, or perhaps it was only a mountain, like this one. It didn't matter. Somewhere on it were other Hmong who called it home.

Fetterman tucked the jump wings carefully in a pocket of his jungle fatigues and buttoned the flap so that he wouldn't lose them. Then he went back outside and returned to the gorge.

"What in hell took you so long?" Updike demanded after Fetterman had successfully recrossed the ravine.

The master sergeant ignored him and spoke directly to Gerber. "They've gone, sir. All of them. I don't think it was the Communists. I didn't see any sign of a struggle. It looks like they simply abandoned the place. A lot of the old fortifications are still there, although they need repair pretty bad. The mine field's still intact. It took me a while to work my way through it."

"Terrific," said Updike. "The people we've come to find are gone. What are we supposed to do now?"

"I think they may have returned to their old village," Fetterman said to Gerber. "At least they may have gone back somewhere near it. They never did like this part of the mountain particularly well. It was too far from their fields, and some of the men said it was the home of bad spirits. The only reason the village moved here was out of respect for the old chief, and the only reason he said they should come was because I asked him to. The Hmong don't much like being too far away from their fields."

"Suppose they've moved down into the valley and joined the Pathet Lao?" interrupted Updike again.

Fetterman slowly faced the man. "These people would never do that. First off, this village hates the Pathet Lao. The Communists have killed too many of their family members. Second, as was pointed out in the briefings, Hmong live only on mountaintops, never in the lowlands. A Hmong won't even stop if he has to cross a valley to get to another mountain. He'll just walk right on straight across."

"All right, then, suppose they've gone to another mountain. How will we find them?"

"They wouldn't do that," insisted Fetterman, "unless something forced them off. This mountain is their home. Their dead are buried here. A Hmong may abandon his house but never his home."

"Tony, if we do find them, do you think you can persuade them to help us?" asked Gerber. "I know you got to be close to them, but six years is a long time. A lot can change."

"If Tou Bee is alive, they'll help us, sir. You can bank on that."

"All right, then," said Gerber. "We go look for them. How far is this other village?"

"About half a day's travel."

"Okay," said Gerber. "Let's find a place to settle in for the night. In the morning we'll go see if we can find the missing Hmong."

"What about the rope?" asked Breneke of no one in particular. "Should we try to recover it?"

"Leave it," said Fetterman with conviction. "We'll be back."

6

THE VILLAGE OF
MUANG XAM TEU HOUA
PHAN PROVINCE LAOS

It was late afternoon when Fetterman, walking point as usual, spotted the village. He had known he was in the general area for nearly an hour, but things had changed. Trees had been felled across trails. The main trail he remembered the villagers using showed no sign of recent traffic and was overgrown in spots. Furthermore, there were new trails crisscrossing the area, which he could have sworn hadn't existed six years before. Some of them showed use, but not recently. It could have been weeks or even months since they had last felt the tread of a human foot.

Slowly the pieces were adding up to a picture that seemed to indicate the Hmong had abandoned this village, too. And then Fetterman found something that made the short hairs on the back of his neck stand on end.

As he edged around a curve in the trail, there, stretched out in two neat rows, running along either side of the path, each one mounted on its own bamboo pole driven into the ground, were the skulls of at least forty men, picked clean of flesh by ants and flies and bleached white by the sun.

It wasn't the grisly specter of human remains that made Fetterman's blood run cold, however. He had seen similar displays before, and worse. What gave the master sergeant pause was the thin line of dark, rust-colored twine stretched across the trail between the fifth and sixth pairs of heads. It was only an inch or so above the surface of the trail, and its color and rough, frayed texture blended so perfectly with the reddish-brown tint of the rocky soil covering the floor of the trail that he nearly missed it, even though he had been looking for something like it. He followed the trip wire to its end and found it anchored to a wooden stake almost ten feet from the side of the trail, then retraced his path in the opposite direction and found that end wrapped around a hand grenade.

The bobby trap was a simple affair, which is often the most effective kind. The very thin trip wire, apparently braided out of three or more strands of long human hair, had been wrapped around the body of a grenade. The grenade had had the pin removed and had been inserted into a tin can, which was lashed to a stake driven into the earth alongside the trail. A tug on the cord would thus pull the grenade from the can, allowing the safety lever to fly free and arm the grenade. Fetterman noted with interest that the grenade was a Soviet-made F-1, similar in design to the U.S. Mark II, better known as the Ridgeway Pineapple, or the British Mills Bomb, and old design with a serrated, cast-iron case, but effective nevertheless. It was the type of hand grenade often issued to the North Vietnamese Army but rarely found in the hands of the VC or Pathet Lao.

The most significant part of the find, however, was the tin can holding it, which had the familiar olive drab paint of an American C-ration. Fetterman eased up to it cautiously and read the label.

Ham and Lima Beans.

Oh, well, he thought, at least they found something useful to use it for, whoever *they* are.

He examined the bobby trap to make sure it wasn't booby-trapped itself, and then decided to have a little fun. Taking a four-inch-long piece of eighteen-gauge wire out of his pocket, he eased the grenade out of the can far enough to insert the safety wire, bending it over at both ends so that it couldn't fall out, then eased the grenade the rest of the way out of the can and secured the safety lever with a piece of ten-gauge wire. Fetterman then untied the cord from around the grenade and resecured it to a small rock, which he placed back in the can.

Whoever came along and tripped over the cord now would have the thrill of a lifetime without having to pay for it with his life, and if the party who planted the grenade came back to check on his trap, he would get a surprise that was sure to make him very uneasy.

It was a good joke, and Fetterman smiled briefly at it. It really didn't matter who had set the trap, or who triggered it, and if the person who hit the cord happened to be a small Hmong child, he'd learn a valuable lesson and would live to pass it on to his playmates.

In the process of arranging the joke, however, Fetterman learned two things that he didn't find at all amusing. First, he found that the inside of the can was still shiny. The fact that it showed no sign of oxidation indicated that it hadn't been there long, and hence, that the trail wasn't as abandoned as it had been made to appear. At any rate, someone had been in the area in the past week or so.

Second, there was something vaguely familiar about the color of the twine. A bit of the rust-colored substance had flaked onto his hands as he worked with the string, leaving a reddish-brown dust. Fetterman sniffed at it and then put his tongue to his fingers. The taste in his mouth was faintly coppery. The twine had been camouflaged with human blood.

Fetterman had an afterthought and unscrewed the fuse from the grenade. Soviet F-1 grenades all had their fuses stamped with a number indicating the seconds the fuse would burn before detonation once the safety lever had been released. The normal delay was anywhere from three to five seconds, although Fetterman had in the past found some with as much as a ten-second delay. This was was stamped 0, indicating no delay. Had the safety lever come off while Fetterman was arranging his little joke, the grenade would have exploded instantly. Presumably it had been designed specifically for booby-trapping. He made a mental note to be careful about inspecting all Soviet grenades in the future before trying to use them.

Fetterman backed up and told the others what he had found.

"Jesus! Who do you suppose did it? The heads, I mean," said Wysoski. "Man! That's really insane."

Fetterman shrugged. "It's an insane kind of war. The villagers could have done it to frighten away the Communists, or the Communists could have done it as a warning to the villagers not to come back here, if they drove them away. It's a Soviet grenade, and a GI issue C-rat can. Take your pick."

"Where would the villagers have gotten hold of American C-rations?" asked Updike.

Fetterman shrugged again. "Maybe we're not the only team in the area. Or maybe they got it from the CIA. The Agency has been running their own operations in Laos for a long time. Hell, maybe they got it off some VC who picked it up off one of our guys or bought it on the black market in Saigon, Luang Prabang or Vietiane. You can pay your nickel and take your choice."

"All right. So what do we do now?" asked Paulsen.

"We go ahead and have a look at the village," said Gerber. "Only we do it very very carefully. Everybody stay sharp in case the enemy's in there waiting for us. But don't get trigger-happy. If there are villagers there, and if they're the ones responsible for those heads on those poles, the last thing we want to do is provoke a war through some misunderstanding. Let's keep in mind that the idea is to get them to help us kill the Communists and not the other way around. We'll proceed to the edge of the village and then Fetterman, Breneke, Paulsen and I will go in and have a look around while the rest of you cover us from the edge of the ville. If anything doesn't look right, we'll pull out fast and you guys can hammer whatever's chasing us. If everything looks okay, I'll signal and you can come on in."

"Captain Gerber, wouldn't it be better to let me take the men in rather than risk yourself?" said Updike.

"If I thought there was going to be any risk. I'd send Fetterman in alone," said Gerber.

"Oh, thank you very much, Captain. I *really* like that idea."

Gerber smiled. "You're welcome, Tony."

"Seriously, John," Gerber said to Updike, "thanks for volunteering, but we'll do it my way. You don't speak Hmong, and I want an experienced officer in charge of the men in case anything does go wrong."

"Yes, sir," answered Updike. "We won't let you down."

"Master Sergeant, may I have a word with you in private before we go in?" asked Gerber.

"Certainly, Captain." When they had walked a short distance away, Fetterman asked, "What was all that crap about, sir? You don't speak Hmong, either, as I recall."

"True," answered Gerber, "but Updike doesn't know that. At least not yet. Beside, I don't need to. I've got you for an interpreter."

"Then why the little charade?"

"Updike doesn't even speak Lowland Lao."

"Again, sir, you don't, either, as I recall."

"No, but I've worked with indigenous people before. He hasn't. He doesn't have the experience to understand that a single wrong gesture or even a grunt at the inappropriate time can cause you all kinds of trouble. Paulsen speaks Lao and has been to the language school to learn Hmong, so he comes with us. Besides, it's his job to set up a network of Hmong agents, so he might as well meet them up front. Breneke comes with us just because I trust him to keep his head. Don't ask me why. I can't say exactly. He caught on pretty quickly when the rope broke back at the abandoned camp, but more than that, I've just got a feeling about him. Anyway, Updike's just a little too conventional in his thinking. I'm surprised he stayed in the Special Forces after his first tour. Besides, I don't entirely trust ringknockers. They're all too worried about their careers for this kind of work. And I wanted to have a chance to speak to you alone without attracting too much attention. I need to ask you the question Updike should have asked, but didn't.''

"I guess you'd better ask it, then, sir," said Fetterman.

"All right. The question is, then, not where would the villagers get hold of American C-rations, but where would they get hold of enough weapons to wipe out a platoon of Pathet Lao and leave their heads on pikes along the trail?"

Fetterman looked away for a moment, then looked Gerber square in the eyes. "Well, Captain, I suppose it's just possible that perhaps not all of that equipment we were supposed to destroy when we pulled out six years ago got properly accounted for."

"I see," said Gerber. "And how much would you estimate got improperly accounted for?"

Fetterman didn't bat an eye. "I'd would estimate half a dozen Thompsons and two cases of M-2 carbines, plus all the captured stock we had on hand at the time. Say about thirty automatic weapons altogether, and maybe a like number of rifles, mostly Chicom Type 53s."

"I see," said Gerber. "Did your recall orders include the destruction of captured stock?"

"The captured stock wasn't specifically mentioned, Captain, although the orders did say all weapons and matériel."

"In that case," said Gerber, "I think it might be best if you made it clear to the village chief that his six Thompsons and ten carbines were captured from the enemy, as well. Preferably after your team withdrew. I'd recommend you do that at the first available opportunity you have to speak with him in private."

"Yes, sir," said Fetterman. He hesitated, then continued. "Captain, I had to do it. I couldn't leave them naked for the Pathet Lao to just walk over."

"Of course you couldn't," said Gerber. "And I haven't the faintest idea what you're talking about. Do what?"

"Yes, sir. Thank you, sir."

"All right, then, let's go in and take a look, shall we?"

"Certainly, Captain."

Heeding the warning of the booby trap, they didn't walk on the trail but paralleled it about a dozen yards off in the brush. The walking was rough, and they moved with extra caution to avoid any other unpleasant surprises. It took nearly forty-five minutes to reach the village that way. Fetterman estimated it would have taken only ten if they had simply walked down the trail, but no one wanted to do that.

When they pushed into the clearing, Fetterman felt his heart sink. The place looked deserted, and the scene was as bad if not worse than the abandoned camp had been. The huts here hadn't simply fallen down from disuse, they had had the walls blown out of them or been burned to the earth. The ground was littered with rusting, spent brass ammunition cases. Inside the village not so much as a dog or a chicken moved.

"Well, I guess we've at least partially got our answer, Captain," said Fetterman. "Somebody fought a hell of a battle here."

Gerber nodded. "Let's check it out. Nice and easy, everybody, just in case it's not quite as deserted as it looks."

They spread out so that there was about three yards between each of them, then the four men walked into the village, weapons ready, but held in a nonthreatening posture. Updike and the others covered them from the tree line.

Everywhere it was the same. The houses had either had their walls blown out, collapsing the roof, probably by some kind of satchel charge, or they had been burned, leaving only blackened ash grown over with weeds. There were no animals in evidence. In the center of the main street was the skeleton of a dog. Like the skulls that had lined the trail into the village, it was bleached white by the sun, indicating that it had been there for some time. At the center they found the village well. It, too, had been blasted with explosives and was filled in by dirt. As they stood there surveying the destruction, Fetterman spoke softly. "Captain, I don't think we're alone."

Fetterman had scarcely spoken when a dozen men appeared at the far end of the village. They were armed with a variety of weapons, including AK-47s, SKS carbines, U.S. M-2 carbines and bolt-action Mosin-Nagant 53 carbines. One of the men carried a tommy gun.

"Stay calm, everybody," Gerber ordered. "Tony, are those your Hmong?"

Fetterman stared. "It's pretty far, Captain, but I don't think I know any of them. They look kind of— Wait a minute. Behind them, sir."

Now Gerber stared. Behind the first group a second group had suddenly appeared. Two men on either side flanked a small, slightly bent figure who walked with apparent difficulty, using the aid of a staff. All were armed.

"Tony, that guy in the middle," said Gerber. "Is it Tou Bee?"

"Let's find out. Stay here please, sir. I'll let you know when it's safe to come forward."

He let his submachine gun hang from its strap looped over his head so that the weapon was across his chest in easy reach. Then, with his hands held out to his sides to show they were clear, he walked toward the men at the far end of the village.

As Fetterman approached, the men raised their weapons in a threatening manner, and he halted with arms still outstretched, then called to them in Hmong, identifying himself as an American and a friend. He hoped that they considered Americans to be friendly.

For a moment nothing happened as everyone stood frozen. Then there was a shout, and the tribesmen lowered their weapons as the figure with the walking stick hobbled rapidly forward. Reaching Fetterman, he threw down the stick and grabbed the master sergeant by both arms, hugging him, then pushed him back and held him at arm's length.

"So!" said Tou Bee Cha. "The White Porcupine has at last returned to us. It is good that you have come back, my son. I felt it always in my heart that you would. Let me look at you."

Fetterman looked, too, but wished he didn't have to. Tou Bee Cha seemed to have aged thirty years since he had last seen him. His face was etched with lines of pain, and a very jagged scar ran along his cheek and down his neck onto his bare shoulder. There was something strange about his left eye, as well.

"You must forgive an old man for not recognizing his son sooner," Tou Bee said, "but I cannot see so very well anymore. The Communist grenade that left me with this scar cost me the use of my left eye. It is still in my head, but it does not see. The spirits have left me with my good right eye to see the sights of my rifle for killing Communists, however."

"Thank you, Father, for welcoming me," said Fetterman. "I didn't know if you would be happy to see me, or even if you were still alive."

"What?" Tou Bee replied. "Should a man be unwelcome in his own home? You are my son. Should a man not welcome his own son when he returns after being gone so long? And as for the rest, as you can see, I am not the man I once was, but I am still alive. The spirits have not claimed me yet, and will not, I think, soon. I am too old and mean to die."

"Father, what happened to the village?" asked Fetterman.

"Bah! It is the work of bad spirits. When you and your friends left us, we remained for a time at the high place in the rocks, as you had told me to do. We should have stayed there. It was a good place to fight the Vietminh and Pathet Lao from. But not all of the men felt as I did. You will remember that there were dissenters even before you left. In time many of them came to feel that we should return here to the village we had left when you persuaded us to go to the High Rock. The dissenters were very persuasive in their arguments, and convinced many others. The High Rock was too far from the fields and had no water of its own, and it was time to harvest the poppy once again. They convinced enough that we should return here to be nearer the fields, and I could not stand against them and remain chief, so we moved back here. It was a mistake. I should have fought them harder.''

"You moved back and the Pathet Lao came," said Fetterman.

"Not the Pathet Lao. It was the Vietminh, the North Vietnamese. At first they did not bother us, and for a time we did not bother them. Two seasons passed, and we had not killed a single one of the sons of dogs. Then one day they came without warning. They blew up and burned our houses. They killed old men, women and children. They killed our cattle and our pigs and chickens. They blew up and burned down our houses and they raped and sodomized our women. They tried to take away our young men. We fought back with the weapons you had left with us, but there were too many of them and they destroyed our village. They tried to kill us all, but they did not succeed. Some of us escaped, and now we kill them."

"I saw some heads along the old trail to the village," Fetterman told him. "Are they our people or the enemy?"

"They are Vietminh," said Tou Bee. "The Communists sent another group back to finish what the first started, but this time we were ready for them. We killed them all and left the sun to whiten their bones. Then we left their heads along the trail as a warning to other Vietminh. Come back if you wish, we say, but know that you will die here if you do. The Communists turned our village into a wasteland. Now we hunt them, and when we find them . . ." He drew his hand across his throat.

"Much has changed," he said, "since you went away, my son. The Hmong of Muang Xam Teu are not so many as we once were, but the Communists have not yet succeeded in exterminating us. Not quite. And before we are gone from this mountain, the heads of many more Communist dogs will join their brothers in lining the trail as you saw before. This mountain has become more than just our home. It is a sacred place to us now because of the memories we honor of those the Vietminh killed here. We have given our mountain a name. We call it Phou Phi Muang Xam Teu.''

"The Mountain of the Spirit of Muang Xam Teu," said Fetterman. "It's a good name. But tell me, Father, is this all that remains of our village and our people? Surely you don't live here."

"No. To remain here now that the Vietminh know of this place would be too dangerous. We have built a new village. It is not far from here and is well hidden. The Communists do not know of it. I will take you there at dark, but we must leave very soon. There you will find the rest of our people."

"How many are left?"

The old man looked thoughtful for a moment. "I was never very good with numbers, the way you tried to teach me to count, my son. There are perhaps ten times as many as you see here, and ten times again. That is all."

Fetterman did some rapid figuring in his head. "Christ! That's less than 350 people left out of fifteen hundred. Father, are we so few?"

"As I say, I am not so good with numbers," answered Tou Bee Cha. "Perhaps there are more, perhaps less. You will see for yourself tonight."

"If the village has moved, what were you doing here?" asked Fetterman.

"Hunting the Vietminh and Pathet Lao. We always pass through here when we are returning from looking for the Communists, so that if they follow us, they will think we are still here. We leave many traps for them along the trails. You are lucky that you did not get caught in one of them."

"Yes," said Fetterman. "I know. I found one of them on the trail with the skulls—a grenade in a tin can."

"The first of many," agreed Tou Bee. "You avoided the trail afterward?"

"I felt it wise."

"It was indeed, my son. The others are not so easy to find. That one, like the skulls, is a warning to the Vietminh. I am glad you were not injured by it."

"Father, the grenade that you used to set the trap, where did you get it?"

"Several days ago we ambushed a small Vietminh patrol. One of the Communist dogs was carrying a whole rucksack of them."

"Are any of your warriors carrying those grenades now?"

"Yes. Of course. We distributed the grenades among our fighters in order to return them to the Vietninh. Minus the pins, of course."

"Has anyone tried to use one of those grenades since you found them?"

"No. The Communists have not dared to show their faces in this area since. We have been looking for them, but unable to find them. Perhaps they have grown weary of the sport. Every time they send a patrol here, the patrol dies."

"More likely they've been too preoccupied with their annual dry-season offensive on the Plain of Jars," said Fetterman. "Listen to me, Father. None of the men should use the grenades until I've had a chance to examine them. Some of them are set to explode as soon as the safety lever is released. If any of our warriors tries to use such a grenade, he will be killed before he can throw it a safe distance. There's a way to tell which grenades are dangerous, but I have to examine each one."

"I understand," said Tou Bee Cha. "I will tell them."

"And now, Father, I've brought some friends with me. They're Americans and have come with me to help us fight the Communists. May I introduce them?"

"Of course."

Fetterman waved Gerber, Breneke and Paulsen forward. "This is Captain Gerber," said Fetterman. "He doesn't speak our language, but he's a good warrior and my friend. He's my American chief, just as you are chief of the Hmong of Muang Xam Teu."

For a moment the old man's eyes flashed with anger. "Is this the one who made you take the weapons and go away from us?"

"No, Father," Fetterman answered quickly. "He's my friend. I didn't even know him then. It was another chief who ordered us to leave. This man has come to help us fight the Communists. He's like a brother to me."

"What's he saying?" asked Gerber.

"He asked if you were the American chief who made the White Star Team leave," Fetterman translated. "Not a popular fellow in these parts."

"I hope you set the record straight," said Gerber.

Slowly the glare on Tou Bee Cha's face subsided. Abruptly he reached out and grasped Gerber by the bicep with his left hand, then shook his right. "Then he is welcome," said Tou Bee.

Fetterman introduced Paulsen, who greeted the village chief in slow but reasonably decent Hmong and requested a private meeting with the chief later so that they could discuss setting up a network of informants to help keep track of the Pathet Lao, VC and NVA. Tou Bee, pleased to find that one of his adopted son's friends spoke Hmong, agreed to discuss the matter but offered the opinion that it would be difficult to do very much because the villagers were so few in number and because the Communists normally kept to the valley, which the Hmong avoided. Fetterman also introduced Breneke, who nodded politely and exchanged a two-handed handshake with the chief. Then Gerber spoke again.

"Please tell the chief that we've come to help him fight the Communists. That if he'll help us, we'll give him weapons and help train his men how to use them, and that we have other men with us, waiting in the forest, whom I'd like him to meet." Fetterman translated, and when the old man nodded his assent, Gerber signaled the rest of the team to come forward and each man was introduced in turn.

Before they set out for the village, White and Portland examined Tou Bee's injured foot and pronounced it infected from a thorn the old man had stepped on. Tou Bee sat stoically while White used a scalpel, probe and forceps to remove the offending object, cleaned and dressed the wound and gave the chief a shot of penicillin. The Hmong, who had no modern medicines and therefore had developed no resistance to antibiotics, often reacted with amazing results to Western drugs, and White expressed the confident opinion that the evil-looking inflammation would be completely cleared up within a week. Gerber then offered to rig a stretcher so that the chief could be carried back to his village, but Tou Bee refused this, stated that he had led his warriors out to fight the Communists and would lead them back home.

The Hmong fighters helped carry the Green Berets' equipment, and with them leading the way, the combined party reached the new Hmong settlement shortly before dusk.

Fetterman, who had felt so depressed by the sight of the deserted fortress and destroyed village was absolutely aghast at what he found in the new village. There were at most fifty houses, and while all were in good repair, the average-size family occupying one of the huts consisted of only four or five people, a small family indeed among the Hmong, who didn't practice birth control, normally lived in extended family groups and were fairly free and open about the practice of premarital sex. A disproportionate number of the villagers were women and children, or very old.

"Many of the young men died when the Vietminh attacked our village," Tou Bee explained. "They fought hard so that the women and children could have time to escape, but we had very few weapons and little ammunition. Many of the women and young girls did not escape, and the Communist dogs abused them and did terrible things to them before they killed them. I did not see these things happen myself, since I had been wounded and was unconscious for a time, but the details were told to me by those who saw it and rescued me, and I saw the results later. When the battle was over, the Vietminh bayoneted the wounded in order to save bullets. Those of our people who were foolish enough to surrender were tortured before they were executed. The men were emasculated and had their organs stuffed into their mouths. The women and girls were impaled on sharpened bamboo stakes forced up their vaginas. The old ones had their heads held underwater until they had drowned, and the infants were thrown into the fires. In all my years I had never before seen such savagery. The men who did it were not men. They were animals. And calling them that is being greatly unfair to the animal world.''

"My captain and I will need to inspect the men and their weapons, Father, so that we may understand what we'll need to fight the Communists,'' Fetterman told him.

"That will not be hard,'' Tou Bee Cha replied. "We have more warriors than we have weapons. Most of those you left with us were lost when the Vietminh attacked the village. Of those that remain many are broken and we could not fix them. We had no spare parts, but some we made to shoot by taking the parts of other weapons that were also broken. Now we have only a few, with little ammunition, and what we can take from the Communists we kill.''

"We've brought a dozen extra rifles with us,'' Fetterman told him. "And we'll be able to get more. Good weapons and plenty of ammunition, as many weapons as you can find warriors for. But first we have to see what we've got to work with.''

"In the morning,'' said Tou Bee. "Tonight there will be a feast to celebrate the return of my oldest son. The village will be glad to know that the White Porcupine has come back to us.''

"We should do it tonight,'' Fetterman insisted. "In case the Vietminh come. We must be ready for the enemy.''

The old man was adamant. "Could you provide these other weapons you speak of tonight? Have you brought with you ammunition to be fired from the Communist weapons we have captured? Do not tell me. I know. The answer to both questions is no. Tonight we will kill a gaur and hold a feast. Tomorrow will be early enough to think of killing. Tonight we celebrate. You have not even seen your brothers."

Fetterman knew there would be no arguing with the old chief. It was useless when he had made up his mind about something, and the old man was right, anyway. There really wasn't anything they could do before tomorrow, and the villagers would insist on a party. The Hmong were a very social people, and almost any excuse was considered a good cause for a celebration. The arrival of twelve Americans bearing gifts of rifles with which to kill the Vietminh would be cause for a minor festival. There was nothing to do but let the event occur and then tomorrow try to get back to the business of running the war.

"Are my little brothers safe and well?" asked Fetterman, letting the matter drop.

"They are well, but not so little now. Both have become warriors in their own right. Tou Yang has claimed the heads of three Communists already, and Tou Lo has killed two of the dogs, one Pathet Lao and one Vietminh. You would be proud of your brothers."

Fetterman wasn't sure that an ability to kill an enemy and then display his head on a pike was a particularly commendable trait in a brother, but he could understand it, given the circumstances. He figured that Tou Lo would be about twenty years old now, and Tou Yang pushing eighteen. That was pretty young to be learning about killing people, but then, he reminded himself, so were the GIs in Vietnam, whose average age was only nineteen. In fact Fetterman himself had been only eighteen years old when he had killed his first man, a German soldier somewhere among the hedgerows of Normandy in World War II.

"You haven't spoken of my mother or my sisters," said Fetterman. "Are they well also?"

The old chieftain's eyes clouded over, and he laid a hand on Fetterman's arm. "Your mother is dead, my son. So, too, is little Tou Mai, and our youngest, Tou Blia, whom you did not know. She was born after you went away. As for Tou Xeng and Tou Ying, they were taken away by the Vietminh. No one has seen them since. Only Tou Pa and your brother's wife, Tou Mali Kue, remain. They look after the family now and tend to the cooking and sewing. I have tried to convince them both to take a husband, but they will not hear of it."

"I'm sorry to hear of the loss of my sisters and of your wife," said Fetterman, meaning it. "And what of my brothers? Has either of them married?"

The cloud in Tou Bee's face was replaced by a quick flash of white teeth. "No, but Tou Yang sees much of Xeng Xiong, and I think they will make their vows soon."

"And Tou Lo?" Fetterman pressed.

The old chief laughed. "Not that one. He is afraid of marriage, I think, but not of making the sex. He has so many girlfriends that half the males in the village are angry with him."

"Sounds like bachelorhood could be a dangerous occupation for him," observed Fetterman.

Tou Bee laughed again. "Maybe so, if he does not soon learn to leave the married women alone. But what can the others do if their women folk seek variety elsewhere? It is not Tou Lo's fault that the spirits have seen fit to endow him so richly that the women cannot resist the temptation of experiencing him."

"Are you saying my little brother is well hung?" asked Fetterman.

Tou Bee cackled and made a gesture with his hands. "Like the elephant. The males call him the One Who Is Too Big for His Loincloth. It is both an accurate description and a jealous complaint."

He laughed again, obviously taking much delight in relating the tale of his son's sexual prowess and dimensions, and

Fetterman laughed along with him, not so much at the story, but because it was good to know that Tou Bee hadn't lost his sense of humor despite all that had occurred.

Arrangements were made to house the team for the night with Tou Bee and two of his neighbors, and Fetterman explained the situation to Gerber, along with the planned celebration.

Gerber wasn't happy about splitting up the team or about the idea that all of them were expected to sit up most of the night getting smashed on Hmong liquor made of fermented corn or rice. He knew, however, that failing to participate fully would be seen as an insult by the villagers and could jeopardize future relations with them. He was forced to violate both the cardinal rule of warfare and all the rules of common sense.

Thus the men of MACV/SOG Special Operations Team Thunderhead found themselves the guests of honor at a celebration in a native village, surrounded by several thousand enemy soldiers, where they proceeded to dine on roast ox and get rip-roaring drunk.

7

PHOU PHI MUANG XAM
TEU, LAOS

Breneke felt the weight of something heavy press against him and snapped his eyes open, groping blindly for his submachine gun while he tried in vain to get the sleep out of his eyes and, at the same time figure out what the threat was. He'd had too much to drink of the fiery Hmong liquor last night, far too much, and he just wasn't functioning right. His head ached like someone had split it open with an ax, and there was a sparkling shower of brilliant pinpoints of light exploding in his brain, like a celestial meteor shower, when he tried to move too fast.

Gradually, as he finally managed to get a hand on the Swedish K, the sparklers settled down enough for him to focus, and he felt something push against him again. He looked down and discovered that he was sharing his bedroll with an attractive young Hmong girl who had snuggled up tightly against his body, pressing her buttocks into his crotch. He sat bolt upright, as if he had been bitten by a snake, knocking aside the blanket, then quickly retrieved it and tucked it around the girl. Although he was still fully dressed, the girl was stark naked.

"Mein Gott!" he exploded, lapsing into his childhood German. "What the hell's going on here?"

"Have a nice nap?" asked Fetterman, grinning broadly.

"What the hell's she doing here?" Breneke sputtered.

"Offhand, I'd say sleeping," remarked Fetterman dryly. "What's the matter, Klaus? Didn't you invite her?"

"I did not!" said Breneke, easing back to a semireclining position. "At least I don't think I did. Jesus, Mary and Joseph! My head hurts. What in God's name was that stuff we drank last night and how much did I have?"

"Just good old-fashioned Hmong corn liquor," said Fetterman. "I can't say for sure, because I wasn't monitoring your intake closely, but I'd say you put away about a fifth all by yourself. As to the young lady, actually, I believe she picked you to sleep with."

"Why me?" Breneke said.

"I believe it had something to do with the color of your hair."

"My hair?"

"In case you hadn't noticed, there aren't too many fair-haired Hmong. Some of the younger children have never seen a person with blond hair, and the rest remember only vaguely the guys on my old team who were blond. If I understood the young lady correctly, she picked you to go to bed with because she figured anyone with blond hair must have been touched by the spirits. She thinks you're very powerful, that you have much magic."

Breneke glanced at the fly of his fatigues and was relieved to see that it was closed. "Uh, we didn't, that is, the girl and I, we didn't happen to do anything last night, did we?"

"You mean other than dancing stark naked in front of the entire village? I'm afraid you'll have to ask her that yourself. I was busy sleeping. You'd better wait until after breakfast, though. Captain Gerber wants a team meeting out in the square in twenty minutes. Oh, and, Klaus, treat the young lady gently, will you? She's my adopted kid sister, and after all, she's only sixteen, although by Hmong standards, that's about two years past the initial marriageability limit."

"My Heidi will kill me," groaned Breneke, thinking of his fiancée.

"It's a customary way to welcome a new guest," said Fetterman. "Especially a strong young handsome one. Surely Heidi will understand you were only trying not to offend anyone."

"You don't know Heidi," insisted Breneke. "She's about as understanding as a gestapo interrogation officer. I'll be lucky if she only castrates me."

"Rather a narrow attitude, I'd say," remarked Fetterman. "Better get a move on if you don't want to eat C-rats. A hot breakfast is now being served on the patio." Chuckling to himself, he left.

Breneke watched him go, not entirely sure the master sergeant had been joking about the dancing naked in front of the village. He did remember dancing with a lot of the villagers last night, but he was pretty sure he had kept his clothes on. At least he hoped he had.

Breneke slipped out from beneath the camouflaged poncho liner blanket, being careful not to wake the girl, and collected his steel pot, webgear and weapon before going outside. He found the others in the square, actually just a wide spot in the village's main street surrounding the community well. There were several cooking fires going in the village, and Dave Dollar, the senior commo specialist, was presiding over a couple of beds of red-hot coals at the edge of the square, where he was stirring up omelets made with ham and fresh eggs. Fetterman had a pot of coffee brewing and was cooking up something resembling bacon in a huge cast-iron skillet he'd found somewhere. The whole scene had a picnic atmosphere and would have resembled a camping trip breakfast if it hadn't been for all the automatic weapons and grenades in evidence.

The meal being prepared smelled good, and Breneke impatiently awaited his turn to be served, surprised at how hungry he felt, despite the excruciating hangover. When he got his food, he shoveled about half of it down before he realized how spicy it was. Without thinking, he grabbed up his coffee to wash down the fiery omelet and nearly scalded his tongue on the piping hot liquid, much to the entertainment of the others.

"Jesus, Dave!" he gasped, his eyes watering and the sweat popping out on his head. "What did you put in there?"

"I just put in a little bit o'red peppers I found growin' on a bush over yonder," drawled Dollar. "If it ain't hot enough fo' ya, I could maybe add some Tabasco sauce. I got me a little bottle in mah pack." That provoked another round of laughter from the team before the men resumed their meal.

The breakfast was a considerably better meal than the men were used to getting while on a mission, and Gerber gave them the extra time to enjoy it, allowing even a few minutes for those who regularly indulged to have a cigarette. Gerber, not wishing to get back into an old and difficult-to-break habit, declined the smoke Fetterman offered him and noticed that the master sergeant, although making a great production of reaming and filling his pipe, didn't light it. Evidently being back here among the tribesmen he had previously worked with had a calming effect on Fetterman's jitters about the mission.

When the last man crushed out his cigarette, many of them having offered a smoke to the Hmong, who politely accepted, men and women alike, Gerber found he didn't need to call the men together. One by one they drifted over and sat quietly on the ground, waiting for him to begin.

"Gentlemen, we've got a lot of work to do," said Gerber when the last man was seated cross-legged in the dirt. "As I see it, our first priority is to see what we've got to work with. Master Sergeant Fetterman and I, along with Sergeants Gunn and Breneke, will conduct a muster and arms inspection as soon as we can arrange with Chief Tou Bee Cha to assemble his men.

"I want Sergeants White and Portland to set up a clinic and see what the state of health of these villagers is. We'll send the men along to you for physicals as soon as we've had a chance to hold muster. You two fellows will have a busy day of it, I'm afraid.

"Sergeants Dollar and Wysoski need to check over the radio equipment and figure out what they'll need to do about stringing antennae so that we can get a message off to C-team at Kontum and let them know we've made contact and the natives are willing to work with us. We'll work out the exact text after we meet again this evening and compare notes so that we know what supplies to request."

"Cap'n Gerber," drawled Dollar, "if ya don' mind ma sayin' so, that might not be such a hot idea, transmittin' from here, I mean. Our defense is pretty thin right now, an' there's no point in giv'n ol' Charlie a good fix on our locale. Wysoski an' I can conduct the survey all right, but I think it might be better ta use a coupla repeater balloons we brought along. We can release 'em after sundown when the wind picks up a might an' set the delay on the recorders ta play back after half an hour or so. That way they'll have time ta drift a half dozen or so miles away from here before they start ta chatterin', an' if ol' Charlie's listenin', it'll give him two separate movin' targets to triangulate on. I'll set the autodestructs ta blow after an hour, so Charlie won't find anythin' other than debris, if'n he finds anythin' at all. We can jus' throw us up an inverted V antenna ta listen for the confirmation."

"Makes sense, Dave," said Gerber. "We'll do it that way. In the meantime, Rawlings and Chavez can have a look around and see what they can do about improving the defenses of this place. If you two can come up with recommendations by noon, we'll talk to the chief and try to get you a work detail organized for this afternoon. I want you to pay particular attention to finding some good sites for OPs and LPs and any remote early-warning systems we may be able to use as an outer perimeter. We've really got to get some decent security established around here as soon as possible."

Gerber turned to Updike. "Captain, that leaves you and Paulsen to figure out drop zones and landing sites for resupply and emergency extraction of the team. I'll ask the chief to supply you with his best scout as soon as possible to serve as a resource. I don't want any on-site reconnaissance patrols conducted yet to confirm the suitability of any locales. Just get his input on probable sites and grease-pencil them in on your map overlays. Some of these people have worked with Special Forces before, so we'll try to find you a scout who can understand maps. After that you can converse with the chief about establishing an intel and E & E net with any nearby villages that might be friendly to us.

"Master Sergeant Fetterman has arranged for some of the Hmong women to provide a hot lunch while we're working. I caution each of you to be careful about eating any raw fruits or vegetables, since we don't want anybody picking up any parasites. We'll all meet back here at 1700 hours to compare notes and plan where we go from here. Dismissed."

The team broke up, with each of the smaller teams going their separate ways to deal with their specific problems. It took about an hour and a half to get the village's fighting force assembled for inspection, the old chief having decided that it was too early for such foolishness after a hard night of partying. After all, he insisted, the men already knew how to fight the Communists and lacked only the weapons and ammunition to do so. With considerable gentle prodding from Fetterman, Tou Bee was finally persuaded that the Green Berets couldn't request the weapons until they knew what was needed, and so the inspection of variously hung-over villagers got under way.

It was a depressing fighting force that lined up along the main street. All told, there were about two hundred males, ranging in age from about thirteen to a few who were almost as old as the chief. Not even Tou Bee knew his own age exactly, but Fetterman estimated it to be close to sixty-five, which was fairly old for a Hmong.

Less than a quarter of the natives were equipped with any kind of weapon beyond a knife and a cross bow or spear, and those that did have a firearm were outfitted with a bewildering array of Chinese Communist, North Vietnamese and American hardware. One nearly toothless old grandfather, who might well have been even older than the chief, was armed with a French MAT-49 submachine gun, which he had lovingly maintained for a decade and a half. All the blueing had been worn from its metal surfaces by years of careful polishing, and not one bit of rust could be found on the weapon despite a total lack of cleaning supplies and oil on the old man's part. Breneke examined the submachine gun carefully, and it appeared to be in good working order, as did the half dozen spare magazines the elderly Hmong had likewise preserved, but the owner didn't have a single round of ammunition for his weapon.

Most of the remaining weapons weren't in as good shape as the French relic. Nearly all were badly rusted and some had considerably pitted bores due to the Hmong's lack of cleaning supplies. Several of them had broken or missing parts, usually springs, extractors, firing pins or operating rods, rendering them useless. There were only two cleaning rods in the entire village. One, for an M-2 carbine, had been bent and more or less straightened back out; the other was for a Chinese Type 53 carbine. There wasn't an ounce of bore solvent or oil in the entire village. By questioning the Hmong warriors through Fetterman, Breneke learned that the Hmong had been using animal fat to grease their weapons and boiling water to clean them.

Tou Bee, who as village headman normally led his soldiers into battle against the Vietminh and Pathet Lao patrols, had done a good job of designating his automatic weapons men and seeing to it that they had more ammunition than the others, but this often meant only a couple of magazines for a captured AK-47. Fetterman had seen to it that several thousand rounds of .45-caliber ammunition was left behind with the six tommy guns the White Star Team had managed to overlook when they withdrew, but less than a hundred now remained and many of those showed such signs of corrosion that none of the

Americans would have wanted to risk firing them, especially in combat. Only two of the Thompsons were still functional, both with badly pitted bores. The M-2 carbines had proven more reliable, perhaps because each had an oiler as part of the sling attachment, and one of the carbine cleaning rods, however bent, had survived. Six of the original ten remained in working condition, although Gunn felt the NRA would have rated them as poor to fair. There were two magazines per carbine, some with bent and crudely restraightened feed lips, and no one had enough ammo left to completely fill both 30-round magazines. Many of the men with Type 53 or SKS carbines had fewer then ten rounds of ammunition. The only thing that was really in good condition or supply was Soviet F-1 type hand grenades, of which there were nearly two dozen, and all of those turned out to be equipped with the zero-delay booby-trapping fuse.

As they inspected the troops, Fetterman recognized a few who had received some training by the White Star Team he'd served with six years previously, and he tapped them out as potential NCOs for the fledgling Hmong strike force. Tou Bee rapidly realized what he was doing, and pointed out others. By the time they finished inspecting the troops, the Hmong had been sorted into three distinct groups.

One group, composed of the very old and the very young, about fifty altogether, would make up the village defense force. A second group of twenty-four Hmong, all with previous training and experience with the White Star Team, would make up the command cadre consisting of four platoon leaders, four assistant platoon leaders and twelve squad leaders. The third group, made up of the remaining hundred and fifty or so Hmong, would be divided into four platoons of three squads each, with each squad having about twelve men. It would be up to the leader of each squad to choose his own assistant, subject to the approval of the chief and the Special Forces personnel. For the time being the twelve Green Berets would serve as company headquarters until the Hmong could learn the ropes.

In addition, each Special Forces officer or NCO would be directly responsible for advising one of the twelve squads. Gerber would also advise one of the platoon leaders who spoke a fair amount of French, while Fetterman and Paulsen would each take a platoon.

It was decided that Updike and Gunn would jointly advise the fourth group, which would become the weapons-and-support platoon when it was determined that one of the Hmong officers had learned German as a boy from some missionary nuns who had once maintained a leprosy asylum about thirty miles away. The Hmong had been orphaned as a boy and had taken a liking to the nuns when a couple of the sisters visited the village nearly twenty-five years ago. With the blessing of the man who was then village chief, he had been allowed to go live with them and had stayed with the nuns until they were driven away by the Communists sometime in the mid-fifties. He had then returned to his native village by foot, taken a bride and reestablished himself in the Hmong community. The man had learned a fair amount of nursing skills from the sisters, as well, and it was felt that he would be of some assistance to White and Portland in training medics, and to Breneke and Gunn in teaching the Hmong how to operate mortars and heavy machine guns.

Gerber didn't know if anyone had ever tried to field a company of largely untrained soldiers utilizing so many languages for communications, but thought that it must be some kind of new record. It was a nearly impossible task that faced them, but one that was typical of the sort of challenges Special Forces soldiers were routinely expected to handle.

The problem, of course, was what to do about Tou Bee Cha. As village chief, it was both his right and duty to lead the Hmong into battle, and while there was no denying that he was remarkably fit for a man his age, Gerber was concerned about his ability to keep up with the younger men under combat conditions. The problem was resolved, at least temporarily, when in a surprise move Tou Bee delcared that Fetterman, as his eldest son, was appointed acting war chief of the village and would lead the warriors against the hated Communists, at least until such time as the chief's foot had healed properly and he could resume his rightful duties.

While Gerber found this amusing, Updike was a bit nonplussed by the notion. He reluctantly had to admit that it made the greatest sense, however, since Fetterman was the only one who spoke Hmong fluently.

Fetterman was also concerned, not only because the chief's decision put him over the two captains, but because he was unsure how well the decision would be received by the chief's natural sons. After receiving assurances from both Tou Lo and Tou Yang that they respected his greater knowledge of modern weapons and would honor their father's wish, Fetterman agreed to accept the post.

Fetterman's appointment as war chief was, of course, deemed sufficient cause by the villagers for another celebration, and plans immediately got under way for a second feast. It was almost enough to make Gerber, who was greatly concerned about establishing some form of real security for the village with outposts and patrols, throw up his hands in defeat, but Fetterman assured him that he would be able to keep things somewhat more restrained, although there was no getting around the fact that everyone would be expected to drink several toasts to the new war chief's health and success against the enemy. Eventually the situation was resolved by the decision to hold two celebrations, one that evening and one the following. That way half the Hmong and half the Green Berets could stand watch while the other half partied. Fetterman, however, as guest of honor, would be expected to attend both nights. It was the best compromise the Hmong would accept, and the Americans wisely decided not to force the issue.

Tou Bee, satisfied with the compromise, exempted the selected Hmong officers and NCOs from participation in the preparations for the festivities, and Gunn and Breneke, acting with Fetterman and Kong Moua, the German-speaking Hmong platoon leader, were able to conduct their first course in firearms instruction that afternoon, using the spare CAR-15s they had brought, as well as the team's weapons, to familiarize the Hmong with the proper procedures for operating, stripping, cleaning and reassembling not only the compact Colt carbines but also the M-60 machine gun. The Hmong proved to be good students and were genuinely interested in learning anything that would make them better killers of Communists. By evening each of the twenty students could properly strip and reassemble both weapons and demonstrate their functioning as well as any basic trainee.

When the team met near dusk for their progress meeting, Gerber felt that some real headway had been made. Despite the fact that the team had few resources with them, and both Chavez and Rawlings expressed the opinion that the village could never be made really fortified in its present location, claymores, grenade traps and a few trip flares had been set out and work was well under way on a punji moat to slow down any enemy advance along the most probable approach to the village. Updike and Paulsen had plotted the approximate location of no less than six possible sites where supplies could be dropped by parachute or a STOL aircraft might be able to get in, all within two days' walk of the village, and had determined several closer sites where helicopters might be able to get in to evac the team in an emergency. White and Portland had completed preliminary physicals on about half of the Hmong recruits and treated a number of the villagers for various ailments. Little progress had been made toward establishing an intel and E & E network, but that was to be expected. The nearest other Hmong village was nearly four days' walk away, and little could be done about setting up a system of informants until someone actually visited it.

When Gerber prepared his message to C-Detachment in Kontum that evening, informing them that the indigenous population had been successfully contacted and the Hmong were willing to help, he added with it an enormous request for supplies. The list included three 60 mm mortars with 120 rounds of high-explosive ammunition, twenty-four rounds of white phosphorus and forty-eight illumination shells. He also asked for four M-60 machine guns with four thousand rounds of ammunition; nine M-79 grenade launchers with 216 grenades; a dozen pistols; 180 CAR-15s; eighty thousand rounds of 5.56 mm ammunition; four more Swedish Ks with suppressors; three thousand rounds of 9 mm parabellum ammunition; a cleaning rod for every weapon ordered, along with a large supply of patches, solvent and gun oil; four additonal PRC-25 radios; fifty claymore mines; two hundred fragmentation hand grenades; two hundred pairs of boots of varying small sizes; and two hundred sets of camouflage fatigues, ranging from size extra small to medium.

He would have asked for a lot more, and a couple of thousand yards of barbed wire, but figured there was only so much the Hmong could carry at one time. Besides, based on Chavez and Rawlings's report about the impossibility of ever adequately protecting the village, he hoped to persuade the chief to return to the abandoned fortress atop the three-sided promontory. If they were to establish a new navigation electronics site for the Air Force, it would have to be there, anyway, and there was no point in ordering a bunch of barbed wire and antipersonnel mines until they were established in a locale where they could make good use of them.

Gerber finished his list by requesting twenty-four compasses and some additional maps, twenty whistles and some signal flares, two M-21 sniper rifles with both autoranging and Starlite scopes, four hundred rounds of match-grade ammunition for the M-21s, and then, just for the hell of it, added a request for two cases of beer, noting that the exact time of the drop and the location of the drop zone to be used would be sent in a few days.

Staff Sergeant Dollar then encoded the message, using the team's preestablished supply catalog and adding a request for additional medical supplies from White, which Gerber had approved. He then encrypted the message onto magnetic tape, using a crypto pad, and burned the sheet of flash paper on which the cipher key had been written. He attached the miniature tape transmitters to two separate black weather balloons, each about eight feet in diameter and armed the autodestruct timers. He then inflated the balloons with helium and set them adrift on the evening breeze. About forty-five minutes later Wysoski reported receiving confirmation of receipt of both transmissions, and a short time later that he had monitored the abruptly terminated marker tones from both balloons, indicating that the self-destruct charges had fired properly.

With the day's business thus concluded, half of Special Forces team Thunderhead, along with about thirty Hmong equipped with the new CAR-15s and their odd assortment of eclectic weapons, set out to establish an outpost and a semblance of a perimeter guard, while the remainder of the Green Berets prepared to receive their second hangover in as many nights.

Having formed a healthy respect for the Hmong liquor, the Americans were more circumspect in their imbibing and only sipped instead of drinking, with the result that when Fetterman indicated they could go off to bed without offering offense to the villagers, they were only fairly drunk instead of riproaring plastered.

Breneke had a bad time of it when Tou Pa indicated her intention to sleep with him again, but as neither Fetterman nor Paulsen were available to interpret his protests, he finally gave up and lay down beside her. He stoically endured her pointedly sexual caresses for perhaps ten minutes, and then, feeling himself beginning to grow aroused, gallantly turned his back to her and lay there in the darkness, trying to go to sleep but painfully aware of her warm presence beside him.

THE TEAM'S SECOND MORNING in the village started as had the first, with a hot breakfast, this one prepared by some of the Hmong women. It consisted of boiled rice and pork, made palatable by the addition of fried eggs washed down with more of Fetterman's campfire coffee.

After breakfast the weapons class resumed with a quick review of yesterday's lesson. In the meantime, other members of the team began combat and general first aid instruction and started a group of Hmong to work learning how to use a map and compass.

Around midmorning Paulsen and Updike, along with Kue Chaw, an assistant patrol leader whom Tou Bee had said was the best scout, and whom Fetterman remembered as being a good pathfinder, set out with a squad of Hmong to reconnoiter the evac LZs and check out one of the nearer potential supply drop sites. Their orders were simple: to evaluate the sites for future use and to avoid contact with the enemy at all costs.

They planned to return to the village shortly after dark, and Updike fervently hoped they would be able to comply with the orders. He felt it likely that the Hmong, who seemed a fairly trigger-happy lot, might well open fire immediately if the enemy was sighted, despite the carefully explained need for secrecy while the newly organized strike force was still in its infancy and very vulnerable to a coordinated Pathet Lao or NVA attack. He did his best to impress upon the Hmong, through Paulsen, that the Communists could muster a much larger and better equipped force than the villagers could field at the present time, and that it was vitally important the enemy not be alerted to their presence, and most particularly to the presence of Americans in the area, until the strike force was strong enough to repel an assault. Despite repeated warnings, he had little faith that the Hmong would heed them if a Communist patrol was sighted, and was greatly relieved that none of the enemy appeared.

Gerber and Fetterman conducted their own survey of the surrounding terrain in midafternoon and slowly came to the inevitable conclusion that Chavez and Rawlings were absolutely correct in their estimation. Although the village could be strengthened with the addition of barbed wire, more mines and weapons bunkers, it was a less-than-ideal defensive position and there was really no way they could ever expect to hold the village against a determined NVA or Pathet Lao assault with only two hundred Hmong soldiers and no real artillery or air support. The inescapable truth was that the only truly defensible position around was the Rookery fortress the Hmong had abandoned. It was also the ideal site for locating the advanced electronic navigational aides the Air Force wanted to put in. It would be up to Fetterman to convince Tou Bee that the village should return there.

It wasn't an easy task. The Hmong had convinced themselves that the Rookery was affected by bad *phi*. There was no natural water supply there, it was far from their fields, and the Americans had abandoned them once before after persuading them to move there. Gerber and Fetterman worked out a plan whereby food could be supplied by regular airdrops, the stone cisterns could be rebuilt and large, collapsible rubber storage bladders, normally used in Vietnam by the Americans for aviation fuel storage, could be brought in to augment the cisterns. That left the problem of filling them, which would require a minor engineering miracle.

After consulting with Chavez and Rawlings, it was determined that a pair of three-inch-diameter plastic water pipes could be installed just below ground level. They would have to run the nearly two-and-a-half-mile distance from the nearest year-round stream, a small river that occasionally dwindled to little more than a creek during the dry season, up the side of the mountain to the Rookery. A system of portable gasoline-powered pumps could be used to suck the water uphill to holding sites, where it could be temporarily stored in the collapsible bladders before being pumped on up the mountain to the rebuilt cisterns and additional bladders. Once the cisterns and bladders at the Rookery were filled, the Hmong would have more than enough water to last them through the dry season should the enemy discover the water line and cut it. The disadvantage was that the Communists might discover the pipe and trace it to the relocated village, but an electronic alarm system could be installed to give warning of discovery, and by then the Rookery would be transformed into an aerielike fortress able to withstand an assault by anything less than an enemy regiment.

The remaining stumbling block was the village shaman. Charged with interpreting signs from the spirit world and exorcising bad *phi*, he was the second most powerful man in the village after the chief. He was also old, stubborn and very much opposed to returning to the rocky promontory. The only means by which Fetterman could hope to persuade the other villagers to return to the Rookery was through the man, whose name was Vas Pao Xiong, and in order to do that Fetterman would have to demonstrate that his magic was more powerful than Vas Pao's, yet do it without causing the elderly shaman to lose face in front of the villagers. It was a challenge that required considerable unconventional thought and a fair amount of outright hocus-pocus.

After consultation with Chavez and Rawlings, the demonstration of Fetterman's power was scheduled for that evening's celebration of his appointment as war chief. After Fetterman had spoken with Dave Dollar, spending nearly half an hour in secret with him, the two demolitions engineers slipped away to prepare the show. They worked all through the late afternoon and into early evening, and Fetterman began to doubt that their little trickery could be ready in time. The celebration was well under way when Gunn finally appeared and gave Fetterman a subtle nod to indicate that all was in readiness.

When there was an appropriate pause in the music and dancing, Fetterman stood and made his carefully prepared speech. "My fellow Hmong of Phou Phi Muang Xam Teu, your new war chief desires to speak with his brave warriors and with all who support them in their war against the hated Vietminh," he intoned gravely.

Gradually the revelers fell silent, anxious to hear what the new war chief had to say.

"After much thought I have reached a momentous decision," Fetterman continued. "We will return to the high place known to the Americans as the Rookery, and which the Hmong of Muang Xam Teu call the High Rock. There we will rebuild our fortress. We will make it into an impregnable place in which the Hmong of our village will be forever safe from the Vietminh and from which we will sweep down like birds of prey to crush our enemies and destroy them."

A low murmur ran through the crowd, and Fetterman could tell that his announcement hadn't been well received. Even Tou Bee wouldn't support him in this.

"My son, you are our war chief by my own hand, and I mean no disrespect, but is this wise?" asked Tou Bee. "The High Rock is a bad place. It is far from our fields. There is no water. And it is inhabited by evil *phi*. Surely it is better to remain here, where the water is good and the soil sweet."

"You are wise, Father," said Fetterman. "I, too, felt as you do. Here the land is better for farming. But the High Rock is a better place from which to kill the Communists. This was revealed to me in a dream last night when the spirits of our fallen relatives, slain at the hands of the Communist dogs, spoke to me. I do not speak to you now with my own voice alone, but with the voices of all their honored spirits. It is they who have shown me the way to victory over our enemies."

"I have received no message from the spirit world to return to the High Rock," said Vas Pao softly. "It is strange that the spirits would speak to you, an outsider, rather than through me."

Tou Bee's eyes blazed briefly. "My son is not an outsider. He is my son and my eldest. He is as much a Hmong as any man here, and I will not have him called an outsider."

"Of course," said Vas Pao quickly. "I meant only that he is not native-born to our people." Then he slyly added, "But the spirits speak through me and I have not heard their voices these past few nights. Perhaps the White Porcupine can explain why this is so?"

The old shaman wasn't going to make it easy, but Fetterman was prepared for him. "The spirits have revealed to me that I was chosen because they see my return to our people as a symbol of our return to the High Rock and as a symbol of our return as a village of great warriors who will strike fear into the hearts of our enemies," said Fetterman. "It has been revealed to me that a sign will be given that the bad spirits have been driven from the High Rock and that it should become our new home. From it we will be invincible in battle and will destroy our enemies utterly."

"And what is this sign to be?" asked Vas Pao.

"In my dream the spirits clearly spoke to me," said Fetterman. "They did not tell me what this sign would be, only that it would come."

"Ah," said Vas Pao. "I thought so."

"They revealed that the sign would come tonight," said Fetterman quickly, "when our great shaman Vas Pao Xiong summoned them from the afterlife to reveal their sign before all the members of our village."

"Bah! This is nonsense," said Vas Pao. "Our villagers are not even all here because you make them stand guard against imaginary enemies when they should be here with us at the celebration. You have divided our village and now you seek to make us abandon it all together."

"You are mistaken, wise one," said Fetterman. "I seek only to protect our village and to do what is good for our people. You do not understand this because the spirits have not yet revealed their plan to you as they have to me. If you will summon the spirits now, I will call in everyone, Hmong and American alike, so that the wish of the spirits may be fulfilled and so that you may see I speak the truth.''

Vas Pao suddenly assumed a crafty look. He was certain that this white devil of an American was up to something, but he couldn't see how he could perform any trickery with the entire village, including the Americans, assembled where he could keep an eye on them. He would go through the motions of summoning the spirits, and when no sign appeared, it would be the end of the matter. Fetterman would never dare to bring up the subject again after suffering such a loss of face. The old chief might even be compelled to remove his adopted son as war chief.

Runners were sent to call in the guards, and the Hmong and Americans gradually assembled around the huge ceremonial fire burning brightly in the center of the village. It was a perfect night for it, clear, and with the moon nearly full, and it was easy to believe that in this place and time the spirit world was close at hand.

The moon lighted the surrounding peaks, throwing high rock ridges and shelves into stark relief as the Hmong crowded in close around the flickering fire, the flames dancing high into the night. There was an expectant air that something, either good or bad, was about to happen as the old shaman rose and slowly took his place near the fire. Carefully he opened the small cloth bag he wore around his neck, which contained the bones, feathers and polished colored stones used for divining the future and summoning the spirits. From an old can of Key chewing tobacco left behind by one of the White Star Team, the medicine man took a pinch of some kind of powder and threw it into the fire, causing it to flare brightly and then burn with a billowing green smoke. Slowly he began his singsong incantation.

''This had better work,'' Gerber whispered to Rawlings standing next to him. ''Otherwise we could be in a lot of trouble.''

"Not to worry, Captain," Rawlings whispered back. "Bernie and I tied in four separate firing circuits, and the Cajun arranged for double backups with his little part of the show. It'll work."

"Who's got the button?" asked Gerber.

Rawlings looked down and Gerber followed his gaze. The Canadian had a small, square transmitter hidden in the palm of each hand, the telescoping antennae running up the insides of his forearms beneath the sleeves of his camouflaged jungle fatigues. "Bernie has the other two," whispered Rawlings. "A signal from any one of them will be sufficient to start the fireworks." As he spoke, he flipped up the safety covers with his thumbs, and a tiny light glowed red over each of the two toggle switches.

Vas Pao rocked slowly back and forth on his heels as he sat cross-legged before the fire, casting and recasting the stones and bones. Gradually his incantations built up to a fever pitch and then stopped abruptly. For a split second there was absolute silence in the camp, broken only by the crackling wood of the fire. The old man turned his face toward Fetterman and smiled the smile of doom.

"There!" shouted Fetterman before the priest could announce the failure of the spirits to appear. The master sergeant pointed at a small but prominent rocky shelf overhanging the side of a nearby cliff.

Instantly a stream of brilliant red tracers shot into the sky from a ridge above and beat down directly on the shelf in a shower of fire. Eerily there was no sound. Then with a great roaring whoosh four LAW rockets leaped from their tubes and arced across the sky like comets, slamming into the ledge and throwing up great white balls of light as the echo of their explosions rolled across the village. From high in the surrounding rocks came a dozen different voices speaking to the villagers in Hmong. The sounds were so amplified that they reverberated from the rocks until they became the garbled cries of hundreds, beseeching the villagers not to forget the spirits of their loved ones but to avenge them against the hated Communists. The cries begged them to return to the High Rock and to follow the directions of their new war chief in annihilating the enemy. Then, in parting, the voices offered their special recognition for the long service of Vas Pao in communicating with the afterworld and sent a demonstration of how the enemies of Phi Muang Xam Teu would be crushed.

As the voices fell silent, there was a shattering explosion and the rock shelf slowly crumbled and slid down the face of the cliff, pulverizing the trees beneath it. A hushed silence followed the awesome spectacle in which even the fire seemed to have grown quiet, and then a low chant began in the crowd.

"Fetterman! Fetterman! Fetterman!"

The Americans quickly took up the chant, and as their voices grew, other villagers joined in until everyone was screaming out the master sergeant's name at the top of his or her lungs. The crowd surged forward, the villagers reaching out tentatively to touch the little Green Beret, now truly one of their own, so that some of his powerful magic might be transferred to them.

Vas Pao sat numbly on the ground, unable to believe what he had witnessed. He was jostled as the throng pressed inward again, still chanting Fetterman's name and interspersing it with cries of "The White Porcupine has returned!"

Fetterman was lifted bodily into the air and twice carried madly around the village by the screaming crowd before he was able to convey his wishes above the tumultuous uproar. Then the crowd also lifted the shaman to their shoulders, now screaming out his name along with that of their war chief. On the third pass around the village, the crowd got completely out of hand, and Tou Bee, along with the other village elders and the entire Special Forces team, suddenly found themselves riding the shoulders of the enraptured throng. The cacophony of noise and the wild parade lasted for nearly an hour before Fetterman was finally able to persuade the Hmong to put everybody back down and restore enough order for something resembling normal speech to occur.

"I have been to the place of the High Rock in the past several days," Fetterman shouted to make himself heard over the noisy assembly. "I visited there before coming here. It is badly decayed from disuse, but with hard work we will restore it to a powerful fortress from which to swoop down on our enemies and destroy them." Fetterman was interrupted by a new round of cheering. "As proof of the truth of my words, I have brought with me a present for my father, our chief. It is an object well known to him, which he lost at the High Rock and which the spirits guided my hand to find there."

There was another round of frenzied yelling, and Fetterman held out his hands until things had quieted down to a dull roar. Then he reached into the pocket of his fatigue jacket and pulled out the paratrooper's wings, holding them high over his head by the thumb and index finger of both hands. "These are wings of silver that no evil spirit can touch," shouted Fetterman. "In the land of my birth they are the symbol of great warriors. They will be that same symbol here, and like the wings of birds of prey, our warriors will swoop down from the High Rock and crush the enemy in our talons. Through all the long years of my absence they survived in the place of the High Rock without being touched by the evil spirits that lived there until the spirits of our relatives drove them away. I give these wings back now to my father so that as long as he lives as chief of our village and wears these wings no harm can come to him or to the people of Muang Xam Teu."

Fetterman knew that he was laying it on a bit thick, but it was his moment. He had them now and he knew how important symbols were to these people. The symbol of a pair of silver wings that had survived six years in the midst of evil *phi* atop the High Rock would be a powerful symbol indeed.

"I give these wings of silver back to my father now and ask him to examine the markings on their back and say if they are not the same wings I once gave him on the High Rock."

Tou Bee pushed himself to his feet, disdaining offers of assistance from those near him, and stood to take the wings from his son. Carefully he turned them over in his hand and squinted with his good eye to examine the numbers on the back in the flickering light of the fire.

"I never expected to see this again, my son," he said softly to Fetterman, the tears sliding down his face. Then he held the wings high over his head as Fetterman had done and shouted in a loud, clear voice, "They are the same."

The crowd went wild, and it took Fetterman nearly five minutes to quiet them. "Tonight you have seen the power of the spirit world summoned by our great shaman, Vas Pao," said Fetterman. "You have heard the voices of our departed relatives with your own ears, telling us that we must return to the High Rock and rebuild our fortress there as a base from which to attack the enemy and as a place where we will be safe from those who would harm us. You have seen proof that I have been to the High Rock and have seen that it is as our departed loved ones say—the evil spirits have been driven from that place. Yet I will not ask you to return to the High Rock with me."

A puzzled murmur rippled through the villagers as Fetterman prepared to take the biggest gamble of his military career. "No, my Hmong brothers and sisters, I will not ask you to go back to that place that we call the High Rock. Not unless our great shaman Vas Pao Xiong, who tonight summoned the spirits here to our celebration, tells you that all that has been spoken is the truth and that it is the will of the spirits that we go there."

Fetterman looked directly at the village priest, and for one long, awful moment was afraid he had gambled incorrectly. Then slowly the old shaman smiled. "It is true!" he yelled, throwing his clenched fist into the air in the warrior's gesture of defiance. "The spirits have spoken and you have heard their words. You have seen their power. We will go back to the High Rock and we will kill the enemy! Long live chief Tou Bee Cha and the villagers of Muang Xam Teu! Long live our great war chief, the White Porcupine!''

There was no restraining them then. The crowd rushed forward, once again picking up Fetterman, Tou Bee and Vas Pao and parading them throughout the village for over an hour.

"If I didn't know it had all been done with a bit of high explosive, a few tracer rounds, a tape recorder and a couple of jury-rigged loudspeakers, I'd swear it was a miracle myself," Updike shouted to Gerber as they were swept off their feet and carried along with the cheering mass.

"You're wrong," Gerber shouted back. "It is a miracle. With the aid of a few tricks and a pair of old jump wings, we've just witnessed the confirmation of the first American Hmong warlord."

"I just hope all the noise doesn't attract the enemy," Updike shouted in return. "We'll never get these guys to go back out on guard duty tonight."

He was right. The celebration lasted until well past dawn.

8

THE ROOKERY
NORTHERN LAOS

Special Forces Master Sergeant Anthony B. Fetterman, war chief of the Hmong of Phou Phi Muang Xam Teu, surveyed his kingdom. In a few short weeks the Rookery, or High Rock as even the Americans had now taken to calling it, had been transformed into a bastion ringed in steel. The bridge across the ravine had been newly rebuilt and was guarded by a bunker containing two M-60s and a Browning .50-caliber heavy machine gun. The bridge had been rigged for demolition, and the large rock shelf leading up to it had been planted with five hundred antipersonnel mines, newly flown in by an Air America Otter from General Vang Pao's big Hmong base at Long Tieng.

The entrance through the rock crevice had been mined with enough high explosives to seal it permanently should the need arise, and the open killing field between the high rock wall and the camp itself sported four rows of a nasty new concertina wire known as razor ribbon. It came in spirals like the old concertina, but the barbs had been replaced with double-edged razor blades stamped directly into the wire.

Another five hundred mines were placed between the wires, along with trip flares and grenade traps, and fifty claymore mines planted just before the deepened and widened punji moat provided a final line of defense explosives. The outer slope of the high rock wall through which the crevice gave access to the camp had been mined, too, to discourage any enemy that somehow managed to knock out the bunker and cross the ravine, then scale the wall to shoot down into the camp.

There was another heavy-machine-gun bunker atop the wall, along with two 90 mm recoilless rifle positions and two more M-60 bunkers. In the unlikely event everything was knocked out, the Hmong defenders could fall back through paths in the mines and razor ribbon to the protection of the high walls of packed earth and rock of the fort itself on the other side of the punji moat.

The ten-foot-high walls of the fort were honeycombed with indivdual bunkers, connecting covered trench lines and more M-60 machine-gun bunkers. At each point of the three-sided fort a heavily fortified bunker contained a .50-caliber machine gun, whose great range made it possible to reach targets on nearby peaks. Gerber's original order for three 60 mm mortars had been augmented by two 81 mm mortars with nearly four hundred rounds of high explosive and white phosphorus shells and a hundred illumination rounds buried in underground bunkers within the fort. A 106 mm recoilless rifle, air-dropped to the team only two nights ago, along with forty-eight rounds of high-explosive ammunition, provided the camp's long-range artillery punch. The High Rock was rapidly becoming the impregnable fortress Fetterman had promised. An NVA or Pathet Lao battalion would find it an impossible nut to crack, despite the small size of the defending force, and Fetterman suspected that even a regiment would find it a difficult meal to swallow without artillery support.

As the complexity of the fort's defenses had grown, it had been necessary for the Hmong strike force to grow along with it. This had posed problems, since all of the able-bodied males were already formed into the single strike company. Eventually, and against their natural prejudices, the Americans had yielded to the inevitable logic of the situation, and the women had been trained to operate the camp's machine guns, mortars and recoilless rifles, thus freeing the men to conduct patrols and raids against the enemy. Even children as young as ten were taught to carry ammunition and to assist their mothers in loading the weapons.

The cisterns had been rebuilt and the rubber bladders installed inside the fort, with more cisterns and bladders in the village beyond the walls. The request for plastic water pipe and portable pumps, which must have brought some blank stares and head scratching back in Kontum had been met, and work parties labored from dawn to dusk, digging in the pipe and leveling spots for the holding bladders with hand tools. In the meantime, Hmong girls carried jars of water up the mountain to keep the villagers and Americans supplied.

Fetterman doubted he had ever seen a more concentrated war effort by a given populace in three wars and half a dozen police actions, yet he knew the effort couldn't be sustained much longer without conducting an offensive operation. So far the entire effort of the village had been directed toward defense, and while the Hmong were well pleased with the gifts of weapons the Americans showered upon them and greeted each new delivery of arms, boots or uniforms with an almost childlike Christmas glee, he had promised them victory over their enemies, and the Hmong were growing restless for their war chief to lead them into battle.

There was also the question of what to do about the problem of Tou Pa. Every night she sought out Breneke and climbed into bed with him. He did his best to ignore her, and she did her best to make it impossible for him to do so. It had been funny to start with, but now it had become a major problem. Her desires, and Breneke's refusal to fulfill them, left both of them irritable, and their crankiness frayed everyone's nerves. The women of the village were beginning to talk about the situation, as gossips everywhere will, and rumors were starting to circulate that Breneke was a man without a penis, or worse, that he had one, but that he felt it beneath him to have sex with a Hmong. In truth, he found Tou Pa very attractive, was flattered by the attention she heaped upon him and wanted desperately to screw her silly, but couldn't bring himself to do it because of his fiancée back in the States and because he knew that sooner or later he, like the other Americans, would have to leave this place.

When the situation finally became so bad that Tou Bee found it necessary to speak to Fetterman about it, the master sergeant realized that something would have to be done. He stretched the truth slightly and tried to explain to his adoptive Hmong father that Breneke was unable to honor Tou Pa's wishes because he had a wife at home. Tou Bee sympathized with Breneke's problem, but the explanation proved ineffective when the chief pointed out that the practice of polygamy wasn't unkown among the Hmong. Fetterman countered with the argument that while that was true, it was usually restricted to the well-to-do. Tou Bee countered in turn by pointing out that by village standards Breneke possessed the wealth of a prince and that, anyway, a promise of marriage wasn't what Tou Pa sought, merely a mating.

Fetterman told the chief that he would discuss the situation with Breneke, but could make no promises. It was the way of the Americans to make their own decisions regarding sex, he told the chief.

Tou Bee gently reminded his son that such was also the way of the Hmong and that Tou Pa had already made her decision. "There is nothing worse, my son, than a Hmong woman who has made up her mind about something. And I fear that your sister is the most stubborn woman in our village."

Fetterman spoke to Breneke as he had promised and was a little surprised by the light-weapons sergeant's answer. "Christ! It's not that I don't want to put it to her, Master Sergeant," Breneke told him. "It's getting so sometimes I can't think about anything else. What if I get her pregnant? You said yourself these people don't practice contraception."

Fetterman assured him that while that was a risk, a child born out of wedlock carried no particular stigma in Hmong society. "It happens all the time," Fetterman told him, but Breneke was adamant.

"Shit, Master Sergeant! I can't do that. I can't leave some little blue-eyed blond Hmong wandering around the mountains of Laos when I go back home. It would be my child and I would never see it again. Besides, how could I live with knocking up my master sergeant's sister?"

Fetterman patted the big German American sympathetically on the arm and told him he'd think on the problem and try to come up with a solution. Finally he came up with one, but he wasn't sure how well Breneke was going to like it. Something had to be done, however, and it was the best solution he could come up with. He hunted up the Teutonic giant and found him with a squad of Hmong, filling sandbags with dirt to be stacked around the newly constructed team house.

"Klaus, how's it going?" Fetterman asked, walking up.

Breneke paused to wipe the sweat from his brow.

"It goes well, Master Sergeant. If we keep at it, we can finish by nightfall."

"It'll be nice to get a good night's sleep without having to worry about somebody dropping a mortar round on our heads," said Fetterman conversationally.

"Those of us who can sleep," Breneke answered pointedly.

"Yes, I see what you mean," Fetterman replied. "I've been giving your problem some thought and I'd like to talk to you about it. Suppose we give the workers a break, okay?"

Fetterman spoke rapidly in Hmong, telling the strikers to knock off but to come back in twenty minutes. When one of them asked how long twenty minutes was, Fetterman slipped off his watch and handed it to the man.

"When this line here gets around to here, you and all the others come back, okay? And don't lose my watch," Fetterman told him.

The man then asked what a watch was but smiled to show Fetterman he was only having a little fun with him. "Do not worry, White Porcupine," the Hmong replied. "I will take good care of your bracelet that counts the passage of the day."

The dozen men of the Hmong work detail ran off in as many directions, and Fetterman sat down on a pile of filled sandbags.

"All right, Master Sergeant," said Breneke. "What is it that's on your mind?"

"Just this," said Fetterman. He reached into the pocket of his fatigues and pulled out a fifth of Beam's Choice and a box of Trojans.

"What the hell's this?" asked Breneke.

"This," said Fetterman, "is a fifth of the finest, smoothest Kentucky bourbon ever distilled. It came with those two cases of beer that Captain Gerber requested. The Captain donated it to the cause to help you overcome your inhibitions. And this," he continued, holding out the Trojans, "is a box of condoms. Surely you've seen them before. I got White to put in a request for them."

"And what exactly am I supposed to do with these gifts?" asked Breneke, his temper flaring.

"Easy, Klaus," Fetterman told him. "Nobody's asking or telling you to do anything you don't want to do. All I'm saying is that they're yours to do with what you want. I don't give a damn if you throw the bottle away and use the rubbers for party balloons, although Captain Gerber might be a little annoyed if his prize bourbon went to waste on a rock. You do whatever you think is right. If you're interested, Tou Pa is in the chief's hut and she's alone. She'll be alone all afternoon, unless you drop by to visit her. I'll be back in twenty minutes, and if you've found something better to do than filling sandbags in the hot sun by then, the Hmong and I will carry on without you. Think it over." Fetterman got up and walked away across the compound, leaving the whiskey and the condoms sitting on top of the sandbags.

Breneke stared after him, seriously considering hurling the bottle at the back of the master sergeant's head, but thought better of it. He stood for a while, feeling the blazing sun growing warm on his body, then wiped his hands on his trousers, picked up the bottle of bourbon and the box of condoms and walked off to find Tou Pa.

A SMILING BUT VERY TIRED Tou Pa emerged from her father's house that evening to the knowing glances of the village women. When Breneke emerged sometime later, also looking tired and more than a little drunk, he was greeted with a chorus of rude cheers from the village men. Fetterman was thankful the German American couldn't translate, although the spirit and intent of the greetings could scarcely have been lost on him.

Breneke ignored them and stumbled through the village and across the compound, singing "Oh Tannenbaum" rather noisily and a bit off-key. Once inside the fort, he stopped twice to shout "Merry Christmas, everyone!" for no readily apparent reason, then lurched his way to the team house and collapsed facedown on his bunk. The bamboo framework creaked ominously under his weight, but the sleeping platform held together. In a few moments he was snoring with a sound that could only be described as the noise made by two rutting rhinoceroses fighting a duel to the death with chain saws.

Fetterman found it fascinating that a man could snore so loudly while apparently lying on his face, and both White and Portland offered the opinion that the phenomenon should be carefully observed and written up for the *Army Medical Journal*, but their enthusiasm wasn't shared by the others trying to sleep. It was noted with satisfaction by all, however, that Tou Pa, for the first time since the Americans had been welcomed into the Hmong village, made no attempt to sleep with the German American but returned to her father's home for the night. She was seen walking very carefully about the village the next day, and it was two more nights before she returned to sleep with Breneke and nearly a week before he was once again called upon to put conscience aside and do the right thing. The rumors regarding his manhood and his prejudice were, however, put finally and firmly to rest.

FOR THEIR FIRST OFFENSIVE operation against the enemy the Green Berets selected the Pathet Lao town of Sam Teu. It was an ambitious target, since the village held several thousand people, but the plan was only to strike at selected portions of the town, namely the docks, the power generating station and the headquarters of the Neo Lao Hak Sat, the political arm of the Pathet Lao. The location of the generating plant, a rather small affair, and the docks had been determined from aerial photographs provided during the preinsertion briefing phase of the mission, and the address of the NLHS had been provided along with them, presumably from information gained from a CIA ground agent or Pathet Lao defector. They would also attack the military police station located across the street.

Two hours before the attack, the weapons platoon, along with one squad from one of the rifle platoons, would attack the Pathet Lao military police outpost in the village of Muong Thong, north of the town. They wouldn't attempt to overrun the outpost, but would destroy it with automatic weapons and mortar fire. It was unknown what sort of communications the outpost might have, but presumably it was connected with the larger town of Sam Teu, either by radio or telephone line, and if so, it was hoped the attack would draw any Pathet Lao or NVA troops stationed in Sam Teu northward out of town, leaving the way clear for the main strike against Sam Teu.

Speed, surprise and firepower were to be the key elements of the assault. It would be a sudden, vicious attack with no quarter given and none expected—a classic raid. The Hmong strike force would sweep in behind a wall of steel and lead, destroy their targets and withdraw before an organized defense could be mounted or troops mobilized to pursue them. There was some concern that two hours was too long a time to allow between assaults, but since intel suggested there was little motorized transport in the region, the idea was to allow any Communist foot soldiers sufficient time to get out of Sam Teu before the real targets were struck.

The raiding party, consisting of nearly the entire Hmong strike company and most of the Green Berets, left the High Rock at dusk and traveled throughout the night in order to be well away from the village fortress by daybreak in case they were discovered by Pathet Lao patrols. They marched throughout the next morning, then slept during the hot part of the day and continued on that evening. While a part of their operational mission assignment was to conduct harassing raids and ambushes in the enemy's rear, they had to be careful not to mount any operations too close to their home base on the High Rock. They had to keep the camp's location a secret from the enemy for as long as possible, both for the safety of the villagers and because they didn't yet know if the U.S. Air Force intended to install their advanced navigational aids there.

While the strike force closed in on their objective, the defense of the High Rock was left to the fifty-member village detachment, composed of Hmong grandfathers and young teenage boys, and to the women and children of Muang Xam Teu. Wysoski had been left behind to guard the radios for any incoming messages, along with Portland to look after the medical needs of the villagers. Updike didn't like being left behind, but understood that it was Gerber's right to go with the troops, and had been placed in a charge of overall village and camp defense. Breneke had been left behind to interpret his orders through Kong Moua, the German-speaking platoon leader.

Tou Bee had offered suprisingly little resistance to the notion that he should remain in the village. Fetterman had simply pointed out to the old man that since he had appointed the master sergeant as war chief, Fetterman must lead the warriors into battle, and the villagers couldn't be expected to follow anyone else's orders as quickly as they would their chief's should an emergency arise.

Tou Bee had seen the wisdom of this and had also wanted to keep an eye on the relationship between Tou Pa and Breneke, which had developed rapidly once the blond American's initial reluctance had been overcome. It wasn't that Tou Bee disapproved of their affair—far from it—he was curious as to how they could spend so much time in bed together without producing any offspring, and he wanted to be around when the announcement was finally made that he would once again be a grandfather.

The chief would have preferred that his white son, Fetterman, take a wife, as well, but a war chief had no time for women, and the White Porcupine couldn't be expected to select just any Hmong female. After all, he had spoken with the spirits and they had shown their power through him. Fetterman was the closest thing to a living god that had ever existed in the village, and that was cause enough for the old man's pride in his adopted son.

By late afternoon of the third day, having covered twenty-five miles through the rugged, winding terrain from their mountain fortress at the High Rock, the strike force split. White and Gunn, who both spoke Vietnamese, went north to hit Muong Thong, along with Ge Yang, the assistant weapons platoon leader, who spoke a bit of the language from two years he had spent in North Vietnam.

With them, they took a thirteen-man mortar squad with three 60 mm mortars, a thirteen-man machine-gun squad with three M-60 machine guns and a thirteen-man rifle squad armed with CAR-15s and two M-79 grenade launchers. Except for the gunners, who wore only side arms, each member of the mortar or machine-gun teams was armed with a CAR-15 and each carried either two 150-round belts of ammo for the machine guns or four 60 mm mortar shells. The Americans did their part, too. White carried a CAR-15 modified with a 40 mm grenade launcher beneath the barrel and a medical kit while humping a PRC-25 radio on his massive shoulders, and Gunn, the team's other giant Teutonic knight, lugged a third M-60 with an additional six hundred rounds of ammunition, enough weight to give a lesser man a hernia.

The main assault force, consisting of Gerber, Fetterman, Paulsen, Rawlings, Dollar, Chavez and the French-speaking Cheu Thao, moved on eastward with two rifle platoons plus a rifle squad from the third platoon, the remaining rifle squad having been detailed to stay behind at the High Rock with the village defense force. The attack force was rounded out by the weapons platoon's second machine-gun squad and a fourth M-60 carried by the detached rifle squad.

It was an impressive amount of firepower, but Gerber knew it was light by Vietnamese standards, where practically every squad had one or two grenade launchers and nearly every platoon carried two or more M-60s. Besides, in Vietnam an American patrol in trouble could get on the radio and count on having air or artillery support in a matter of minutes. Here in Laos their own mortars were their artillery support, and while Royal Lao and U.S. pilots did occasionally fly air support missions for the Royal Lao Army or for General Vang Pao's Hmong guerrillas fighting down on the Plain of Jars, they could expect no help from the air here, and the nature of their orders precluded even asking for any. When it came to fighting the enemy, they were truly on their own.

By 1800 hours the main attack force was in position to begin the assault on Sam Teu, and at 1830 hours Dollar, carrying the main group's PRC-25, recieved word via his Hmong assistant that White and Gunn's team was ready to hit Moung Thong. To help keep the enemy confused about the presence of Americans in the area, all voice radio traffic took place in Hmong if possible. Either the Pathet Lao or the NVA would pay a reward worth more than a year's salary to the average Laotian for the head of an American and considerably more for one captured alive.

At 1845 hours the force under White and Gunn attacked the Pathet Lao outpost at Moung Thong, raking the haphazardly sandbagged, flimsy wooden structure with a heavy volume of automatic weapons fire and plastering it with thirty-six rounds of high-explosive and white phosphorus mortar shells. The assault didn't last more than ten minutes, during which the Hmong and their American advisers received very little return fire. The accuracy of the Hmong gunners was good, and only a few nearby structures were hit by stray rounds.

The team then withdrew by a route different from the one they had taken to the village, swinging first away to the northwest and then dropping back south to throw off any pursuing enemy. When they were sure their trail was clear, they angled back toward Sam Teu and set up their mortars in a position where they would be able to support the main assault force if needed. There were still twelve rounds available for each of the mortars, and they had accomplished their task, destroying the target and setting it ablaze.

While the Hmong were disappointed that they didn't have the opportunity to engage in any trophy taking, they took heart in the fact that they had finally met the enemy in battle and defeated them utterly, and that the only casualty they had sustained was when one of the loaders had cut his hand on a piece of safety wire arming a mortar round.

Just outside Sam Teu the main attack force waited, now split into two teams. One group, consisting of Gerber, Chavez, Paulsen, Rawlings and Cheu Thao, with four rifle squads, including the one carrying an M-60, waited near the riverbank north of town between Sam Teu and Muong Thong, ready to hit the power plant and docks. The second group, under Fetterman and Dollar made up of two rifle platoons and the machine-gun squad, waited south of town to attack the NLHS headquarters and the Pathet Lao military police headquarters.

It was nearly half an hour after White and Gunn had announced they were beginning their attack on Muong Thong when Gerber's group was surprised to hear the sound of heavy engines approaching. They hadn't expected that the Pathet Lao would have any significant motorized transport available, but the noise was unmistakably that of truck engines. He listened while they ground their way up the narrow, rutted dirt path not more than a hundred yards from the river, then had Cheu Thao send a runner to check with the three men he had left to watch the roadway.

In a moment Kue Chaw, the Hmong's top scout, appeared and reported through Cheu Thao that he had seen both large and small trucks filled with soldiers driving northward toward Muong Thong. Gerber asked how many of each and got a second surprise when the Hmong answered him directly in broken but understandable English.

"One little. Have four wheel. Three Vietminh ride. Others big. Have many wheel each side." He held up three fingers. "Like so. One and one and one. Many Vietminh ride."

"How many big trucks?" Gerber asked.

Kue Chaw held up three fingers again "Many Vietminh ride," he insisted.

"Sounds like a GAZ field car and three ZIL army trucks," Gerber told Paulsen, who had come over to see what all the fuss was about. "Looks like our intel was wrong about the Pathet Lao not having any motorized transport."

Kue Chaw shook his head violently. "No Pathet Lao! No Pathet Lao!" he insisted. "Vietminh! Many Vietminh!"

Paulsen fired off a string of rapid Hmong phrases, and Kue Chaw responded in kind, gesturing rapidly with his hands as he traced first a square and then a star in the dim light.

"Captain," said Paulsen, "he says they weren't Pathet Lao. They were regular NVA. He saw the flag painted on the doors of the trucks as they passed by. A red flag with a yellow star in the middle."

"Great," said Gerber. "Just frigging wonderful. There weren't supposed to be any NVA in the town, and now suddenly there's enough of them to send a whole platoon running north in trucks to check out the trouble in Moung Thong. There could be a whole damn company of them in Sam Teu. We'd better let Fetterman know what's going on.''

Gerber tried for a full five minutes to raise Fetterman on the PRC-6 radio, but had no luck. Either the little radio wasn't working right, Dollar's PRC-25 wasn't receiving them properly or something was blocking the signal.

''I figure we've got about forty minutes, tops, before the bad guys get to Muong Thong, find out the show is over and start back. The damn village just isn't that far away. Say an hour before they can return, and they could be carrying anything from a platoon to a light company in those trucks, depending on how they packed them in.''

''Which means they could have anything from a couple of platoons to a couple of companies left in town,'' said Paulsen. ''And if they've got radios, they could be back sooner than that if somebody in Sam Teu hollers at them.''

Gerber made a snap decision. ''We can't wait. If we're going to go at all, we've got to do it now.''

''Captain, if I may,'' interrupted Rawlings. ''If Bernie and I were to string a wire across the road and tie it to a couple of claymores, it might slow their return down a bit. Won't take but a jiff to set up, and it could purchase us some time.''

''Do it!'' said Gerber. ''You've got five minutes. It's all we can spare. Go! Paulsen, you go with them and bring in the road watch. We've got to move fast.''

Gerber rapidly shrugged off his pack and dug out three of the aluminum-cased, hand-launched signal flares from underneath the flap, identifying the proper ones by their position beneath the flap and then confirming that he had the correct ones by using his red-lensed flashlight to read the labels printed on the sides of the tubes. He cupped his hand around the lens so that the light couldn't be seen from any appreciable distance and remembered to close one eye before he switched on the flashlight. That way, if he had forgotten to put the red lens into the flashlight, he wouldn't lose his night vision in both eyes. He hadn't, and quickly confirmed that he had the right flares. Laying them out in proper order on the ground in front of him, he switched off the flashlight, tightened the flap on his pack and struggled back into the shoulder harness. Then he unsnapped the little leather cover and lifted it from the face of his watch.

Gerber watched the self-luminous hands of the watch tick off the seconds. He figured he'd allowed Chavez and Rawlings about two extra minutes beyond what he'd promised them, but he had no intention of shorting them. Wiring up a couple of claymores to a trip wire could be a tricky business, especially in the dark, and he didn't want to startle the men at the wrong time by suddenly sending a flare streaking skyward. He couldn't wait forever, either, and when the hands of the watch said exactly five minutes had gone by since he'd first looked at it, he uncapped each flare and fitted the tops of the aluminum tubes to the bottom of each container so that the firing pin mounted in the cap would be positioned over the primer in the bottom of the tube. With the signal flares thus ready for firing, he held the first one in his left hand, the tube pointed skyward. But still he didn't fire.

When Gerber saw the other men running toward him from his position at the top of the embankment, he waited until they had slid down on the river side of it and made sure everyone was accounted for. "Close your eyes," he said, and Paulsen repeated the order in Hmong.

Gerber allowed a couple of seconds for the order to be passed up and down the line of men, then slapped the bottom of the tube sharply with his right hand. The firing pin in the cap placed over the bottom of the tube crushed the primer, initiating the propellant charge, and the signal flare whooshed out of the tube and broke high overhead in a red star cluster. Quickly grabbing up the other two tubes in turn, Gerber fired each of them, both green star clusters. Had his decision been to abort the raid instead of beginning it immediately, he would have fired a green followed by two reds.

Gerber retrieved the three empty tubes, not wishing to leave any clues behind for the enemy to discover later, and stuck them into the left thigh pocket of his fatigues. "That's it!" he yelled, getting to his feet. "Come on! Let's go!"

Paulsen repeated in Hmong the order to move, and the troops swarmed over the embankment and raced toward the town. As he went with them, Gerber mouthed a silent prayer. "For God's sake, Tony, keep our head down and don't do anything stupid."

FETTERMAN SAW the red star cluster break over the town at the same time Dollar pointed it out to him, followed rapidly by two green star clusters. "Something's gone wrong," he said. "That's the attack signal, and it's almost an hour and a half ahead of schedule."

"Why d'ya'll suppose they didn't use the radio?" asked Dollar.

"Must have had a reason," said Fetterman. "You try to raise them on the move. We're going in."

He looked at the men nearest him, their camouflaged faces painted in hideous war masks of green and black. They knew nothing about the alternate signal and were plainly edgy. "My brother warriors," he said, addressing them in Hmong, "something has gone wrong. We must not wait but attack now. The colored stars are a sign from our brothers north of town. Be ready for anything, but do not be afraid. Follow me to victory."

As Fetterman stood, the nearest Hmong reached out to touch him for luck, and then they were all up and running toward the town. "For Christ's sake, Captain," Fetterman muttered under his breath, "be careful."

THE FORCE WITH GERBER swept into the town, passing first through a district of bamboo-and-wooden houses where only lamplight showed through the windows. Evidently electrification didn't extend to the entire community. As they passed deeper into the town, streetlights and the more or less steady glow of dim electric bulbs began to appear in windows. They kept as much as possible in the shadows and continued to parallel the riverfront until they reached the docks. Here Gerber detached Rawlings and Paulsen, along with two rifle squads who had been briefed on what to do, while the rest of his raiding party proceeded across the docks to the adjacent power generating station.

The power plant was surrounded by a high wire fence, but it was neither barbed nor electrified, and a couple of Hmong with wire cutters made short work of it, opening a large hole through which the men poured. The locked door of the plant was made of wood, which splintered and yielded under a short burst from the M-60, and Gerber and Chavez, along with Cheu Thao and one squad, pushed their way inside while the squad with the machine gun set up security outside.

The Hmong knew what they were supposed to do and quickly searched the building, finding only a night watchman who wasn't even armed and a skeleton crew of three technicians and six stokers for the ancient, coal-fired boilers that generated steam for the turbines the French had installed prior to World War II.

The Hmong, disappointed at the lack of an expected fight, wanted to take the civilians out and shoot them, and Gerber had some difficulty persuading them through Cheu Thao that the prisoners weren't soldiers and probably not even Communists, facts which Chavez, who spoke lowland Lao, quickly confirmed before setting about the business of rigging his charges to destroy the plant. Although Gerber didn't like leaving behind anyone who had seen Americans, he couldn't bring himself to permit the execution of unarmed civilians, and he finally succeeded in persuading Cheu Thao that it would be more effective if the workers were left alive to tell how the plant had been destroyed by Hmong warriors. Cheu Thao finally decided that would be a good idea and settled for only roughing the prisoners up a bit. They were then taken outside where they could be watched until the raiding party was ready to leave.

In the meantime, Chavez worked frantically with a few of the Hmong helping him to rig the small plant for demolition. He would normally have used TNT blocks for a job like this one. Since it was a more cost- and energy-effective use of high explosives, but C-4 was easier to shape, and being more powerful, required less tamping and permitted less to be carried to do the same job. It wasn't as sterile as TNT, which was used by practically every army in the world in some form, but the whole mission of Thunderhead was looked on as more covert than clandestine, and he didn't figure the enemy would be left with a whole lot to analyze once it detonated.

The boilers were easy enough to rig, but hot, so Chavez used shaped charges with standoffs set to punch holes in them with a jet of superheated gas when they detonated. The coal storage bins were doused with diesel fuel and packed with thermite charges to set them ablaze. He also took time to plant cutting charges on a few key I beams supporting the roof in order to collapse it onto the building and make fighting the fire or salvaging anything useful a more difficult prospect.

The real challenge was the generators themselves. He would have liked to pack the armatures with C-4 but settled for increasing the charges by half and placing them on the armature covers, then tamping them with sacks of rice that the Hmong carried in from the dock outside. Cutting the turbine shafts was another tough project. Two of them he handled easily by doubling the charges and tamping them over the shaft covers; it really didn't matter whether they were cut completely or simply so badly bent as to be unusable.

The third turbine had had the cover removed sometime in the past, and since it was one of the two that were running, it had to be shut down before he could pack C-4 around the shaft, plunging a large section of the town into darkness. The move was sure to attract unwanted attention that would rapidly focus on the power plant, and it would probably take him a while to figure out exactly how to shut the thing down, so he left that one until the very last.

Outside, Rawlings was busy with a demolition problem of his own. Charge calculations had to be rapidly figured and blocks of TNT primed and placed on the proper pilings below the waterline. There was also an ancient gasoline-powered donkey crane to be destroyed, and he handled that quickly by placing a single one-pound block of TNT beneath the engine and wrapping a few yards of detonating cord around the latticework of the boom. While he was doing that, one of the Hmong found several steel drums containing what was identified as gasoline, and these were punctured and used to soak down the wooden planking of the docks. He had just finished tying the piling charges together with detonator cord when Gerber and the others came out of the power plant.

ENTERING SAM TEU from the south, Fetterman and his group didn't fare quite as well as Gerber's. They had barely entered the town when a ZIL truck full of soldiers came wheeling around a corner. The entire group of Hmong immediately opened fire, riddling the truck with bullets and killing everyone inside it before it clipped off a wooden lamppost and plowed through a house, finally coming to rest. There were no other trucks following it, but the strike force attack on Sam Teu had been rather noisily announced to anyone in the town who had ears. With the need for stealth now eliminated, the men charged down the dirt streets to their objective, and Fetterman initiated the assault by blowing the doors off both buildings with LAW rockets.

A sandbagged guard post outside the military police headquarters with an RPD machine gun mounted in it barely had time to open fire before it was silenced by several well-placed 40 mm grenades from M-79s. Other grenades were then fired through the windows and blown-open doorways of the two- and three-story concrete buildings. Then the Hmong split into two teams and charged inside, leaving the machine-gun squad to cover the street.

There was no question of civilian noncombatants here. Anyone found inside either building at this hour was considered to be either Pathet Lao or NLHS political cadre and shot on sight. The Hmong moved from room to room in the old French colonial structures, kicking in doors and tossing in grenades before entering, then spraying the room with automatic weapons fire.

Fetterman would have liked the opportunity to take a few prisoners for interrogation, figuring that either Pathet Lao military policemen or political officers might be full of all sorts of useful information about the area, but the Hmong had no facilities to keep them, and taking them to the High Rock would jeopardize its location if one somehow managed to escape. Besides, they couldn't afford to be burdened with the excess baggage of prisoners during their withdrawal. Trying to drag a bound and blindfolded prisoner through the high jungle and rugged hills would only slow them down, and Fetterman had seen enough of the truck they had shot up on the way in to know that there were regular NVA troops in the area. That was probably what had caused Gerber to launch the assault early, and was more than enough to convince Fetterman that they didn't want to be slowed down in their retreat.

The three-story NLHS headquarters was virtually deserted, and after clearing it, Dave Dollar and several Hmong who had been carefully briefed by Fetterman prior to the mission set about collecting at least one copy of every document they could get their hands on, piling the others up in the hallway for burning. Those not occupied with searching for papers busied themselves with smashing up typewriters and the printing press found in one of the downstairs rooms.

Across the street in the military police headquarters a short, sharp firefight ensued. There had evidently been a dozen or so Pathet Lao in the building, most armed with AK-47s, and they put up stiff resistance, fighting from room to room and slowly retreating back along the narrow hallways. They had to be blasted out with grenades.

As the process of clearing the building continued, it developed that the structure contained several cells in a basement. The locks were shot off the cell doors when no key could be found and the occupants, if any, helped to the street and given the chance to run away into the night without regard to whatever crime they were being held for.

One cell, which had a heavy steel door secured with a mammoth padlock that had to be blown off with a small quantity of C-4, proved to be an interrogation room. A middle-aged Laotian woman was found inside, stripped naked and bound to a wooden chair with wire. She had been badly beaten, and the Pathet Lao had apparently been working on her with a heated poker and a pair of pliers. The woman could barely stand, let alone walk, when released from the chair. Her crime, she said, when Fetterman questioned her, was simply that she had dared to voice the opinion that North Vietnamese soldiers didn't belong in Laos. Fetterman gave her his poncho liner blanket to cover herself and saw to it that she was helped outside. It was all he could do for her.

As Fetterman ascended the stairs back up to ground level, he passed a pair of Hmong attempting to hack the head from the body of a Pathet Lao militiaman. He stood for a moment and watched the grisly spectacle with a curious sense of detachment. He didn't approve of the mutilation of enemies killed in battle, but he had seen it often enough to be unmoved by it.

He had witnessed the taking of trophies by virtually every army fighting the brutal war that raged throughout Indochina and had seen the mutilated bodies of Americans left beside the trail or roadside by the NVA and Vietcong. It had been going on for so long that it was impossible to know which side had started it, although he suspected it had gone on long before the Americans had arrived.

At the top of the stairs Fetterman was presented with an unexpected prize. Some of his Hmong warriors had found a Pathet Lao hiding in a broom closet and had brought the man forward so that the master sergeant could have the honor of killing him personally.

Fetterman was appalled by the notion. He would have killed the man instantly in a firefight, or in cold blood if he had been a sentry guarding a facility Fetterman needed to infiltrate, but he had no intention of murdering a prisoner. The man was babbling his innocence and protesting that he was only a policeman and not even a member of the Communist Party. He spoke Lowland Lao of course, and the Hmong couldn't understand him, but Fetterman knew what he was saying clearly enough.

Fetterman was suddenly sick of the whole thing. He was about to tell the Hmong that they could turn the man loose or kill him as they saw fit, but that he wouldn't shoot him, when he noticed something heavy sagging in the man's pocket. Fetterman reached in and fished it out. It was a bloody pair of pliers.

The image of the tortured Laotian woman flashed before his eyes, and without even thinking about it, Fetterman drew his short-barreled Smith & Wesson .44 Magnum revolver and shot the man once between the eyes. The 240-grain semiwadcutter slug entered just at the bridge of the nose and blew the back out of the man's head, splattering blood and brains on the wall behind and showering with bits of tissue and bone the Hmong holding him.

As the deafening roar of the revolver died in the room, the two Hmong released the prisoner, and the Pathet Lao slumped slowly to the floor. One of the Hmong, unaware of the motivation behind the action, immediately offered to cut off the head for Fetterman.

Instead, in a show of utter contempt, Fetterman spit on it. "The White Porcupine," he said, "does not take trophies from those who torture women. They are unworthy even to have their heads displayed on a stick."

For a moment no one spoke or moved in the room. Then, one by one, the Hmong, too, threw down their trophies and spat upon them. Slowly they turned their backs, shouldered their carbines and walked out. Without realizing it, Fetterman had set a precedent. There would be no more trophy-taking by the Hmong of Muang Xam Teu. Their warlord had spoken, and such an act was beneath the dignity of those who would follow him into battle.

A BURST OF AK-47 FIRE from the far end of the docks alerted Gerber that somebody had finally come down to see why the lights had gone out in half of Sam Teu. As the AK was answered by half a dozen CAR-15s and an M-60, several more AKs added their protest of the unauthorized occupancy of the docks and power station to the very noisy night Sam Teu seemed to be having. It was time to go.

"You guys ready?" Gerber yelled at Chavez and Rawlings. Both men held thumbs up. "Whenever you are, Captain."

Gerber gave a couple of the prisoners a shove.

"Di! Di!" he shouted at them. *"Di di mau lien!"*

He didn't know if any of them understood Vietnamese or not, but they got the message and started to run toward the northwest corner of the riverfront. One of the Hmong raised his CAR-15, but Gerber pushed it aside.

"Cheu Thao! You tell them not to shoot, damn it!" Gerber demanded.

Cheu Taho translated, and the Hmong slowly lowered his weapon.

"All right, then," said Gerber. "Let's get the hell out of this place before more company comes." He spoke first to Paulsen, then to Cheu Thao in French, telling them to have the men fall back past the power plant and along the river until they could cut inland. "Fire 'em!" he yelled at Chavez and Rawlings.

"Fire in the hole!" said Chavez, using the old mining blaster's lingo.

"Fire in the hole!" Rawlings echoed.

Both men pulled the pins on two M-2 weatherproof fuse igniters to start the twin dual-firing trains burning. Then they ran for all they were worth.

The Americans and Hmong were still uncomfortably close when the roof of the power plant caved in and the exploding boilers lifted it back up again, plunging the entire town into total darkness. Whoever had been firing the AK-47s from the north end of the docks was entirely too close when the pier lighted up like a burning pine tree and then blew itself into the air in a shower of flaming timbers, twisted steel crane parts and human bodies.

FETTERMAN WAS NEARLY out the door of the police station before he realized that no one had checked the files. Since there had been no written Hmong language until American and French missionaries had developed one for them in the 1950s, it was hardly surprising that none of the Hmong could read and write, except for Cheu Thao and Kong Moua, and they could only read and write in French and German respectively. Someone had to check the police files for interesting information, and as the resident expert on Lowland Lao, Fetterman was elected.

Telling a couple of the Hmong to return with him, Fetterman went back inside and began pawing through the filing cabinets and index cards until he found a drawer marked Informants and a second drawer marked Politically Unreliable. Figuring those two would contain the most useful information, he bundled the files up and stuffed them into two large cloth sacks and gave them to the Hmong to carry outside. Then he dumped the other files into a pile on the floor and set them on fire with his Zippo.

He was just going down the front steps and could hear a distant exchange of gunfire coming from the dock area when heavy firing broke out a few blocks up the street. He easily recognized the various distinct sounds of AK-47s, CAR-15s, and RPD and an M-60.

Fetterman told one of the Hmong to get Dollar and tell him to torch the NLHS building and pull out, then realized the commo expert wouldn't be able to understand the Hmong, and went himself. Asking directions of the Hmong in the building, he found Dollar on the second floor, seated in the middle of a big pile of papers with lots of reports and files littering the floor around him.

"Y'all won't most likely believe this stuff," said Dollar. "Lots of propaganda an' bullshit like that of course, but some of it is absolutely priceless. I got me here the name an address of pretty near every single NLHS member in Laos. I guarantee."

"Terrific," said Fetterman, "but you'll have to read it some other time, Dave. The Indians are coming. Bring what you can carry and burn the rest. We've got to go."

"It's a cryin' shame," said Dollar. "I don't reckon I've got through more'n about half of it." He stuffed two laundry bags completely full, then dragged them toward the door. "See if'n y'all can get a coupla the boys ta help carry this stuff outside while I put a match ta the place, will ya, Master Sergeant?"

Fetterman called out, and two Hmong came running. He sent one of them upstairs to make sure everybody was out of the upper floor, and the other to check the rest of the second floor. When they gave the all-clear, he handed each one a laundry bag and told them to drag it outside.

As they did so, Fetterman followed them down. Behind him, Dollar, with another load of papers tucked under one arm, paused at the doorway to pull the pin from an incendiary grenade with his teeth, a practice recommended neither by the American Dental Society nor the U.S. Army. He tossed the grenade into the room and hurried down the stairs after the others.

Outside, Fetterman quickly organized his troops to reinforce the Hmong fighting up the street. They had just reached the embattled force and Fetterman was being advised of the situation by the Hmong noncom in charge when a series of explosions ripped the night air and the entire town was plunged into blackness.

Using the cover of darkness, Fetterman ordered the Hmong to break contact with the enemy and withdraw to their preplanned rally point. Making sure that all his men were accounted for, Fetterman was the last man to leave. Then popped two CS grenades behind him as he ran to discourage any enemy soldiers who might give chase.

Fetterman caught up with the others as they ran through the darkened dirt streets, and just at the edge of the town, the raiding party ran right into an enemy patrol. There was no time to deploy fire teams properly and the range was far too close to use grenades. The fighting instantly erupted into hand-to-hand.

Carbines and machine guns were next to useless at contact range, and the knife and machete ruled the day. For five long, awful, bloody minutes the two groups of opposing soldiers struggled in the darkness, and then the enemy's resolve broke and they ran. For a moment it was a gun battle as the range widened enough for the two sides to use their AKs and CAR-15s, but Fetterman yelled to the Hmong to stop firing, since their muzzle-flashes were only giving away their positions to the enemy. Amazingly the Hmong heard him above the noise of battle and did as he commanded. The enemy, whether Pathet Lao or NVA, was glad to be free of whatever monster it had run into and had no interest in pressing a counterattack. They simply ran away, and Fetterman let them go.

They reached the rally point without further incident and linked up with Gerber's group, then withdrew to the second rally point and joined up with White and Gunn's group, which had attacked Muong Thong. By daylight they were well clear of the objective, with no sign that anyone was following them.

They were tired, but pressed onward in the daylight, wanting to put as much distance between Sam Teu and themselves as possible. Behind them, as they climbed out of the valley and into the forest-covered hills, a dark smudge below marked the still-burning docks.

The Hmong were jubilant. They had expended most of their ammunition and grenades during the raid, but it wasn't the loss of weight that put a spring in their step. Their new uniforms hung in tatters and they were bloody. They had gone nearly forty-eight hours without rest. Several of their number had been wounded in the hand-to-hand fighting. But no one had been killed.

Out of the entire raiding force of nearly a 150 men there hadn't been a single American or Hmong fatality, and they had accounted for the deaths of at least forty enemy soldiers.

Gerber felt that they had been extremely lucky. But the Hmong of Phou Phi Muang Xam Teu knew better. The magic of the White Porcupine was strong. No harm could come to them as long as their war chief was there to lead them into battle.

9

THE PLACE OF THE
HIGH ROCK PHOU PHI
MUANG XAM TEU LAOS

On April 7, a week after President Lyndon Johnson had announced a halt to all bombing in the northern two-thirds of North Vietnam, the very area in which the secret Air Force facility at Lima Site 85 on Phou Pha Thi had so effectively directed air strikes before being overrun by the 766th NVA Regiment, the raiders returned from their strike on Sam Teu.

They found they had visitors waiting for them in camp, lounging around the top of the wall—six new Americans wearing brand-new Vietnam leaf-pattern camouflage fatigues, well-polished boots and jaunty scarlet berets with matching silk neck scarfs that were as out of place in the field as they were useless. They had shiny new M-16s and .38-caliber revolvers on their hips. And every single one of them was wearing a pair of Air Force-issue sunglasses.

"One of you guys Gerber?" asked one of the dandies.

"I'm Captain Gerber," said Gerber, looking the man up and down. "Mind telling me just who the hell you are and what you're doing here?"

The talking dandy flashed a perfectly practiced and completely insincere smile and popped a stick of chewing gum into his mouth before answering. "I'm Captain Bruce Murdock," the gum chewer said between chomps. "And this is Lieutenant Sammy Bauer, Master Sergeant Virgil Mince, Staff Sergeant Craig Carnes, Staff Sergeant Tim Kettelsen and Sergeant Denny Davorski." He waved his hand vaguely at the others in a gesture of introduction. "We're your team."

Gerber noticed the large chunk of silver wrapped around the man's finger. Good Christ! he thought. Just what we need around here, another goddamn ringknocker. And a Zoomie to boot. "And what kind of team is that?" he asked patiently.

"Combat Air Control team, of course," said Murdock. "Christ, doesn't anybody know anything around this place?"

"I know that right now you're dangerously close to a charge of insubordination," said Gerber. "Now, then, would you care to try again?"

Murdock's smile vanished, and he came to attention and snapped a crisp regulation salute. "Sorry, sir. Captain Bruce Murdock and Combat Air Control Team Tango Alpha Charlie reporting as ordered."

"Christ's sake, you idiot, don't salute. All that does is identify officers for any enemy snipers who happen to be watching. Just tell me what this is all about."

Murdock looked puzzled. "You're Captain MacKenzie Gerber, Army Special Forces?"

"I think we've already been through that one. Now, are you going to tell me what this is all about, or are you just going to stand there? Because if so, I've got better things to do."

Murdock was really flustered now. "Captain Gerber, we're combat air controllers. We've been sent to make an evaluation of the suitability of this place for installation of a TACAN site. Weren't you advised of our coming?"

"When was I supposed to have been advised?" asked Gerber.

"Saigon sent the message out five days ago, two days before we were parachuted in. One of your men was there to meet us with a bunch of these Laotians, so you must have gotten the message.''

"That would be Sergeant First Class Breneke, I imagine," said Gerber.

"That's right," answered Murdock. "He's the one who met us. Big blond fellow. Got kind of a German accent."

"Well, Captain Murdock, it's kind of like this," Gerber explained. "I've been out in the field for the past six and a half days. I wasn't here to receive any messages that Saigon might have sent and I get my orders out of Kontum. Also, we don't normally rebroadcast messages to troops in the field unless they're related to the mission under way. It bothers them unnecessarily and gives the enemy an opportunity to get a DF fix on our transmitters, not generally a good idea, and especially not when we're this far from friendly territory. When I checked in before entering the perimeter, I was told we had visitors, that's all. So I'm afraid you'll have to forgive my not knowing to expect you."

"No apology necessary, Captain."

"That wasn't an apology," said Gerber. "We were told during our preinsertion briefing to find a site that might be suitable for that navigation equipment you're talking about, but nobody said anything about sending us a team of combat air controllers to make an evaluation."

"I'm sorry, sir. I didn't know that," said Murdock. "Saigon led me to believe you'd been fully briefed."

"Just exactly who in Saigon are we talking about?"

"The Joint Unconventional Warfare Task Force. My team and I were detached to them from TAC."

Gerber shook his head. "I'm afraid that once again the military's right hand doesn't know what its left hand is doing. It would be nice if just once the Puzzle Palace East let everybody know what the rules of the game were instead of just shuffling the cards.

"If you don't mind, I'd like to get my men checked in, see to it that the wounded are looked after and get a shower and some clean clothes. We can talk then unless you've got something else pressing. Is that okay with you, Captain?"

"Certainly," said Murdock, but he looked anything but certain.

"Fine. I'll meet you at the team house in about an hour. Do you know where that is?"

"Yes, sir."

"Outstanding. See you then."

Gerber walked off. He was being unnecessarily rude to the newcomers, and he knew it, but he didn't care. There was something about them that just rubbed him the wrong way. He took care of the business at hand and then hunted up Updike to find out what he knew about the situation before heading for the showers.

Updike didn't know a whole lot. Wysoski had copied a message from JUWTF at MACV HQ in Saigon shortly after the raiding party had left. It advised them to expect a special paradrop and specified the date and time and the drop zone to be used. That was all. Sensibly Updike hadn't relayed the message because it didn't seem related to the mission under way. He'd sent Breneke along with Kong Moua as interpreter and a squad of Hmong to meet the plane, and they'd come back with the six Air Force types.

Since their arrival the Air Force personnel had mostly complained about the poor food and lack of beer, although they had enjoyed the party the Hmong insisted on throwing in their honor when they arrived in the village. Updike had gotten the villagers to construct a house for them, and the Air Force people were now ensconced in it, complete with hammocks, little folding camp stools and about a thousand pounds of electronic equipment and radios they'd brought with them.

The Air Force commander, Murdock, had explained that they were there to evaluate the High Rock as a TACAN site, and indicated that he had sealed instructions that he had orders to hand over to Gerber only. Since he wouldn't give Updike the envelope, Gerber's XO had simply seen to it that the

Air Force personnel were quartered and fed, then left them alone, with one exception. Wysoski had picked up some high-powered radio transmissions on his gear the day after the Air Force team arrived, and a check showed that the Air Force people were sending a transmission. Since it wasn't a burst transmission and was being sent from the middle of the camp, Updike had ordered them to stop. The Air Force people hadn't been too pleased about that, but had complied when Updike threatened to confiscate their equipment if they didn't cease and desist. Wysoski had later sent the message for them, using one of the balloon-borne transmitters, and gotten back an acknowledgment that seemed to mollify the Air Force people.

Gerber complimented Updike on his handling of the situation and then went off to take his shower. After six and a half days in the field, he needed it, some clean clothes and a shave, rather badly.

When he finished, Gerber felt ten times better and decided there was a lot of truth in the old axiom that in the middle of a bad day nothing can improve your attitude like a pair of dry socks. He bundled up his dirty clothes and gave them to the Hmong woman whose turn it was to do the team's laundry, a questionable honor, but one in which the villagers took considerable pride. Then he set out to find Murdock.

For his part, Murdock was greatly relieved to see that Gerber didn't resemble a Mexican bandit quite as much now that he was cleaned up. Murdock had heard stories about these Green Berets. Some of them got a little too unconventional on these covert operations and went native. You never knew what they might do if they took something you said the wrong way, and the natives they worked with followed their orders as if they were some kind of god. Piss one off and he might have you taken out and beheaded. And this bunch looked as if they would do it, too. They were a ragged, unshaven, unkempt lot, and one of them, a wiry little guy whom Murdock had first mistaken for Gerber because of the way the natives acted toward him, looked as if he'd taken a bath in blood.

Gerber came up and flopped down on the sandbags beside Murdock. "Captain Updike says you've got some papers for me."

Murdock nodded and produced a small manila envelope. Gerber tore it open and took out the single sheet of paper inside. It was in code, of course, and he gave it to Dollar and asked him to run it over to the commo bunker and decipher it.

Murdock thought Gerber should have done it himself, but didn't press the issue. There was no point in adding fuel to the fire, and Gerber didn't seem to care much for the Air Force, anyway.

"Okay," said Gerber. "Suppose you fill me in on exactly what your mission is while Sergeant Dollar is playing with the code books."

"Like I said earlier," said Murdock, "we're supposed to evaluate the site for a TACAN installation, then make a recommendation."

"And that's all?"

"That's it. Just look things over, and if they check out, we file our report and we're out of here. Somebody else takes over the actual installation and operation of the equipment."

"And have you completed your evaluation?"

"Pretty much. We've got a few more tests we need to run, but your exec made such a fuss the last time we tried to use our gear, I thought it best to wait until I had a chance to talk to you."

"My exec was right to raise a fuss," Gerber told him. "One of the things that keeps us safe here is that the enemy doesn't know about this place. Updike says that according to one of my radiomen, your people were putting out high-powered radio waves. We're only a couple of dozen miles from North Vietnam here, and while the Pathet Lao may not have the kind of equipment necessary to nail down a high-powered transmitter, the North Vietnamese sure as hell do. This isn't Vietnam. Different rules apply here, and if you forget and break them, the whole village could wind up dead. You'd have been making your transmissions just about the morning after we hit several Communist strongholds in Sam Teu, right when every enemy soldier in this part of the province was looking for us. I only hope none of them were listening, too, because if they were, they'll have a pretty good idea of where to find us."

"So what?" shrugged Murdock. "If they find us, we just call in an air strike and blow the hell out of them."

"Like I said," repeated Gerber, "different rules apply here. This isn't Vietnam. We don't have TAC air on standby. We've got no air support at all, and no artillery for that matter. All we've got is a couple of hundred Hmong and some mortars and recoilless rifles. That valley down there is full of North Vietnamese Army regulars as well as Pathet Lao, and they've got real guns—85 mm and 122 mm stuff. If they decide to shell this place with that kind of punch, they can muscle us right off this rock."

"We were told that Ravens were directing close air support for Hmong operations in Laos," said Murdock.

"Jesus! Who told you that?" Gerber shook his head in disbelief. "Sure there are FACs, and from what I understand, they do a damn good job when they can get the Royal Lao Air Force to fly, but they're in the Plain of Jars supporting Vang Pao's guerrillas, not up here. Hell, we're not even supposed to be here."

"I never heard of mounting an operation without air support," said Murdock.

"Welcome to Laos, Captain. We do it all the time here," Gerber told him.

Murdock shrugged. "Well, it's your war. My job is just to make the survey and submit a recommendation. After that it's back to Vietnam and directing air strikes for the grunts."

"How long have you been in Vietnam?"

"About four months."

"And before that?"

"The whole team deployed together from Forbes Air Force Base in Topeka, Kansas."

"So how come you're not out driving a Phantom?" asked Gerber.

"I flew an F-105 during my first tour," said Murdock. "Eighty-five bombing missions over the North, and one MiG kill—a seventeen. Then I took some flak and lost my cabin pressure. Cost me an eardrum and a couple of pieces of steel in my right leg. The leg's fine, but the eardrum knocked me off flying status. Air Force wanted experienced pilots for controllers, and since I couldn't fly, I couldn't FAC, so I went to a CAC team. It's not as bad as you might think, and it let me take up parachuting."

For some reason Gerber found himself beginning to like Murdock, despite his initial impression. Anybody who liked jumping out of airplanes enough to come back for a second tour in Vietnam couldn't be all bad. He just wished the man didn't act like a fighter jock. "So what do you think? Does the place qualify?"

"Still have to finish those tests to be sure, but I'd say offhand that it'll do nicely. We can probably finish in a day or two once you give the okay to go ahead. After that I'd imagine they'll move the equipment in as soon as possible. You know about what happened at Phou Pha Thi?"

"We were briefed."

"Then you know they'll want to get an alternate site in operation as soon as possible," said Murdock.

"How much equipment are we talking about?" asked Gerber.

"You mean once the site is fully operational? I'd say up to a 150 tons all told and about thirty or forty technicians."

"That's a hell of a lot of equipment," said Gerber. "I hope they don't expect us to pack it all up the mountain."

"It'll be helicoptered in," Murdock told him. "We've got a special squadron of CH-3s based at Udorn to do the job."

"That's still a hell of a lot of equipment."

"Figure about sixty trips in all to lift it in," agreed Murdock. "That's figuring a maximum load of two and a half tons per helicopter per flight, and it doesn't account for the construction personnel or their equipment."

"The bad guys are sure going to notice that," said Gerber.

Murdock shrugged again. "That's the way the numbers add up. Not much I can do about them."

"Cap'n Gerber, I got yer message decoded," said Dollar, walking up. He handed Gerber the original and the translated copy, and Gerber read it.

Personal to CO Thunderhead. Operation Hard Rain moved forward due to increased enemy use of Ho Chi Minh Trail. Imperative new Air Nav site established ASAP. Afford all possible assistance to Air Force team sent to evaluate. Suspend all other operations until further notice to prevent enemy detection of site. Acknowledge receipt of message.

Signed CO JUWTF.

"Wonderful," said Gerber. "Well, the message is clear enough. I just wish it had arrived before we pissed off every Pathet Lao and NVA within thirty miles of here. Go ahead and complete your tests, but please keep them as brief as possible. I'll inform my men."

When he was given the news, Fetterman expressed the opinion that the whole thing was a very bad idea. The enemy, he felt, was sure to notice all the activity going on atop Phou Phi Muang Xam Teu, and while they could probably hold out against the first few units sent to investigate, the Hmong couldn't stand forever against a determined enemy assault.

His concern was only somewhat relieved by Murdock's promise that once the Air Force began erecting the facility, they would be able to rely on air support. Fetterman requested that Gerber relay his concerns to high command, and the captain did so, seconding the opinion of his team sergeant.

In Saigon the protest was noted, considered and then ignored. The importance of the TACAN facility to accurate aerial bombing of North Vietnam and the Ho Chi Minh Trail was simply too great, and the study conducted by the Air Force Combat Air Control team sent to survey the site indicated that Phou Phi Muang Xam Teu was an almost perfect location. The go-ahead was given, and on April 15, five days after the North Vietnamese had agreed to open peace talks in Paris, the first fifteen tons of equipment, along with a dozen technicians and about two dozen Air Force construction specialists, arrived on the High Rock at Phou Phi Muang Xam Teu.

The Hmong watched all the goings-on with great curiosity. It was the most activity anyone could remember in the history of Muang Xam Tue. They didn't watch with great enthusiasm, however. They had already had their first taste of combat against the Communists with their new weapons and under their new war chief and they simply couldn't understand why they should stop fighting and help build the strange monument of metal going up in the middle of their fortress. Fetterman did his best to explain it to them, but was less than successful. A bullet from a rifle fired into an enemy's head the Hmong could understand, but using invisible beams to direct invisible bombers against invisible targets was beyond their capacity for patience. In the Hmong view, if the enemy was out there somewhere, you should go look for him, and once you found him, you should shoot him.

The work pressed ahead at a frenzied pace. The navigation facility was now officially known as Site Alpha Lima Tango, a name derived from Alternate Laotian TACAN Site. The men who worked in sixteen-hour shifts around the clock to build it simply called it Site ALT or Site Alternate.

Every two or three days another flight of helicopters would arrive, carrying up to twenty tons of equipment and supplies. For the most part they came at night, the pilots navigating by instruments and using infrared vision equipment, as well as radio and light signals from the reception committees to guide them in to a safe landing. Still, the enemy could hardly fail to notice all the activity going on atop a previously insignificant mountain.

In an effort to avoid being caught unaware by any surprise Pathet Lao moves toward Site Alternate, the sloping mountainous jungle that afforded the only ground approach to the High Rock was planted with over a thousand highly sophisticated electronic warning devices, including sensitive microphones disguised to look like plants, trip wire-activated alarms and buried geophones sensitive enough to detect a footfall at a distance of ten yards. A ring of infrared lamps, the concept borrowed from the security system of an American museum, surrounded the outer perimeter of the camp with a network of invisible beams, which if broken sounded an alarm. It took eighteen Air Force technicians working in three shifts just to monitor all the intruder-detection systems.

As the bunkers, vans and antennae arrays of Site Alternate grew, crowding the tiny fortress, new personnel arrived with such frequency that even the Hmong grew weary of hosting a celebration for every new arrival, so they abandoned the practice. Diesel generators brought the magic of electrification to Muang Xam Teu, and banks of modified aircraft landing lights mounted on poles stood ready to illuminate the perimeter in case of a night attack by the Pathet Lao.

An Air Force major named Beeson arrived to assume command of the high-tech facility, but Gerber's team was left in charge of providing security for Site Alternate. The Air Force would provide the alarm systems, but it was up to the Hmong and Green Berets to provide the muscle if trouble developed. Murdock and his boys, who had hoped for a quick trip back to Saigon as soon as they had completed their survey, found themselves ordered to stay to provide direction for air support should it become necessary.

The Hmong strike force, under the direction of their war chief the White Porcupine, expanded their system of outposts farther down the mountain, and found it necessary to garrison the water pumping stations that now ran ten hours a day to keep the holding reservoirs, cisterns and rubber storage bladders full, as well as meet the increased demands for potable water.

They also expanded their patrol schedule, continually running reconnaissance and security patrols in a wide area over the mountain. When they encountered enemy patrols, they shadowed them, and if the Communists found nothing, they were allowed to leave unmolested, an arrangement that didn't sit well with the Hmong, but which they adhered to because it was the will of their war chief. When the enemy had the misfortune to stumble across one of the lower pumping stations, the entire twenty-man Pathet Lao patrol was wiped out in a sudden, brutal ambush as they attempted to retreat down the mountainside.

In order to draw attention away from Phou Phi Muang Xam Teu, Gerber gave Fetterman permission to conduct patrols on other nearby mountains. The Pathet Lao would certainly mark the disappearance of the patrol that had found the pumping station, so Gerber reasoned that he might as well give them several places to look instead of making it easy with just one.

While one of the recon teams dotting the mountainsides might be as small as five or six Hmong scouts and a Special Forces adviser, the ambush patrols were made up of two or three heavily armed squads and usually two advisers. The almost constant patrolling required took on a killing pace. With so many patrols out at any one time, the Special Forces men were getting only four or five hours rest before going back out into the field. The long hours, difficult conditions and lack of sleep were draining the men, and Gerber doubted they could keep it up much longer.

Meanwhile the Air Force personnel got eight hours of sack time every night, took a hot shower every day and slept in the air-conditoned comfort of their metal vans, where they could listen to their stereo tape decks or watch a movie when they weren't working on their equipment.

At the start of the last week of April two Air Force cooks and a portable field kitchen arrived, and the Air Force people, who kept to their own part of the compound, breakfasted on scrambled eggs and ham and ate steaks and baked potatoes for dinner, while the Green Berets dined on C-rations or ate rice, pork, chicken and monkey with the indigenous troops. The only exception was Murdock's team of combat air controllers, who soon found they had more in common with the Special Forces men than they did with their brothers in blue, and occasionally ventured out of the Air Force compound to visit the Green Berets, sometimes even accompanying them on patrols.

The combat air controllers learned quickly from Gerber's men, and soon abandoned their jaunty red berets and silk neck scarves in favor of more functional boonie hats, which the Green Berets provided for them. Gone, too, were the shiny insignias and qualification badges from their uniforms. When they went into the field now, their faces were covered in camouflage makeup and their sunglasses stayed in camp.

On May 8 Air Force Lieutenant Samuel Bauer, a twenty-four-year-old graduate of the AFROTC program at Texas A&M, went out with Klaus Breneke on a patrol to recon a previously ignored section of an adjacent mountain. The six-man recon patrol stumbled across a group of nearly thirty Pathet Loa, and in the two-and-a-half-hour-long running firefight that ensued, Bauer distinguished himself in a manner that earned him a recommendation for a Bronze Star for Valor, not for his actions as a combat air controller, but as an infantryman fighting the enemy in the oldest of ways—one-on-one and hand-to-hand.

At one point during the battle the recon team was pinned down by heavy fire from an RPD machine gun. Unable to call for assistance, their Hmong radio operator having been killed and his PRC-25 smashed in the RPD's initial burst, Bauer rose to his knees, exposing himself to enemy fire in an effort to direct Breneke on target with the M-79. When that proved ineffective, Bauer got to his feet, disregarding the withering enemy fire, and charged the machine-gun position, firing his M-16 in short bursts as he ran. When he got within throwing range, he dropped to the ground, just as the Pathet Lao gunner raked a row of tracers over him.

Breneke thought the young Air Force officer had been killed, but Bauer immediately sat up once the bullets had swept passed him and pitched two fragmentation grenades on top of the enemy. As soon as the grenades exploded, Bauer got back onto his feet and rushed the position, finishing off two of the three wounded enemy soldiers he found there with his M-16 and dispatching the gunner with his survival knife. The grenades had stunned the enemy and peppered them with shrapnel, but hadn't killed any of them. Had Bauer not assaulted the enemy position the recon team would have been held up by the murderous fire until the other Pathet Lao could outflank them.

While Sam Bauer was risking his life to save an Army Green Beret and three Hmong strikers, the Johnson Administration was debating the seriousness of the North Vietnamese offer to negotiate and whether or not to go ahead with a very expensive and possibly unncessary navigational installation on top of a mountain in northern Laos. A carrot-and-stick approach had already been agreed upon in dealing with the North Vietnamese, halting the bombing of Hanoi and Haiphong as a gesture to get them to the peace table, while stepping up the bombing of the Ho Chi Minh Trail. The approach seemed to be working, albeit slowly, but it was too early to tell yet if the North Vietnamese were serious or just playing for time. After much discussion the decision was reached to go ahead with Site Alternate, but to proceed at a reduced pace.

On Phou Phi Muang Xam Teu things slowed down for the Air Force personnel and they began working ten-hour days instead of sixteen. For the Green Berets and Hmong guarding them, however, there was no rest. The patrols continued to go out, both day and night. Some of the nearby mountains were heavily patrolled, while others were left completely alone in order to keep the enemy guessing.

During the remainder of May the Americans and Hmong ambushed five more enemy patrols, four Pathet Lao and one NVA. Three of those patrols resulted in the complete destruction of the enemy forces, all three without the loss of a single Hmong life. Those three patrols were led by Master Sergeant Anthony B. Fetterman.

The legend of the White Porcupine was growing.

10

SITE ALTERNATE PHOU
PHI MUANG XAM TEU
NORTHERN LAOS

On May 31, 1968 the TACAN facility on the High Rock was three-quarters finished. There were nearly forty Air Force technicians, another twenty-five support personnel and Murdock's six-man combat air control team. Eighty-two Americans in all, including Gerber's Special Forces team, inhabited the mountain enclave along with a 175 Hmong strikers and about 250 Hmong women, children and grandparents, a total population of about 510 people. Site Alternate consumed nearly a ton and half of supplies each week. Flown in by helicopter, it consisted mostly of petroleum products for the Air Force generators, spare parts and food for the Air Force mess hall.

All the men of Special Forces team Thunderhead had been working almost around the clock for two months now. They were worn out and their nerves were wearing thin. Gerber was especially concerned about Fetterman. The master sergeant led more patrols than any member of the team, and although he showed it less, he was the oldest man on the team and the strain had to be mounting on him. Outwardly Gerber had never known Fetterman to show any sign of being stressed out, but he knew that every man had his breaking point, and Fetterman had been pushing harder than the rest. Gerber had already picked up on what he took to be a couple of disturbing clues.

For one thing, when Fetterman was in camp, which was seldom, he was spending less and less time with the team and more and more time with the Hmong. Frequently he didn't return to the team house to sleep, but instead stayed with Tou Bee Cha, his adoptive father and the village chief. He was cordial enough when around, but simply seemed to prefer the company of the Hmong to that of his fellow Americans.

For another, Fetterman had stopped wearing his helmet on patrols. This lapse of dress code wouldn't have concerned any other member of the team, most of whom preferred a boonie hat to the uncomfortable weight of a steel pot and liner and also left theirs behind when going out with a patrol, but the others didn't know Fetterman the way Gerber did. The fact that he *was* wearing a helmet had saved Fetterman's life as a young soldier in World War II and had prevented serious injury or death twenty times over throughout the years. Fetterman swore by the things and had once said that he and his helmet were inseparable. Even when he wasn't wearing it, he always kept it close at hand, as he did his weapon. And now he'd taken to leaving it in camp, an act that was almost at odds with the character of the man Gerber knew so well. It made him wonder if Fetterman had started believing the stories the Hmong told him about being both invulnerable and invincible in battle. If so, it was time for Gerber to order him to take a rest before he did something fatally stupid.

Gerber found Fetterman squatting outside the door of Tou Bee's hut. It was a position the Hmong used to rest or engage in conversation, but one which Gerber found excruciating. Fetterman was dressed only in a pair of tiger-stripe fatigue pants that had been cut off to make six-pocket shorts. His neck was hung with a heavy necklace of Hmong silver and polished stones, and the leather straps of the shoulder holster in which he wore his ever-present .44 Magnum revolver crisscrossed his sunburned back.

Gerber had always considered it a curious handgun for a man of Fetterman's small size, but then there were many things that were unique about Tony Fetterman. The master sergeant's Swedish K was nowhere in sight, but as Gerber approached, he spied it leaning just inside the doorway of the hootch.

"Morning, Captain," said Fetterman, taking the briar pipe from his mouth and starting to rise.

Gerber motioned him to stay put and sank down beside him, sitting cross-legged rather than squatting. "Something bothering you again?" asked Gerber, nodding at the pipe.

"Not at all," Fetterman replied mildly. "In fact, I don't really remember ever feeling more content than I do here. It's good to be back. I was just having myself a little think-it-over, that's all. Care to join me in a smoke?"

"I think I'd better not," Gerber replied. "That last one I had in Kontum tasted too damn good. So what's the great war chief of the Hmong thinking about this morning?"

Fetterman smiled. "If you mean me, I guess you could say I'm thinking about life. About how good it feels to be back here. About how much I love these hills and people. And about what's going to happen to them when we abandon them someday. We will, you know, despite all the promises you've made them and I've made them and all those fork-tongued politicians back in Washington have made. It's in the nature of things.

"The Hmong don't understand the outside world. They don't know about stoplights and flush toilets and gas ranges and washing machines. They've got no use for them. This is their world here. These mountains. This village. That's all there is. If the outside world would leave them alone, they'd be quite happy with leaving things just as they are for another couple of thousand years.

"But the outside world won't leave them alone. The Chinese drove them out of their homeland in China, and the Communists will drive them out of here, or if not the Communists, the Laotians will one day, although I suspect the Lowland Lao better pack a lunch and bring some friends when they're ready to try it. You see, Captain, this mountain is all they've got, but it's enough.

"The problem is, the Hmong also don't understand treaties and borders and political parties. They don't understand public opinion polls and election-year politics. And most especially they don't understand deceit and lies and what it means to fight a war you've got no intention of winning. They're good people, but they'd never make good Americans because they're too honest. We're like an alien life-form to them. And because they don't understand broken promises and expediency, one of these days when somebody else wants to take their mountain from them, we'll abandon them because it's the expedient thing to do."

"That's quite a dose of philosophy for this early in the morning," said Gerber. "I didn't think it was our job to make them into good Americans, just help them hang on to what they've got."

"That was never our job, and you know it, sir. We might like to think it is, but our job was to find a new site for the flyboys' big electronic marvel so that we could expediently bomb hell out of the North Vietnamese. I really wish we could do some real good for these people, but as long as we're in the business of doing what's expedient, we aren't helping these people. We're just using them."

"Maybe what they need is somebody to teach them," said Gerber, "so they'll know enough not to trust people like us."

"Maybe," said Fetterman thoughtfully. "Maybe so. But what good would it do? Look around, sir. There's fewer than four hundred of them here. Four hundred left out of the fifteen hundred that were here six years ago. What are four hundred Hmong with a bunch of rifles going to do against the North Vietnamese Army when they decide to push us off the hill? What are they going to do when the politicians decide it's time for us to pack up our kits and go home and let the NVA just walk in here and take the place? No, sir, Captain. I love it here, and I love these people, and I wish to God I'd never come back. We won't do them any good. We'll use them and then we'll turn our backs on them. When that happens, I don't know if I'll be able to face it."

"What else can you do?" asked Gerber.

Fetterman shrugged. "I don't know, but there ought to be something. There just has to be."

"So how are Tou Pa and Breneke getting along?" asked Gerber, shifting the subject.

Fetterman grinned. "The situation's getting desperate. Klaus is nearly out of rubbers. If White doesn't get a new supply in pretty soon, Breneke may have to introduce the young lady to oral sex."

"Do you think the Hmong world is ready for that?"

"Question is, is Klaus?"

"Say, Tony, where's your helmet at?" Gerber asked casually.

"Where's yours, sir?" countered Fetterman.

"Hanging back in the team house," Gerber admitted.

"So's mine. Captain, you don't have to try to be cute about it. You order me to and I'll sleep in it. But the Hmong don't have helmets, and until we get them some, their war chief can't very well hide his head beneath one, no matter how good an idea he might think it is."

Gerber sighed. "I see what you mean. Just don't get stupid and go native on me, okay?"

"Who, me?" said Fetterman innocently. "What do I look like?"

Gerber eyed him up and down. "Right now you look like a cross between Ernest Hemingway and Robinson Crusoe."

"And you look like Jungle Jim," said Fetterman.

Gerber took a look at himself and decided Fetterman had a point. He was wearing a jungle jacket with the sleeves ripped out of it, had a Browning and a machete belted around his waist, a pair of binoculars hanging around his neck and an Australian-style bush hat on his head. The only thing missing was a big, scoped, bolt-action rifle, say a .300 Holland and Holland or a .460 Weatherby maybe. The little CAR-15 just didn't cut it. "You planning on taking out a patrol today?" asked Gerber.

"Tonight," said Fetterman. "Today I rest. Unless you've got something special in mind?"

"No. Nothing at all. In fact, I came down here to tell you to take the day off."

"Why's that?" asked Fetterman suspiciously. "You starting to worry about the old man?"

"I always worry about my friends. Especially when he's also my team sergeant. I just figured we can't keep going on at this pace without killing ourselves. People have to sleep sometime. You get today off. Tomorrow it's Paulsen's turn, and so on. It's only one day out of twelve, but it's something. Besides, I've got a special treat planned for dinner."

"And you want me to cook it, I suppose?"

"I was hoping you might. If I let Dollar do it, he'll put so much hot sauce on it nobody will be able to eat it."

"What is it? Not another snake, I hope. I really can't do much with snake without some lemons."

"Oh, ye of little faith. Tonight we dine like kings of the realm. Murdock pinched us a dozen steaks from the Air Force mess, and one of the Hmong found me some baking potatoes. I've even got twelve cans of Miller beer I've been hoarding to wash it down with. It isn't cold, of course, but it *is* beer."

"In that case, sir," said Fetterman, "I'm going to bed. I'll need my strength to lift my knife and fork. You put the fire on about 1600 and I'll be there around 1700 to do the honors."

"Don't be late, or I won't save you an appetizer."

"What sort of appetizer?"

"Beam's, of course. I've been hoarding a bottle of that, too."

"In that case, I'll be early. sir."

IT WAS A PLEASANT EVENING. There was a cool breeze moving down the mountains and the men were pleasingly stuffed with good food, which Fetterman had cooked to perfection. Murdock had shown up just after supper, bringing two dozen ice-cold beers with him to add to the warm ones Gerber had furnished, and the men were enjoying the company of their peers as only those who have fought the enemy together understand. It was good to be here, in this place and time, and to be alive and with friends. It was the first time in many weeks that all the team had been in camp, and the atmosphere was almost festive, in a quiet, relaxed sort of way. The time was getting on toward eight o'clock, time for the men who normally rose early to begin thinking about getting ready for the next day's patrols, and then bed, but no one moved to enter the team house. It was almost as if no one wanted to break the spell.

At 7:58 p.m. there was a distant rumble of thunder from the valley below that might have marked the beginning of a shower had there been any clouds in the sky. Fetterman was the first to react. "Incoming!" he yelled, rolling off his ammo-crate stool and diving for the ground.

A few seconds later the High Rock shook as four shattering explosions rocked the ground beneath the men and flames leaped up in the village beyond the wall of the camp. In the valley at the base of the mountain, five companies of Pathet Lao guerrillas and two battalions of the NVA 770th Regiment, a combined force of nearly eleven hundred men, began their attack on Site Alternate atop Phou Phi Muang Xam Teu.

"Christ! What in the name of hell were those things?" asked Murdock, dusting himself off and then dropping back into the dirt as a series of four more explosions split the night, tearing chips off the face of the east cliff.

"Hundred and twenty-two millimeter howitzer from the sound of it," Fetterman yelled back. "Looks like the bad guys finally got tired of all the late-evening flights and decided to enforce the noise abatement ordinance."

"Dollar! Wysoski! Alert the outposts. Tell them to stay sharp and to be ready to pull back if necessary. Gunn, you've got the FCT with me," shouted Gerber.

"Is there anything I can do?" asked Murdock.

"Now would be a good time to start working on some of that air support your people promised us," said Gerber. "I think we can assume the enemy knows we're here, and sooner or later we're going to need it. If it turns out we need it tonight, it'll be a whole lot better if it's on standby when we call for it than if they have to wake up the flight crews first."

"I'll see if we can't get them out of bed," said Murdock.

"Fetterman—"

"I know, Captain. Paulsen and I will roust out the Hmong and get them on the wall."

Gerber nodded and turned. "White, Portland, get the dispensary ready, then lend a hand on the 81 mm pits until we start taking casualties. Chavez, Rawlings, you take the corner bunkers on the northwest wall. Breneke, you get Kong Moua and get out to the outer ridge. Make sure our people up there know what they're doing."

As the men ran off in various directions, more shells smashed into the hilltop. Incredibly, in the Air Force compound, airmen came walking outside in their stocking feet and stood looking around, as if wondering what all the fuss was about. Murdock pushed past them, nearly knocking one to the ground. Gerber shouted to them that the base was under attack, then left them to fend for themselves and followed Gunn up the ladder of the fire control tower.

For ten minutes the enemy pounded the camp and mountaintop village with artillery, firing 160 high-explosive shells onto the High Rock, then the firing tapered off to about four rounds a minute. While the village had been heavily damaged, the camp suffered surprisingly little. Some of the hootches were destroyed and several of the stone cisterns damaged, and one 60 mm mortar pit had been destroyed, killing the four Hmong in it. But the bunkers had been sturdily constructed, and barring repeated direct hits, they could take considerable punishment. Most of the villagers had escaped serious injury, fleeing the village as soon as the shelling had begun and taking refuge in the deep bunkers of the camp.

"You don't suppose they're running out of ammunition?" quipped Gerber when the firing began to subside.

"More likely just letting the guns cool," said Gunn. "Those big 122s can manage about four rounds a minute with a good crew, but they can't keep it up very long. Judging from the salvos, they've apparently got four howitzers down there. So my hunch is we can expect to take about four to eight rounds a minute while they soften us up some, then about a ten- to twenty-minute barrage just before they attack, say from a hundred and fifty to three hundred rounds. Of course, they may just plan on sitting down there and blasting the hell out of us for the next couple of weeks, depending on how much ammunition they brought with them. Could make it kind of hard to sleep around here. We're lucky there's no high ground for them to get a good observation post above us. Probably accounts for why most of the salvos hit the village. A good forward observer who can see the target really well and talk those big guns in on it can ruin your whole day."

For five hours the shells kept coming as the enemy fired over twelve hundred rounds, dispelling any notion that this was a simple harassment shelling. Things settled down to a fairly regular pattern. A salvo of four shells would hit either the camp or the village, the defenders would wait until the dust had settled, then get up and go about their business, taking cover before the next group of four smashed into the mountains. The enemy guns, wherever they were, were either so well hidden or far enough out of range of the camps mortars and recoilless rifles that there was little the Hmong and Americans could do but crouch in their bunkers and wait.

Gerber knew that if they could hold out until daylight, they would be okay. With the coming of the sun, Murdock's team would be able to get a Raven overhead to look for the enemy cannon and direct air strikes against them, giving the defenders of Site Alternate some relief. The problem was, the enemy knew that, too, and unless they simply intended to reduce the camp by artillery fire, they would have to attack before sunup. Air support would make hamburger out of any enemy infantry trying to move up the sparsely covered slope of the mountain, once they got out of the trees.

At about a quarter to one in the morning, Night Light 21, a C-47 flare ship flown by Air America pilots, arrived onstation and began dropping flares to light up the valley. About twenty minutes later the field telephone in the fire control tower connected to the communications bunker buzzed, and Gerber answered it.

"Captain, this is Wysoski. We just heard from outpost number seven. Sergeant Dollar told me that Cheu Thao says the outpost reports the valley is full of enemy soldiers."

Outpost seven was the farthest one out, nearly two-thirds of the way down the mountainside.

"Any idea how many?" asked Gerber.

"It's hard to get a good answer out of these Hmong, sir. All we can find out is 'many many many many.' Cheu Thao sure seems pretty excited, though. He keeps asking if the outpost can pull back. Says there's too many Pathet Lao."

The captain considered the situation. The Hmong hated the Communist enemy, and it wasn't their way to run from a fight. If the Hmong soldiers in outpost seven wanted to pull out, the enemy force must be sizable.

"All right," said Gerber. "Tell him to have them drop back to outpost three, and pull in five and six, as well. Tell them to drop back to outpost four."

He rang off and turned to Gunn. "Enemy in the valley. Lots of them. I think we're going to have visitors. Lay the mortars to cover the area between outposts five and six. When they start up the mountain, we want to be able to give them something to think about."

Gunn picked up another phone to talk to the mortar pits, and Gerber buzzed back down to the commo bunker. "Is Captain Murdock down there?" he asked.

"Yes, sir. He's talking to the flare ship pilot right now. Night Light says he's got movement in the valley. Lots of it. He also says he's going to have to orbit higher. He's taking some pretty heavy double A. Twelve-sevens and a zeep, he thinks."

"Tell Murdock to give Night light our thanks and ask him to stay in the area as long as possible. Then tell Murdock that if he's going to deliver that close air support he keeps promising, now is the time to do it."

Gerber hung up and buzzed the forward command bunker on the northwest wall.

"Fetterman," came the immediate response.

"Tony, take some men and drag the 106 to the top of the northwest wall. It's not doing us any good just sitting there in the middle of camp. We've got nothing to shoot at on the neighboring hills and we're liable to need it when they hit us. The flare ship says the valley is crawling with enemy. I've pulled in outposts five, six and seven."

"Understood, sir."

Gerber hung up, and Fetterman immediately took a dozen men with him to help drag the heavy 106 mm recoilless rifle to the top of the wall. It was difficult to move the ungainly weapon on its cumbersome, small-wheeled mount, but with the assistance of the gun crew and some Air Force volunteers, they succeeded in lugging the monster up the sandbagged wall to the top of one of the bunkers. Once there, they piled a ring of sandbags around it to afford some protection for the gunners, then set up a relay chain and started passing ammunition up to it. Most of the Air Force personnel had taken shelter in the bunkers shortly after the shelling had started when one of the rounds had plowed into the van containing their kitchen and scattered their gourmet food all over the landscape. For the most part, they'd stayed in the bunkers, not wanting to

venture outside where it could be unhealthy. But the group
that helped Fetterman move the 106 mm recoilless volunteered to stay topside and help carry ammunition to the gun
crew.

Gerber heard somebody climbing the ladder into the FCT
unannounced, and mindful that the tower was a favorite target for enemy sappers who had infiltrated a camp in Vietnam,
whirled, covering the top of the ladder with his CAR-15. The
uninvited guest turned out to be Beeson, the Air Force major
in charge of the Site Alternate navigation facility. He was fully
attired in fatigues, flak jacket and helmet and armed with both
an M-16 and a .45 pistol. Gerber lowered his weapon and
helped the man over the top of the sandbags.

"You really ought to announce yourself, sir," Gerber told
the senior officer. "The men are trained to shoot anybody who
doesn't. Victor Charlie likes to slip a few men with satchel
charges into a camp before an attack, and the fire control tower
is usually one of the first things they hit."

"Sorry," said Beeson. "I never thought of that. Just wanted
to see what was going on. There's nothing for us to do over at
the site except make sure any fires that get started get put out,
and I've got men watching for that sort of thing. I just can't
stand cowering in some bunker while the enemy drops can-
nonballs on my head. Is it okay if I stay and watch?"

Another bloody tourist, thought Gerber. "You can stay if
you like sir," he said, hoping the man wouldn't, "but please
stay out of the way."

"You won't even know I'm here," Beeson assured Gerber.

Major, you almost weren't, thought Gerber, but he kept it
to himself and just nodded.

Twenty minutes later the phone from the commo bunker
buzzed again. It was Wysoski, calling to tell Gerber that Murdock had a flight of two A-1 Skyraiders ten minutes out with
a full load of snake and nape, a mix of high-explosive iron
bombs and napalm.

"Tell Murdock to ask the flare ship pilot if he can make another pass over the valley at the foot of the mountain to light it up for them, then have the Skyraiders drop everything they've got on the valley. Maybe we can break this up before it gets started," Gerber told him.

Murdock did as asked, and the flare ship pilot complied despite the heavy ground fire. The two Skyraiders, flown by American air commandos, rolled in behind the C-47. In the harsh glare of the parachute flares dropped by the Goony Bird, the A-1 pilots saw the valley below Phou Phi Muang Xam Teu choked with the black shapes of men moving steadily toward the base of the mountain. They dropped their entire eight tons of bombs and napalm on the first pass and then returned to strafe the valley with their 20 mm cannon. The Skyraiders made three more passes, firing the four 20 mm guns each plane carried in its wings before heading home. The valley below the High Rock was now marked with fires from the fiercely burning napalm, which in turn marked the charred bodies of dead men.

At a quarter to two in the morning, despite the efforts of the Skyraiders, the enemy attacked with three companies of Pathet Lao and an NVA battalion. Outposts three and four were quickly overrun and destroyed, while the occupants of outpost two fell back to outpost one, which guarded the cleft in the rock wall at the ravine. As the enemy surged up the mountainside, the flare ship kept the slopes illuminated, and the camps mortars laid down a deadly barrage of HE and white phosphorus, which the enemy steadily advanced into. As the Pathet Lao and NVA fought their way through the rain of steel and fire, the enemy gunners intensified their bombardment of the mountaintop.

Gunn did his best to keep the mortars on the leading edge of the enemy thrust as they drove up the mountain, calling in corrections to the mortar pits, which Murdock relayed from the flare ship orbiting overhead. The enemy, meanwhile, blasted the hilltop with over eight hundred shells, heavily damaging the Air Force complex and setting its fuel storage bunker on fire, which exploded like a giant Roman candle, showering the interior of the camp with great balls of fire.

The enemy surged up the mountainside like a rising tide, reached the limit of tree cover and were stopped by the mine field and ravine. They withdrew to the protection of the trees under heavy fire from outpost one, the .50-caliber machine-gun bunker guarding the cleft on the opposite side of the ravine, and from the Hmong strikers strung out along the top of the rock wall with Breneke. The enemy deployed among the trees and directed their fire at the defenders. Five T-28s arrived and plastered the tree line with five-hundred-pound bombs and .50-caliber machine-gun fire, forcing the enemy partway back down the mountain and into Gunn's waiting mortars.

At 3:30 in the morning the flare ship pilot reported that more enemy troops were massing in the valley. The enemy renewed its artillery barrage and reattacked from the tree line, using mortars and B-40 rockets to clear a path through the mine fields.

It was some of the most heroic and senseless slaughter Breneke had ever witnessed. The Pathet Lao, reinforced by two fresh companies, swarmed across the open killing ground under murderous fire from the rock wall and outpost machine-gun bunker. The enemy used the bodies of their dead, throwing them ahead of them to clear a path through the mines missed by the mortars and rockets.

Breneke requested permission to blow the bridge across the ravine if the enemy reached it and received permission to do so from Gerber. A full company of Pathet Lao charged across the open ground, and when they reached the edge of the ravine, Breneke blew the bridge up in their faces. Undaunted, the enemy began throwing lines with grappling hooks across the chasm while using intense automatic weapons fire and rocket-propelled grenades to keep the defenders' heads down.

Then, suddenly, the Communist artillery fire lifted as the fighting at the ravine intensified. Gerber barely had time to wonder why the enemy had stopped shelling when flares and mines started popping in the inner perimeter and the cry went up—"Enemy in the wire!"

"How in hell did they get there?" Paulsen asked.

Fetterman shrugged. "Maybe they grew wings." He shouted to the Hmong to open up, and the entire northeast wall began firing.

Breneke's group was now in a very bad way. Besides being pounded by heavy mortar fire, they had to keep sweeping the enemy off the other side of the ravine, and now had enemy troops between them and the camp. To make matters worse, some of the outgoing fire from the fort was being directed too high and was hitting the rock wall where Breneke and his platoon of Hmong were trying to hold the Pathet Lao at bay. The German American light-weapons specialist radioed the camp and requested permission to fire the charges to seal the cleft in the rock wall. He also requested that the outgoing fire be lifted and that he be allowed to abandon his position and attack the enemy in the inner perimeter from the rear and fight his way through to the camp. Permission was given, and the charges were lighted as Breneke and the Hmong withdrew.

The enemy, it seemed, had had no real intention of trying to reach the wall of the fort, but had intended to hit Breneke's party from the rear. The two groups quickly closed, and as the charges set to seal the entrance through the rock exploded, Breneke and the Hmong with him fought their way through the Pathet Lao in bloody hand-to-hand fighting.

Inside the camp the defenders had their own problems to worry about as the corner bunker facing the village was suddenly blown apart by a satchel charge and heavy firing broke out from the village beyond the fort walls. In a daring display of raw courage, two companies of specially selected and trained North Vietnamese commandos had succeeded in doing the seemingly impossible. They had scaled the sheer rock faces of the three-sided cliff and swarmed into the village to attack the fort from the rear. In minutes they had succeeded in knocking out two more machine-gun bunkers and were swarming over the walls and into the camp. The punji moat, which ran only on the northwest side of the camp, was no help, and the fort's defenders, preoccupied with the fighting occurring to the northwest and pinned down by the intense artillery bombardment, had been caught off guard.

The fighting along the southern half of the southwest and northeast walls was hand-to-hand, and dozens of NVA troops armed with AK-47s, grenades and satchel charges poured into the camp at the shattered south bunker. Quickly they split into three groups, two of them running along the inside of the walls to fire into the backs of the defenders, while the third group ran forward to hurl explosives into the open mortar pits and attack the communications bunker.

Gerber, Gunn and Beeson stood in the fire control tower, firing their weapons down into the enemy troops. Then there was a shattering explosion beneath them as a satchel charge blew one of the legs out from under the tower. The FCT leaned abruptly to one side and then crashed to the ground in an avalanche of sandbags that included Gerber and the other two men.

Fetterman, quickly realizing what had happened, stripped every other man from the northwest wall, and leaving Paulsen in charge of the defenses there, the war chief of the Hmong led his soldiers in a counterattack to push the enemy out of the fort.

Hearing the firing and explosions outside in the camp itself, Wysoski grabbed his CAR-15 and started up the steps of the commo bunker to station himself where he could guard the open doorway. He had just reached the top of the stairs when a deafening explosion rocked the bunker. The young communications sergeant had been hit directly in the chest by an RPG-7 round intended to be fired into the bunker. The explosion blew pieces of Wysoski all over the interior of the bunker, covering the men and equipment inside with bits of bloody flesh and bone chips.

Murdock shoved off his chest the lifeless body of Cheu Thao, killed by fragments of the same exploding rocket grenade that had practically disintegrated Wysoski, and grabbing his M-16, pushed himself to his feet. He couldn't see out of one eye and was covered with blood, but he didn't know if it was his, Cheu Thao's or Wysoski's. There was a ringing in his ears, and he seemed to have gone suddenly deaf. He gained his feet just as an NVA soldier with an AK-47 came down the steps into the bunker. Murdock emptied a full 20-round magazine from the M-16 into the man, nearly cutting him in half from his crotch to his head, then drew his .38-caliber revolver and put three rounds apiece into the other two NVA who tried to follow the first one down.

The camp's small dispensary had begun to fill up with casualties hours ago, most of them wounded either by shrapnel or secondary missile fragments from the exploding artillery shells. Portland and White had long since abandoned the mortar pits to treat the wounded. That fact alone saved them when the NVA sappers reached the pits and hurled in their grenades and satchel charges, knocking out most of the camp's mortars and killing or wounding the crews, along with several women and children who had been helping carry ammunition to the mortarmen. It didn't help them when an NVA sapper hurled two satchel charges into the dispensary, killing Sergeant First Class White and three patients and critically wounding Staff Sergeant Portland and several others. Two NVA then forced their way into the dispensary and machine-gunned the survivors of the blast with their AK-47s.

Outside, Gerber struggled to crawl out from beneath the crushing pile of sandbags. Gunn and Beeson were dead, buried beneath the sandbags intended to protect the occupants of the exposed tower from shrapnel and bullets. Gerber managed to get the sandbag off his chest but was held fast by those pinning his legs. He had lost his CAR-15 somewhere, buried under the sandbags, he supposed. With difficulty he succeeded in getting his 9 mm Browning Hi-Power pistol out of its holster, and taking two grenades from his webgear, he straightened the pins slightly so that they would pull easier and laid them out on the ground next to him.

Let the bastards come, he thought. At least I'll take a few of them with me.

Gordon Rawlings had died when the bunker at the south end of the northwest wall was blown up as the NVA commandos began their assault. The twenty-four-year-old Canadian, who had voluntarily chosen to serve in the Army of a country not his own and fight in a war most of his countrymen didn't agree with, had given his life for a cause he believed in, fighting the secret war in Laos.

Fetterman and his platoon of Hmong fought their way through the camp, clearing the enemy from the bunkers and mortar pits. Slowly they forced them back into the corner and out through the gap where the shattered south bunker containing Rawlings's now-unrecognizable remains had stood. Twice the enemy tried to surge back through the gap, but they were pushed out and kept out by the Hmong. Although the Hmong suffered heavy casualties, they seemed to take no note of them. Despite the bad situation, they were assured of victory, for they followed their war chief, the great White Porcupine, and their chief, his father by choice, fought at his white son's side.

To the northwest of the camp, Breneke succeeded in fighting his way through the Pathet Lao and reached the safety of the fort's walls with just two of his men. They crossed the bridge over the punji moat and entered the camp only to find that they had survived one battle to be thrust into the middle of another. Enemy sappers had somehow gotten inside the fortress and were running along the walls, throwing explosives into the bunkers and shooting defenders.

Breneke gunned down one of the enemy just as he was about to hurl a satchel charge into the 106 mm recoilless rifle position atop the wall. The charge rolled backward down the sandbags and exploded, peppering Breneke with shrapnel. Bloodied and hurt, but still able to function, he staggered back onto his feet and was about to lead his men onward when he saw Tou Pa running toward him, bleeding badly from a jagged cut on the side of her face. A moment later he saw the Chinese stick grenade, hurled by one of the NVA still inside the fort, land in the dirt between them.

Without hesitation Breneke hurled himself onto the grenade, shielding Tou Pa from the blast with his body. The grenade detonated with a muffled *crump*, and he felt an intense heat and saw a blinding flash of light in his head that curiously reminded him of the hangover he'd had the first morning he'd found the Hmong girl in bed with him.

Breneke lived long enough to die cradled in the arms of Tou Pa, whose language he couldn't even speak, and whom he had tried desperately to drive away. As he looked up at her torn, bloody face, he thought she was the most beautiful creature he had ever seen and was sorry he had been so stupid for so long. He had begun by wanting to have nothing to do with her, and in the end had grown to love her more than life itself. He hoped that his Heidi would understand.

Taking Tou Pa's hand, he slid the silver ring with the Special Forces crest on it from his finger and placed the heavy, ridiculously oversize object on her hand. Then he smiled at her and closed his eyes.

Updike had been wounded by a fragment from an artillery shell that knocked him unconscious as he ran along the bunker line of the northwest wall shortly after the shelling had begun. He had been taken to the infirmary and had lain there unconscious for several hours. When the satchel charges had been hurled into the dispensary, he had been shielded from the blast because he was lying down. He had escaped death a third time when the two NVA sprayed the room with bullets because he was protected by the bodies of those now lying on top of him. Digging his way out from underneath the dead, he confirmed that both Portland and White were gone, then found a weapon and went outside.

The camp was in a shambles. There were fires burning everywhere. The FCT was down and there was heavy firing going on along both the northwest wall and the southern corner of the camp. There seemed to be some isolated pockets of fighting going on inside the camp, too. The multimillion-dollar Air Force facility was in ruins.

Updike found some Air Force technicians hiding in a bunker with some of the Hmong women and children, and got them organized. The technicians weren't afraid to fight, only afraid of dying, as any sensible man would have been. This wasn't their kind of war, and they didn't know what to do until someone showed them how to do it. He got them to go with him, found some others and, with about thirty cooks, construction workers and electronics techs, helped to plug the gap in the south corner of the fort.

Dave Dollar gradually realized that he wasn't dead, and not yet ready to be so. He checked out the commo bunker and found that Murdock was the only one besides himself alive. Dimly he became aware that somebody was trying to talk to him on the radio. It was Night Light 21.

Dollar answered the radio and was informed by the pilot of the flare ship that he had two A-26 Invaders inbound and that the pilots would like to know where to drop their ordnance.

"Light up the mountaintop an tell 'em ta drop it anywhere outside the wire," said Dollar. "We're bein' overrun down here."

There was a long pause, and then the flare ship pilot answered. "Ah, roger, Thunderhead, understand you're being overrun. I'll tell the pilots to bomb outside the perimeter. Good luck to you guys. Keep your heads down."

The flare ship pilot, in a display of flying that would have brought credit to a FAC, brought the ancient Goony Bird down low over the mountaintop and lighted up the countryside surrounding it like a Christmas tree. The two Invaders came in even lower, right behind him. One of them dropped his entire load right in front of the northwest wall, less than thirty yards from the punji moat. The second A-26 unloaded on the Hmong village, now peopled exclusively by the enemy. A hundred NVA were turned into roast meat as sixteen thousand pounds of napalm burned them off the mountain.

Night Light 21 then radioed the camp. "You fellows still alive down there, Thunderhead?" he asked.

"Some of us are still kickin'," Dollar told him. "Y'all tell those A-26 boys thanks fer us."

"Thunderhead, I'm going to have to leave you now," said Night Light 21. "I'm flying this thing on fumes now. The A-26s will stay on-station as long as they can. They're fresh out of napalm, but they've still got a lot of .50 caliber left. You can talk to them direct on Guard channel two. Call sign is Nightrider. Just try to hang in there until daylight. We'll try to get some choppers in to take you out. Good luck again."

It was Paulsen who found Gerber and dug him out of the pile of sandbags. With the Pathet Lao assault outside the northwest wall broken, and with all the telephone lines inoperative and no one answering the radio except the commo bunker, he'd felt it prudent to take stock of the situation in the camp and had left Chavez in charge of the wall's defense.

"How bad are we?" asked Gerber.

"Pretty bad, Captain. The main walls awfully beat-up. We've got no mines left and only about a dozen claymores, as near as I can figure. I've got no idea what kind of shape the firing circuits are in. We've lost the outer wall and we've apparently got a pretty good-size hole in the south wall near the corner. The village is a write-off."

"Casualties?"

"I haven't had time to get a count. Heavy, I know that much. A bunch of the Air Force guys bought it when the sappers got inside the camp. Breneke's dead. I saw his body. And Wysoski bought it when they hit the commo bunker. I don't know about the others."

"Gunn and Major Beeson, too," said Gerber, nodding toward the rubble that had been the fire control tower. "Maybe Rawlings. I think he was in the bunker that got blown right at the start. Perhaps it would be more useful to ask who's still alive."

"Chavez is holding down the wall, although I don't know how well his Hmong are holding out. I think it's pretty well limited to shoot here or shoot there. I reckon right now that's probably enough. Dollar still has a working radio, and we've got two A-26s upstairs just aching for someone to shoot at. We've lost our flare ship, though. Dollar says if we can hold out till dawn, they're going to try to get some choppers in here to pick us off this rock."

"Who's they?"

"They, them, the CIA, the Air Force, or maybe even Special Forces. Who knows? Does it really matter as long as we get out of this place? The bad guys have stopped hitting us for the moment, but if they decide to hit us again, we haven't got a thing to stop them with."

"How long till dawn?" asked Gerber, looking at his watch. It was broken, the crystal cracked.

"About two and a half hours, I guess," said Paulsen.

"All right, then, I guess we'd better have a look and see what we've got left to work with." He glanced around and spied Beeson's M-16 sticking out from beneath a sandbag. Gerber rolled the sandbag off it, picked up the weapon and checked its functioning, then stuck a fresh magazine into the magazine well. ''We'll start with the corner nearest the village and work our way back up to the front wall.''

11

SITE ALTERNATE PHOU
PHI MUANG XAM TEU
NORTHERN LAOS

The Hmong village was a smoking wasteland, their houses smashed flat by the NVA artillery, their furnishings splintered and broken. The stock pens that had held chickens, pigs and cattle had been blasted open, the animals killed. And then the enemy had pulled themselves up the cliffs and poured into the village to attack the fortified camp from the rear. An American warplane had responded and turned the ruins of the Hmongs' lives into ash. As the flames leaped high into the early-morning sky, not so much as a dog moved in the streets of the village of Muang Xam Teu.

Before the A-26 had delivered the air strike that broke the back of the NVA assault, the fighting had been vicious. The attacking enemy had outnumbered the defenders by over five to one, yet the Hmong had ignored the odds and pushed them back, winning a hard-fought battle to eject the invaders and hold them outside the wall until the A-26 could finish the job.

Fetterman had been at the vanguard of the Hmong counterattack, not ordering his men to repulse the enemy, but showing them how it was done, leading by example. He had rushed forward yelling not out of fear but out of anger, firing his submachine gun in short, controlled bursts. He didn't even pause to take cover while reloading, but did so on the run, heedless of the bullets flying about him.

When an NVA soldier suddenly came up off the ground at him as he was switching magazines for the third time, Fetterman didn't even break stride. He smashed the man in the face with his weapon, then drew the big Magnum revolver from under his jacket and shot the sapper in the chest as he pushed past him. Pivoting like a quarterback putting on a display of broken-field running, Fetterman wheeled to meet a new threat, and firing the Smith & Wesson double-action, dispatched five more NVA with a single, well-placed shot apiece, before using the heavy pistol to beat a seventh NVA repeatedly in the throat, crushing the man's trachea.

As the North Vietnamese commando collapsed wordlessly to the ground, his face purpling as he clawed at his throat with his hands in a futile effort to get air into his lungs, Fetterman grabbed the man's AK-47 and jerked back the bolt, making sure a round was chambered in the Communist weapon. He shot down three more men before the magazine ran out of ammunition, then beat another one to death with the rifle, splintering the wooden stock in the process. Only then did he pause, and then just long enough to kick out the empties and stuff six more rounds of ammunition into his revolver.

The Hmong followed the example of their war chief and fought like the savage barbarians the Chinese had named them. When their weapons ran out of ammunition, they either reloaded and continued firing, or if there wasn't time for that, they would pick up an enemy's weapon and use it, as the White Porcupine had done, or simply swing their own like short baseball bats, as though visualizing the enemies' heads as balls and aiming to hit a homer clear out of the park. Their attack was so sudden, so unrelentingly fierce, that the NVA commandos, themselves crack troops, crumbled before the Hmong assault and were chopped into bits and pieces.

The Hmong spread out on either side of their war chief and formed a cup-shaped pocket, almost a V with Fetterman at the point, trapping the NVA in the cup and driving them back. They reached the wall and fought their way up it, forcing the enemy ahead of them over the ruin of the corner bunker and back into the village out of the camp.

Fetterman reached the top of the wall with an empty revolver in one hand and his knife, an old Case VS-21 combat dagger, in his other hand. He sorted among the weapons he found lying there, looking for something usable, but couldn't find anything loaded. One of the Hmong brought him his Swedish K, having picked it up from where Fetterman had dropped it in the heat of battle, but it was too badly bent to work properly. Finally the master sergeant spotted a dead Hmong and stripped the man of his CAR-15 and ammunition.

Fetterman rearmed himself just in time to direct his men in repulsing an NVA counterattack, then inspected the debris filling the shattered bunker and determined that the .50-caliber Browning was still functional. Between NVA counterattacks he and a few of the Hmong succeeded in getting the gun set back up and into operation, and they held the gap in the camp's wall against two more assaults until the A-26 delivered its load of napalm and put an end to the enemy threat.

Then spine-chilling quiet settled over the camp. For the moment, the Pathet Lao and NVA effort to take the High Rock had ceased and the enemy artillery was still. The defenders of Site Alternate had won an important if not decisive victory, and for the time being they still held the camp. It had, however, been a victory with considerable cost. Half of the Special Forces team lay dead in the ruins of the camp. Nearly twenty-five of the Air Force personnel had been killed, too, and the three-sided fortress was littered with the bodies of dead Hmong strikers lying among the NVA. The body of Tou Lo, one of the chief's remaining sons, was among them.

When Gerber and Paulsen found Fetterman, the master sergeant was seated on the ripped leaking sandbags of the south bunker, sorting through various American and North Vietnamese weapons, trying to select those that were most serviceable, while the Hmong scoured the battlefield looking for others and shooting the NVA wounded.

"We really shouldn't be letting them to that," said Gerber.

Fetterman looked up at him wearily. His uniform was torn and there was a bullet hole through his sleeve where an AK-47 round had just missed his arm. His face and hands were covered with cuts and scratches, and his clothing was drenched in blood and sweat.

"You want to try to stop them, Captain, go ahead. Be my guest. I won't do it. First off, we've got no facilities to care for them and no place for holding prisoners. I doubt whether or not we've even got enough medical supplies to care for our own wounded. Second, I'm not sure I don't agree with them. And third, I don't think we're in any kind of shape for humanitarianism. Take a look around you. This place is a mess. If the NVA want this place, they can probably march a troop of Boy Scouts up the hill right now and take it. Rawlings is dead. What's left of him is under those sandbags right over there. You needn't bother looking. There's nothing anybody can do for him now, and there's not all that much left to see. White and Portland got zapped, too. Updike told me."

"Updike? I thought he was in the infirmary."

"He was until the NVA sappers blew it up. He's down the wall a piece with some Air Force types, trying to figure out how many Hmong we've got left."

Gerber looked at the Hmong executing the wounded NVA for a moment longer and then looked back at Fetterman. "You okay?" "Nothing serious. I'll live, if we can get down off this damn rock before they throw the kitchen sink at us."

"I thought they'd already done that," said Gerber. "Breneke and Gunn have both bought it, too. So's Wysoski. I haven't got a head count on everybody else yet."

"So what's the plan?"

"There's no plan," Gerber told him, "except to hang on until sunup. Dollar says they're going to send some choppers in to lift us out of here."

"All of us?" asked Fetterman pointedly. "Or just the Americans?"

Gerber sighed. "I honestly don't know the answer to that, Tony. All I know is that they've written the camp off. The TACAN site has been rendered permanently inoperative. Major Beeson is dead, and the helicopters will be here sometime after sunup."

"I won't leave my Hmong behind, sir," said Fetterman. "Not again. Either everybody goes or I don't go, either."

"Don't try to be funny."

"I'm not trying to be anything, sir. I'm just telling you how it is. For Christ's sake, Captain, look around you. How long do you figure these people can hold out? There's no way off this rock except by going down the hill were the enemy is."

"I'm sure every effort will be made to extract the locals, too," said Gerber, but he didn't even say it with enough conviction to convince himself.

"That isn't good enough, sir. You said yourself the place is a write-off, and you know the procedure as well as I do. They'll get a couple of birds in here to take out the Americans and leave the locals to make their own way. What the hell do they expect them to do? Walk over to the edge of the cliff and jump? I won't leave without my Hmong, sir, and that's final."

"Goddamn it, Fetterman! They are not, *your* Hmong," Gerber suddenly exploded. "You're an American, a master sergeant in the U.S. Army, not some native warlord in some damn episode of *Terry and the Pirates*. What the hell's the matter with you? Have you forgotten why we came here?"

"No, Captain," said Fetterman quietly, "I haven't. Have you?"

Gerber stared for a moment. "We'll talk about this later," he said finally. "Right now we've got more important things to worry about, like how we're going to stay alive until those choppers get here."

"For what it's worth," said Fetterman, "the .50 here wasn't damaged. As to the rest, we've got more weapons than we've got men. The question is how much ammo we've got. The sappers blew up number three ammo bunker. I don't know about the other two."

"All right. I'll have Chavez check on the ammo situation. Get me a head count on the Hmong right away and try to do something about plugging this hole back up. I don't think the enemy has time to try scaling the cliffs again, but we want to be ready for anything. We've lost the outer wall, and with the flare ship gone, I think we can safely assume the enemy will use the cover of darkness to try to get across the ravine and hit us from the northwest."

Gerber could hardly have been more prophetic. The Pathet Lao and NVA had noted the departure of the Air America flare ship, and although the sound of their engines warned them that the two bombers were still in the area, without the flare ship to light the way for them, the A-26s would be like bats without radar. Under cover of darkness the remaining two companies of Pathet Lao and the second battalion of the 770th NVA regiment moved up the side of the mountain and into attack position.

Twenty minutes later Gerber called a team meeting near what was left of the fire control tower. When the others had arrived, he stood waiting for a few moments, then realized that everyone was present. The other six members of the team were dead. Murdock was there with his team and they were a bit light, too. Sergeant Davorski had been seriously wounded, and Master Sergeant Virgil Mince had joined the ranks of the departed. He had been a little late ducking between salvos during the shelling and had been caught in the open by a 122 mm round. The burst from the explosion had blown the career Air Force NCO right out of his boots but had left his feet still in them. It mattered little. The blast had also decapitated him.

"The walls are in pretty fair shape except for the southwest corner where the breach was made," said Gerber without preamble. "We've lost the outer wall at the ravine, of course, and I assume the enemy can cross it at will. I also assume that most of the mines between the inner wire and the moat have been lost, either when the Pathet Lao initiated them or when the A-26 napalmed in front of the main wall. A few of the claymores are still in place, but I've got no idea about the reliability of their firing circuits. Numbers, gentlemen."

"We've got about a hundred Hmong still fit to fight," said Updike. "That doesn't count eight medics. They've got their hands full trying to take care of the wounded. Unfortunately Portland and White didn't have much opportunity to teach them a whole lot beyond some pretty basic first aid and how to start an IV. The Air Force medic is doing what he can to help them out. I think you can assume the more seriously wounded aren't going to make it. Some of the rest won't either, unless we get them to a real surgeon. There's only so much that lactated ringers and normal saline will do for you."

"How many wounded?" asked Gerber.

"About fifty strikers and fifteen of the Air Force personnel. I'm only talking about the seriously hurt ones, you understand. Somebody with a hole or a piece of steel in them or a broken bone. People with cuts and bruises we don't have time to worry about right now. I'd say maybe twenty of them are critical cases. Probably half of those will be dead before the choppers get here. There's about twenty civilian casualties, as well, and thirteen dead villagers."

"How are the medical supplies holding out?"

"What medical supplies?" snorted Updike. "Most of them got blown up with the dispensary. The medics scrounged some from the rubble and found some odds and ends the Air Force had, but other than what they had in their bags, that's about it."

"Weapons?" asked Gerber.

"Three-fiftys are still in working order," said Fetterman. "We've got five M-60s, two 90 mm recoilless and the 106. CAR-15s are no problem. We've also recovered fifty-two AK-47s in pretty decent shape and two RPDs. I've divided up the captured ammunition so that there's four magazines with each of the AKs and about four hundred rounds with each of the two RPDs."

"Mortars?"

"Two 60s are still operative. The 81s are gone," said Paulsen.

"We're down to two 60 mm mortars?" asked Gerber in disbelief.

"Yes, sir. The sappers really did a number on the mortar pits."

"Ammunition?" asked Gerber.

"Down to about eighty thousand rounds of 5.56, Captain," answered Chavez. "Still ten thousand rounds of 7.62 remaining for the machine guns, and the two hundred rounds of match stuff we got for the M-21s. There's also 250 grenades and about three hundred rounds of the 40 mm stuff for the M-79s."

"Issue it all," Gerber told him. "What about mortar rounds?"

"The NVA blew up the main 60 mm bunker. We're down to a hundred rounds plus whatever's still left in the pits. We've got loads of 81 mm stuff, but nothing to use it in. Most of the recoilless rounds were in the main 60 bunker, so we lost those, too. We've got sixty rounds for 90s and forty-eight for the 106."

"What about heavy-machine-gun ammo?"

"Thirty-two hundred rounds remaining, not counting whatever's still in the bunkers. "We've also got about ten thousand rounds of 9 mm for the pistols and submachine guns."

"Pass it all out. Everything. Clean out the ammo bunkers. If we get hit again, we're going to need it all, and there's no sense leaving anything behind for the enemy when we pull out. Chavez, you rig up something to blow the 81 mm stuff. Make the fuse fairly short. Say five minutes. We'll fire it just before we leave.''

"Captain, I've been thinking about that," said Chavez. "We don't have a lot of time to improvise anything really fancy with the demolition supplies we've got. To beef up our defense, I mean. But we could take a bunch of those 81 mm shells and lay them out in front of the moat, then tie them together with det cord. I could fire the cord either electrically or mechanically. If Master Sergeant Fetterman could get some of the Hmong to help me, we could do it in, say, twenty or thirty minutes."

"I don't know if we've got that much time," said Gerber. He looked at Fetterman, who nodded.

"It's worth a try, Captain."

"My people can help, too," said Murdock, "and maybe some of the other Air Force personnel. Just tell us what to do."

"Captain, my first MOS was demolitions," said Paulsen. "I could help Chavez rig the detonators."

"All right," said Gerber. "Do it. Updike, you pass out the ammo. Fetterman will get the Hmong lined up and send them over to you. Captain Murdock, I'd like two of your men to help Captain Updike with the ammunition. The other one should round up as many of the Air Force personnel as possible and get them to help Paulsen and Chavez with rigging the mortar rounds. Have him caution them to keep to areas that have been cleared by previous explosions or fire. There may still be some live mines out there. Also see what the Air Force has to fight with, if anything. The time for spectators is past. Let's get moving, people. We don't know how much time we've got."

The Pathet Lao and NVA knew exactly. In a little over two hours it would be daylight, and the enemy atop the mountain would be able to call in air support, something they had already demonstrated the ability to do. The American warplanes would have little difficulty spotting their targets in daylight. If the enemy base was to be taken, it would have to be done before dawn. Pathet Lao troops already held the rocky ridge on the other side of the deep ravine that protected the enemy camp, and several lines had been placed across it. Driven by a sense of urgency, the Communist troops forced their way up the mountainside and crossed the ravine on ropes. On the broad shelf beneath the sheltering wall of rock they waited for the signal to attack.

IT WAS DANGEROUS WORK, placing the mortar shells and tying the detonating cord around them. The mortar rounds themselves were safe enough, as was the det cord until fired, but the distance to the rock wall held by the enemy was at most four hundred yards, and the men working in the open, although concealed by the darkness, were well within range should the Communist troops open up. Nevertheless, nearly two hundred high-explosive and white phosphorus shells were placed on the open ground and laced together with the explosive-filled, plastic-covered cord.

"Do you know where I wish I was right now?" Paulsen asked as he and Chavez rigged firing trains so that they could detonate the mortar shells in ten-round groups.

"I'd settle for anything but here," said Chavez.

"I suppose I would, too," said Paulsen. "But right now I wish I was in Albuquerque. There's this little restaurant right outside the gate at Kirtland Air Force Base, a real hole-in-the-wall greasy spoon called Magill's. It serves the best damn burrito smothered in green chili you ever ate. I haven't been there for a couple of years, but I sure do wish I had one of those burritos right now."

"An Irish restaurant that serves Mexican food?" asked Chavez.

"Naw. The owner's a Mexican American guy named Mike. You know, Magill."

"Paulsen, you'd better stick to Hmong. Your Spanish is lousy. It's Miguel's, not Magill's. What were you doing in Albuquerque, anyway?" asked Chavez.

"Believe it or not, I was on detached service to Sandia National Labs there. I told you my MOS used to be demolitions. Well, the Army and the Air Force were doing this joint study on the penetration characteristics of various designs of bombs. Me and a couple of civilians used to take these bombs up in a cargo plane, fly over a bunch of sandbagged bunkers built out in the desert and push the dud bombs out the door to see how well they'd penetrate."

"They needed a demolition expert to drop duds?" asked Chavez.

"Course not. They needed somebody who could design the bunkers to be as bombproof as possible, otherwise it wasn't a fair test. Then, when they were done measuring the penetration depth and stuff, the Air Force would give us a live bomb. We'd get a truck and drive it out into the desert and put it in one of the bunkers, and then I'd blow it up for them so that they could measure the blast effects and stuff."

"Why didn't they just have a plane fly over and drop it on the bunker?" asked Chavez. "Seems to me that would have been a lot simpler and a fairer test."

"Those civilian eggheads are all number crunchers. They'd spend days setting up all their instruments and stuff to measure the explosion under just so-so conditions. They didn't want to go to all that work and have some flyboy buzz by at five hundred miles an hour and miss the target."

Chavez shook his head. "It still seems pretty dumb to me. What good's a bomb if you can't hit the target with it? If the bombs aren't accurate, they shouldn't be using them."

"Ah, you just don't understand how the government defense bureaucracy works," said Paulsen.

"Maybe not," allowed Chavez, "but I know how these things work. I hope you do, too."

"Not to worry, amigo. I know what I'm doing."

"Say, Paulsen, why didn't they just use an Air Force EOD man?"

"I was already assigned to the project. I guess they figured there was no point making work for their own people when I could do the job."

"Yeah, but I mean, why assign you at all? Why not just use an Air Force guy to begin with?"

"Like I said, they wanted somebody who knew how to build bunkers the Army way. Besides, the Army wasn't about to let the Air Force conduct a study of how to blow up Army bunkers without having an Army representative involved in the project. It doesn't look good in Congress."

"Your tax dollars at work," said Chavez.

"You get what you pay for," agreed Paulsen. "You about done?"

"Almost."

"Well finish it up, will you? We don't want to be caught out here in the open when the shooting starts."

Paulsen had no more than got the words out of his mouth when the enemy renewed his artillery barrage. Both men ducked instinctively as the rounds smashed into the camp behind them.

"That's it!" yelled Chavez. "No more time. Everybody back to the camp."

The Hmong and Air Force personnel who hadn't finished placing their shells left them where they were and ran for the bunkers in the wall of the fort. Paulsen and Chavez followed, unrolling the firing leads behind them.

For ten minutes, the NVA gunners pulled out all the stops, pounding the camp with over two hundred artillery rounds. Several of the shells landed in the village, indicating the enemy still didn't have an accurate idea of the defenses atop the High Rock. The camp's defenders crouched in their bunkers and covered their ears, alternately cursing or praising the quaking roof beams over their heads. Many prayed to whatever god or spirits they believed in, including some Americans who had never set foot inside a church in their lives. Most simply gripped their weapons and waited.

Then, as suddenly as they had begun, the Communist guns stopped firing. For a moment it was deathly quiet, and then the air was filled with the sound of bugles.

"That's it!" yelled Gerber. "They're coming. Everybody topside. Fetterman! Paulsen! Get the Hmong out of the bunkers. Get them up on the wall."

12

**SITE ALTERNATE THE
HIGH ROCK PHOU PHI
MUANG XAM TEU, LAOS**

The Americans and Hmong scrambled from their bunkers and up the steps in the side of the wall to their firing positions.

"Everybody hold your fire until I give the order!" shouted Gerber.

Fetterman and Paulsen translated.

"Tony! Illumination!" Gerber yelled.

Fetterman had already picked up the telephone connected directly to the mortar pits and he now spoke rapidly into it. Within seconds the camp's two puny 60 mm mortars fired and twin parachute flares broke open overhead. Lighted by the sickly yellow-green glare of the flares, a black horde of men washed over the outer rock wall and flooded down onto the open ground.

"Sweet Jesus, we're dead," said a young Air Force technician crouched next to Fetterman.

"Airman, you're not dead until I tell you you're dead," said Fetterman. "Nobody dies until I say so. That's an order."

The scared youngster looked unbelievingly at Fetterman, then looked past him at the Hmong standing next to him. They seemed utterly calm, as though they didn't have a care in the world. The enemy was pouring through the outer wire, and they hadn't even lifted their weapons yet. The airman swallowed hard and tried to pretend he wasn't scared, either.

"Wait for it," said Gerber. His voice, like the Hmong, was calm. "Wait. Wait."

Fetterman spoke into the phone, and more illumination shells burst overhead. The front ranks of the enemy were at the second wire now and they had begun shooting.

"Not yet," said Gerber as the enemy bullets began snapping past and thudding into the sandbags. "Wait."

More flares popped overhead. The enemy was nearly to the third line of razor ribbon.

"Updike! Hit the lights!" called Gerber.

Updike threw the big switch on the junction box, and fifty aircraft landing lights, mounted on poles along the wall and powered by batteries that had been kept charged by trickle chargers run by the Air Force's diesel generator, turned the night into high noon.

"Fire!" yelled Gerber. "Open fire!"

The entire wall erupted in gunfire. As the lead element of the Pathet Lao and NVA ran abruptly into a wall of hot lead, the heavy machine guns and recoilless rifles, sited on the rear of the enemy assault, began sweeping men from the top of the rock wall as they climbed up the far side and found themselves with a face full of steel.

Paulsen and Chavez each detonated twenty of the mortar shell mines, and the air was suddenly filled with flying men and body parts as the forty 81 mm shells exploded almost simultaneously. Fetterman, meanwhile, had ordered the mortar crews to switch to high-explosive shells, and they were dropping charges, too, on the top of the rock wall and just behind it as fast as they could drop the rounds down the tubes.

But the enemy just kept coming, and the Americans and Hmong kept piling them up on the open ground. In the space of three minutes the killing ground, already littered with bodies from the previous Pathet Lao assault, was covered with an additional 150 dead or dying.

The Hmong, too, were taking casualties from the intense enemy fire, but it was nothing compared to the withering fusillade that greeted the attackers. The NVA and Pathet Lao were dropping like flies in a room filled with DDT, but there were too many of them. The enemy attack faltered, then surged ahead. Along the wall of the camp, Hmong women and small children worked frantically, bringing more ammunition to their husbands and fathers. There were so many dead soldiers lying on the ground outside the fort that the enemy was tripping over their own dead and wounded as they fought their way through the last of the wire, some soldiers carrying ladders to throw across the punji moat and scale the walls of the camp.

In the tree line beyond the ravine the NVA commander committed his reserves, the previously unused third battalion of the 770th regiment, another four hundred men.

Chavez and Paulsen fired the remaining mortar mines. The attack crumbled and the enemy was hurled back to the wall. For a moment the firing died to almost nothing, then another company of NVA came pouring back over the rocks, and the firing grew to a deafening roar.

With the pole-mounted landing lights illuminating the open ground between the rock wall and the camp, the A-26 pilots now had something to shoot at, and they roared in low over the mountaintop, firing the eight .50-caliber machine guns each plane carried in its nose. Once again the enemy assault dissolved.

Three more times the NVA tried to break through to the camp, and three more times they were turned back by the combined firepower of the fort and the A-26s. The enemy then switched to a new tactic and began mortaring the camp as they assaulted once again. The A-26 pilots, now out of ammunition, nevertheless made another pass over the mountaintop in an effort to fool the enemy into withdrawing. Miraculously it worked, and the enemy withdrew behind the rocks and intensified their mortar barrage.

The A-26s were by now running low on fuel, as well as having exhausted all their ordnance; they could do no more. Murdock thanked them for their help, and the pilots wished the men on the ground luck and encouraged them to hold on.

With the aircraft gone, and dawn rapidly approaching, the enemy tried again, sending fresh troops into the fray. The Hmong gunners returned the enemy fire as the NVA advanced, shooting their weapons until the barrels of the .50-caliber machine guns became so hot that they turned plastic, wildly spraying the battlefield like garden hoses suddenly turned on without anyone holding them. Hmong women poured dippers of water on the superheated barrels of the Brownings and M-60s in an effort to cool them. It did little good. The water was transformed into steam as soon as it hit the hot metal.

The enemy fought their way through the hail of death and reached the punji moat, throwing ladders across and heaving the bodies of their own fallen men into the pit to provide something safe to walk on. As the NVA began to swarm across the moat, Fetterman picked up a flare and fired it into the pit. The diesel fuel from the supplies for the Air Force's generator that hadn't been destroyed by the shelling had been poured into the bottom of the moat by the Hmong, and it ignited, filling the early-morning air with the smell of the burning fuel and the sickly sweet odor of charred flesh.

Staff Sergeant Dollar appeared, dragging a PRC-25 up the sandbagged wall. He had been ordered by Gerber to remain in the commo bunker and await word of the rescue on the long-range radio equipment.

''Cap'n Gerber!'' he yelled over the noise of the firing and the exploding mortar rounds, both incoming and outgoing. ''Choppers an' air support are on their way in. Be here in twenty minutes. We gotta hold till then.''

''I hope to hell we can,'' Gerber shouted back.

Dollar gave Murdock the frequencies for the inbound aircraft, and both men tuned their radios and began trying to raise the rescue team.

Having been beaten back yet again, the NVA retired to the rocks and kept up a heavy volume of small arms and machine-gun fire while continuing to rain mortars on the camp. Fetterman armed himself with one of the camp's two sniper rifles, the range being too great for his submachine gun to be effective, and busied himself by taking potshots at the enemy gunners. While it was impossible to tell if he actually killed anyone, he was so effective that two of the NVA machine guns fell silent and didn't fire again.

Murdock finally reported that the helicopters and their escort were only seven minutes out and that the helicopters had requested landing instructions.

"Tell them to use the clear area at the far end of the village, just before the cliff," Gerber told him. "And advise them that the LZ's going to be hot. Very hot." Gerber turned to Fetterman. "Tony, we need to secure an LZ. The pickup team is on their way in. Take a squad of Hmong and make sure the village is clear. We'll use the open area near the cliff."

"They'll only be able to get one bird at a time in there, Captain."

"You got a better spot in mind let's hear it."

"No," said Fetterman. "I haven't."

"Then go."

Fetterman tapped on the shoulder a number of Hmong near him, and they left their positions and followed their war chief.

Gerber turned and grabbed one of the Air Force personnel, recognizable by his baseball cap and M-16. He saw the single bar pinned to his collar as he turned the man around and realized that he was a first lieutenant. "Lieutenant, do you know where the dispensary is?" Gerber asked him.

The man nodded.

"All right, then, get your people off the wall. All the Air Force personnel. Take them to the dispensary and help the people there move the wounded to the far end of the village, right up near the cliff. Master Sergeant Fetterman and some men will be waiting for you there. Helicopters are coming to pick us up. Do you understand?''

The lieutenant nodded again, grabbed some Air Force types nearby and took off down the line of men on the wall. He didn't have to be told twice that it was time to get the hell out of there. He had no illusions about the camp withstanding another assault.

Murdock suddenly grabbed Gerber's arm. "They've got a gunship with them. An AC-119 Shadow. Four miniguns and two 20 mm Vulcan cannon. It'll be overhead in about two minutes."

"Tell them to put everything they've got on the backside of the rock ridge," said Gerber.

"I already have."

"Then get your team together and move to the village. The far side near the cliff. Choppers will pick you up there."

Murdock nodded. "The helicopters have two A-1s flying cover. They've got rockets and napalm. I could ask them to drop the nape between the rocks and the camp. Give us all time to pull back."

"Do it," said Gerber, "but not before the choppers come in. Once we leave the wall there'll be nothing to hold back the enemy except for the air cover."

Murdock nodded. "See you when this is over. I'll be in the bar."

"I'll just follow my nose," Gerber assured him.

Murdock turned and ran.

The Shadow gunship lumbered overhead ninety seconds later, dropping half a dozen flares to light up the area beyond the camp's lights, then came around in a tight circle and began firing. The sight was awe-inspiring, the tracers from its four machine guns and two multibarreled cannons, one tracer every fifth round, seemed to draw six, steady red lines to the ground. The rocky ridge just short of the ravine where presumably most of the enemy soldiers were still gathered disappeared in a cloud of dust and exploding 20 mm shells.

"Fall back to the village!" yelled Gerber. "Abandon the wall and fall back to the far edge of the village."

Paulsen repeated the order, and the Hmong and Special Forces soldiers stopped firing and dropped down to the ground below the wall. You couldn't really call it a retreat. They just plain ran.

The enemy mortars, hidden in the trees across the ravine, were still dropping shells on the camp and village, and Gerber and the others had to dodge the explosions as they withdrew through the camp. If someone went down, there was no time to think about treating his injuries. He was just picked up by those nearest him and carried toward the village. If he was obviously dead, he was left where he fell. There was no way to tell if any wounded were left behind.

The gunship made another pass, chewing up the rocks and sweeping NVA from the shelf into the ravine, then broke to orbit outside the battle area while the Skyraiders zoomed in to drop their napalm just in front of the camp.

An Air Force CH-3 Jolly Green Giant was sitting at the edge of the village when Gerber reached the cliff. Fetterman was arguing with the crew chief while the Hmong tried to get their women and children aboard.

"What's the problem?" asked Gerber.

"There's not enough room for everybody," Fetterman told him. "They only brought five choppers."

"Then fill this one with as many women and kids as you can get on board. Put the Air Force personnel on the next one and fill the two following with wounded and dependents. We'll take the last one out and as many of the Hmong as we can."

The crew chief started to protest again, but Gerber cut him off by jacking back the cocking piece of his borrowed M-16.

"Sergeant, you argue with me and I'll shoot you. Then there'll be space for one more," Gerber told the man.

The Air Force crew chief looked at Gerber, decided he meant it and started helping the civilians on board. The surviving Air Force personnel were put aboard the next helicopter and the load was balanced out with children. The evacuation continued as the Skyraiders rocketed and strafed the enemy positions between firing passes by the gunship. The final helicopter was inbound when Tou Bee appeared, limping badly and stumbling along, a shattered arm hanging loosely along his side.

Fetterman broke back toward the village to help the old chief along. As he reached him, the old man suddenly slumped to the ground. Try as he might, Fetterman couldn't lift the frail body. He was simply too exhausted.

"Captain, help me!" he called out, struggling to get the Hmong chief up on his shoulder.

Gerber ran to help his friend, took one look and laid a hand on Fetterman's shoulder. "You can leave him now, Master Sergeant," said Gerber. "He's dead."

"No, he's not," protested Fetterman. "He just passed out. Help me carry him."

"Tony, the man's dead. He's got a hole in his back the size of my fist."

Fetterman looked and saw that it was true. Dazed, he stood and stared at the Hmong gathered around him, saw the concern in their faces.

"Come on, Tony," said Gerber. "The chopper's landing. We've got to go." He pulled Fetterman after him by the wrist.

They had almost reached the helicopter when Fetterman yanked free. "No, sir, I'm not going."

"Tony, don't be an idiot. You've done all you can here. Get aboard the chopper."

"I'm sorry, Captain. I can't do that. These people need me. I can't leave them again. It's been a pleasure serving with you, sir. You'd better get aboard yourself."

Gerber smiled and took Fetterman's hand. "I understand, old friend. Good luck to you, Tony. Before I go, though, there's something I want you to understand, too."

"What's that, sir?" asked Fetterman, shaking Gerber's hand.

"Just this," said Gerber. He buttstroked Fetterman under the chin with Beeson's M-16, breaking the stock. He hoped he hadn't broken Fetterman's jaw, as well. "Put the master sergeant on the helicopter and keep him there," Gerber said to Paulsen and Chavez. "Sit on him if you have to. If he wakes up, hit him over the head with something if you have to, but keep him on that chopper."

Chavez and Paulsen grabbed Fetterman beneath the armpits and dragged him over to the CH-3. The crew chief helped them haul him aboard.

Gerber ordered Dollar and Updike to board, stuck his head in the helicopter and saw that there was still room for a few more. He glanced around and saw Tou Pa and her brother Yang standing near the edge of the crowd of remaining Hmong. He went over and told them to get aboard the helicopter, but, of course, they didn't understand him. He pushed them both toward the chopper and was looking for one more passenger when an NVA mortar round landed near him.

The explosion had a ringing quality to it, like the sound of someone hitting the outside of a boiler with a sledgehammer. Gerber could feel hot metal burning into his back. Everything seemed to shift into slow motion as he turned toward the chopper. There was a rushing sound in his ears, and everything turned gray around the edge of his field of vision, then slowly faded to black.

EPILOGUE

UDORN, THAILAND

Gerber stared out the window of his hospital room at the sprawling American air base outside. Udorn was one of the busiest bases in Southeast Asia. American warplanes, mostly F-105s and FB-111s, flew out of it regularly to bomb targets in North Vietnam and along the Ho Chi Minh Trail in Laos and Cambodia. F-4s operated out of Udorn, too, as did air commandos flying clandestine missions into Laos. All the traffic made it hard to sleep, and he was having a tough enough time doing that already.

The Air Force doctors who had operated on him had taken thirty-seven pieces of steel out of his back, hips and legs. There were a few pieces still in there, but the doctors thought that in time they would work their way out from beneath his skin on their own. Meanwhile he was ordered to rest, drink all his liquids and enjoy the pretty round-eyed nurses who worked on the floor. When he was well enough, he could look forward to a stateside leave. The wounds he had suffered had been serious, but not serious enough to get him thrown out of the Army. He still had a career if he wanted it. It was small comfort.

Paulsen had been in to see him and told him what had happened. The mortar round had hit between himself and Tou Pa and Tou Yang. Both Hmong had been killed. Paulsen and

Dollar had left the helicopter, picked him up and carried him aboard, thinking him already dead. He had only vague recollections of his first week in the hospital as he drifted in and out of a morphine-induced stupor.

The NVA had finally succeeded in overrunning the High Rock after the Americans had pulled out. A Raven pilot who had flown over the area in the late afternoon had reported seeing several bodies hanging from ropes on the sides of the cliff where the remaining Hmong had apparently tried to let themselves down the mountain. Of those left behind there were no reported survivors.

In order to keep the NVA from getting their hands on the Air Force's high-tech electronics and turning it over to their Soviet allies, the Air Force had bombed the High Rock for three days straight. The rock had finally collapsed under the bombardment, and about half of it had slid down into the valley below.

The others had been by to see him, as well. Dollar and Chavez had dropped in a couple of times, and even Updike had wheeled himself up from his room to pay his respects. He claimed he didn't really need the wheelchair, but the nurses insisted on it. He was still suffering from a mild concussion and blurred vision. Murdock and Bauer had stopped by, too, the former offering a rain check on his bar date with Gerber. Only Fetterman hadn't come to call. Gerber couldn't really blame him, but had hoped his friend would understand.

Just then there was a knock at the door, and Gerber turned in his bed to see the master sergeant standing there, a large adhesive bandage stuck to his chin.

"Come on in," said Gerber. "I was hoping you'd stop by."

Fetterman stood awkwardly in the doorway for a moment, then came in and stood by the bed.

"Have a seat," Gerber told him.

"No thanks. I'll stand if you don't mind, Captain. I've just had my butt kicked up between my shoulder blades where it belongs."

Gerber raised a questioning eyebrow. "How so?"

"I had a little talk with Paulsen. He told me how you tried to save Tou Pa and her brother. I just wanted to say thanks and to tell you that I'm sorry. I'm still mad as hell about what you did, but I understand why you did it. It was the right thing to do, even if I didn't agree with it. You saved my life. If I'd stayed, I'd have been killed along with the rest. For that I thank you."

"So," said Gerber, "are you going to stay mad forever, or are we still friends?" He offered his hand, knowing full well that Fetterman might refuse it.

Fetterman stared at it for a moment, then stuck out his own. "Sure," he said, "as long as you promise not to hit me on the chin again."

"I've got a little something here for you," said Gerber, rummaging in the drawer of his bedside stand. "Paulsen picked it up. He thought the White Porcupine might want it."

Gerber leaned over, grimacing with the effort, and passed the object to Fetterman. The master sergeant looked down at the thing in his hand, then as understanding dawned, he turned it over and looked for the date on the back. "My jump wings."

"Tou Bee must have dropped them. They were lying next to him."

"I told him that as long as he wore them the village would be safe."

"It was until he dropped them," said Gerber. "The war chief of the Hmong kept his word."

"Did he, Captain? The war chief of the Hmong is dead. He died on the place of the High Rock when his people died."

"But Master Sergeant Anthony B. Fetterman is still alive," said Gerber. "I'll settle for that."

GLOSSARY

A-1 SKYRAIDER—Piston-engined, singleprop aircraft of post-World War II and Korean War vintage. It carries four 20 mm cannons and up to eight thousand pounds of bombs and rockets.

A-26 INVADER—Improved version of the World War II successor to the A-20 Havoc. A twin-engined, propeller-driven aircraft, it has a top speed of about 350 miles per hour. The A-26 used in Vietnam and Laos typically carried eight .50-caliber machine guns and up to eight thousand pounds of bombs and rockets.

AA—Antiaircraft fire. Also called double A. The term triple A means antiaircraft artillery and usually denotes heavier guns or missiles.

A-DETACHMENT—Basic ten- to fourteen-man operational unit of Special Forces, popularly called an A-team. The size could vary considerably, but in Vietnam the number was usually twelve.

AIR AMERICA—CIA-owned airline in Southeast Asia. It flew both clandestine/covert missions resupplying mercenary strike forces and overt bona fide passenger and freight trips. The team was also generally used to describe any CIA air asset, including helicopters and clandestine ops transports and gunships.

AIR COMMANDO—U.S. Air Force pilots and crews who flew special operations aircraft, mostly propeller-driven fighter-bombers and modified transports such as the AC-47 gunship, known as Spooky or Puff the Magic Dragon, and A-1, A-26 and T-28 aircraft. They conducted various classified and clandestine missions, especially in Laos.

AK-47—Standard shoulder arm of Communist troops in the latter part of the Vietnam War. It is a selective-fire assault rifle, using 7.62 mm ammunition.

AO—Area of Operations. The geographical area in which a military unit conducts operations against the enemy.

ARVN—Army of the Republic of Vietnam. The South Vietnamese Army. Sometimes disparagingly called Marvin Arvin.

B-40—Communist Chinese version of U.S. 3.5-inch rocket launcher, better known as a bazooka. The B-40 was widely used by the Vietcong.

BAR—Browning Automatic Rifle. U.S. 30-caliber automatic rifle. Introduced during World War I, it was the standard U.S. squad automatic weapon of World War II and Korea and also saw service in Vietnam. It was replaced by the M-14.

BLOOD CHIT—Piece of cloth sewn to the back of an aircrew member's jacket, displaying the American flag. It asked for help for the wearer and promised a reward for anyone who did so. The message was written in several languages.

BOOM BOOM—Term used by Vietnamese prostitutes to sell their product.

BOONIE HAT—Floppy, wide-brimmed cloth hat with side vents and chin strap popular in Vietnam. It kept the sun and rain off the wearer's neck and shaded his eyes. Also know as a jungle hat or go-to-hell hat.

B-TEAM—Special Forces Operational Detachment-B. Typically a twenty-three-man detachment headed by a major, designed to provide immediate adminstrative logistic and communications support to several A-Detachments.

C-47—World War II-vintage propeller-driven, twin-engined cargo plane much used in Southeast Asia.

C-119—Fairchild Flying Boxcar. Derived from the earlier, similar C-82 packet, the C-119 is a twin-engined transport with distinctive twin tail booms.

C-123 FAIRCHILD PROVIDER—Twin-engined, propeller-driven aircraft capable of flying over a thousand miles with a fifteen-thousand-pound payload. It has a top speed of about 230 miles per hour.

CAR-15—Officially the XM177E2 Colt Commando submachine gun, a carbine version of the M-16 with a shortened barrel, improved flash suppressor/noise reducer, telescoping buttstock and redesigned forward handguard. Developed originally as an aircrew combat/survival weapon, the CAR-15 was much used by Green Berets and the Hmong tribesman who fought under them.

CARIBOU—Twin-engined, propeller-driven, fixed-wing transport aircraft.

CH-3—U.S. Air Force Sikorsky S-61R heavy-lift transport and cargo helicopter.

CHARLIE—From the phonetic alphabet, Victor Charlie for VC. The Vietcong. Generically used for both the VC and NVA soldiers, and for the Pathet Lao or LPLA.

CLAYMORE—U.S. Command-detonated mine employing a thin sheet of plastic explosive to fire a fan-shaped cloud of 750 steel balls up to 250 yards.

CO—Commanding officer of a military unit. Also known by his radio call sign as the six.

COMSEC—Communications Security. Techniques used to prevent an enemy from hearing or understanding messages passed between friendly units.

CONCERTINA—Barbed wire in an accordion or spiral-like coil. It was easy to deploy or take down, and if cut, it tended to spring back and snag the cutter because it was staked out under tension.

CONTROL—CIA case officer in charge of field agent or team.

CS—Powerful form of tear gas available as a powder for dusting trails or tunnels, or in grenade form. Widely used during the Vietnam War.

DA—Department of the Army.

DEUCE-AND-A-HALF—U.S. Army two-and-a-half ton six-wheel-drive truck.

DF—Direction Finding. The process of using one or more radio receivers equipped with directional antennae to fix the direction or location of a radio transmitter.

DZ—Drop Zone.

E AND E—Escape and Evasion. An E and E net is a network of indigenous allies who assist friendly personnel, particularly downed fliers, in avoiding the enemy and returning safely to friendly forces.

F-105—Republic Aircraft F-105 Thunderchief. A single-seat, single-engined jet fighter-bomber that bore the brunt of the U.S. Air Force bombing missions in Vietnam.

FCT—Fire Control Tower. An elevated structure, usually of wood and reinforced with sandbags, similar to a U.S. Forest Service ranger tower, from which to direct the fire of a camp's weapons and observe the enemy. It was a prominent feature of most Special Forces A-camps in Southeast Asia.

FIREFLY STROBE—Pocket-size but very powerful battery-operated strobe light used as an emergency beacon and for signaling aircraft.

FOB—Forward Operating Base. Also short for Special Forces Operating Base.

GRUNT—Infantry man. Originally a foot soldier but also used to indicate those soldiers, whether foot soldiers or not, who did the actual fighting in Vietnam.

GW—Guerrilla Warfare.

HE—High Explosive. May refer to shells, bombs or demolition charges.

HELIO COURIER—Single-propeller, piston-engined STOL aircraft capable of carrying five people.

HOOTCH—Almost any structure from permanent to temporary designed for habitation. Most generally a native hut, or one's own quarters.

IN-COUNTRY—Said of U.S. troops serving in Vietnam. They were all considered in-country.

INDIAN COUNTRY—Enemy territory.

JP-4—Enhanced kerosene used as jet and helicopter fuel.

KIP—Laotian monetary unit.

LAAGER—Circular-shaped defensive position used by troops, especially at night.

LANGLEY EAST—CIA Far East Division, which included Southeast Asia. So called because CIA headquarters was located in Langley, West Virginia. See *Pentagon East*.

LAW—M-72 66 mm Light Antitank Weapon.

LENSATIC COMPASS—Highly precise, liquid-filled compass with jeweled bearing.

LP—Listening Post.

LRRPS—Long-range Reconnaissance Patrols lasting several days or weeks and conducted deep behind enemy lines. Also elite troops specializing in such missions. LRRPs are often conducted by U.S. Army Rangers.

LZ—Landing Zone.

M-1 GARAND—U.S. .30-caliber rifle. The main U.S. shoulder weapon of World War II and Korea.

M-14—Standard U.S. shoulder weapon from the late 1950s through the early Vietnam War. Uses 7.62 mm ammunition.

M-16—Selective-fire 5.56 mm assault rifle used by U.S. and South Vietnamese troops. It eventually replaced the M-14 rifle and became the standard U.S. shoulder weapon of the Vietnam War.

M-21—Special heavy-barreled version of the M-14 rifle fitted with a bipod, Sionics sound suppressor and quick-change mount, allowing the use of either a Starlite scope or Automatic Range finding Telescope. It fires selected lots of match-grade 7.62 mm ammunition and was used by U.S. Army snipers in Vietnam.

M-60—A 7.62 mm, general-purpose machine gun, usually used with a bipod in Vietnam, but which could be mounted on a tripod or pital mount.

M-79—Single-shot, break-open, reloadable 40 mm grenade launcher resembling an extremely short-barreled, overgrown shotgun.

MAAG—Military Assistance Advisory Group. The name of the U.S. advisory effort in Vietnam prior to the establishment of MACV.

MACV—United States Military Assistance Command Vietnam. The headquarters of the U.S. Advisory effort located in Saigon. It replaced MAAG in May 1964. MACV was also known as Pentagon East and Puzzle Palace East by the troops.

MAT-49—French-manufactured 9 mm parabellum submachine gun similar to the Swedish K and U.S. M-3 grease gun.

MP—Military Police.

MPC—Military Payment Certificate. Issued to U.S. troops in Vietnam in lieu of real money, supposedly to keep the American dollar from flooding the economy.

NCO—Noncommissioned Officer. A corporal or any of the various ranks of sergeant as distinguished from a warrant officer or a commissioned officer.

NCOIC—Noncommissioned Officer In Charge. An NCO in charge of a unit or body of men in the absence of any commanding officer.

NLHS—Neo Lao Hak Sat, also written NLHX, Neo Lao Hak Xat. The Lao Patriotic Front. Laotian Communist political organization formed in 1956, of which the Pathet Lao was the military arm.

NUBIES—Short for know-nothing nubies. Youngsters. Referred to the flood of unqualified personnel who swelled the ranks of the Special Forces in the late 1960s.

NVA—North Vietnamese Army.

OP—Operation.

OTTER—Large, single-engined, propeller-driven, high-winged monoplane used for supply duties in forward areas, communications duties and as a utility transport.

PATHET LAO—Military arm of the NLHS. After October 1965 it become officially the Lao People's Liberation Army or LPLA, although the term Pathet Lao continued in general use.

PCOD—Personnel Coming Off Duty. The PCOD lounge, known at Nha Trang as the Playboy Club, was a sort of combination officers' and NCOs' club for Special Forces personnel.

PENTAGON EAST—MACV Headquarters in Saigon. Also known as the Puzzle Palace East.

PHI—Spirit(s). According to popular Lao and tribal Tai beliefs, everything has a spirit, and *phi* inhabit various features of the landscape as well as dwelling within animals and people.

PIASTRE—South Vietnamese unit of money worth slightly less than one cent.

PILATUS PORTER—Single-engined, turboprop STOL aircraft capable of carrying ten people.

PLF—Parachute Landing Fall. Technique used by parachutists to lessen the impact of landing and reduce the chances of injuring themselves.

PSP—Perforated Steel Plate. Metal planking with holes drilled in it, used to surface runways, roads, helipads and even sidewalks in Vietnam.

PRC-10—U.S. Army portable radio. In use since World War II, the PRC-10 was gradually replaced in Vietnam by the lighter PRC-25, which offered simpler operation and more channels.

PUNJI STAKES—Sharpened bamboo stakes placed in the ground and usually camouflaged so as to penetrate the foot when stepped on. The VC frequently coated them with feces or buffalo urine to ensure the spread of infection.

Q COURSE—Qualification Course. The course of instruction that qualifies a soldier to wear the Special Forces tab.

RA—Regular Army.

RAAF—Royal Australian Air Force, or one of its members.

RADIO INTERCEPT OPERATOR—Radio operator or technician who listens in on various radio frequencies in the hope of overhearing enemy radio transmissions and gathering useful Intelligence from them, or fixing the location of the transmitter.

RANGER—U.S. elite troops specially trained in patrolling and raiding. They conduct long-range patrols and attack difficult targets.

RAVEN—U.S. Air Force pilots who flew light, single-engined, slow-moving, propeller-driven aircraft over Laos and served as Forward Air Controllers, directing air strikes against targets on the ground.

RINGKNOCKER—Graduate of either the U.S. Military Academy at West Point, the U.S. Naval Academy at Annapolis or the U.S. Air Force Academy at Colorado Springs. So called because of the class ring they all wear. A less than flattering term.

RP—Rally Point or Rendezvous Point. A designated place for meeting after a parachute drop, raid or other troop movement.

RPD—Soviet Bloc squad-level light machine gun firing the same 7.62 mm round as the AK-47, but fed from a 100-round nondisintegrating metal link belt housed in a round, drumlike carrier.

RPG—Rocket Propelled Grenade. Usually refers to the RPG-5 or the later model RPG-7. A Soviet antitank weapon somewhat similar to a bazooka, used against vehicles and bunkers by the VC, NVA and Pathet Lao.

RTO—Radio Telephone Operator.

RTTY—Radio Teletype communications. Radio communications involving a keyboard for entry of the message into the transmitter and a printer linked to the receiver.

SKS—Standard Communist shoulder weapon used early in the Vietnam War. A semiautomatic carbine firing the same round used in the AK-47.

SMOKE ROUNDS—See *WP*.

SOG—Studies and Oservations Group. Cover name for MACV covert and clandestine special operations.

SPOOK—Slang for a spy.

STEEL POT—U.S. general-issue protective headgear in use since World War II, consisting of an outer steel cover and an inner liner of compressed fiber with a web suspension system and chin strap.

STOL—Short Takeoff and Landing. Refers to aircraft with leading edge slats, large flaps or other modifications to enable them to operate from very short, usually unimproved airstrips.

STRAIGHT KEY—Telegrapher's key. A spring-loaded switch for intermittently completing an electric circuit.

STRIKE FORCE—Body of indigenous troops paid, trained and directly led into combat by Special Forces or CIA advisers.

STRIKER—Indigenous soldier employed as a mercenary by CIA or Special Forces.

SWEDISH K—Karl Gustav Model 45B submachine gun. A 9 mm parabellum weapon similar to the U.S. M-3 grease gun, popular with Special Forces soldiers and Navy SEALs in Vietnam. It was often fitted with a sound suppressor.

T-28—Designed in the late 1940s as a single engine, propeller-driven, high-performance trainer for the U.S. Navy and U.S. Air Force, the T-28 was later modified for counterinsurgency duties in the Congo, Algeria and Southeast Asia. It carried two .50-caliber machine-gun pods and about two thousand pounds of bombs or rockets on six underwing attachment points.

TAC—United States Air Force's Tactical Air Command. Provided air superiority over the battlefield and close air support to ground troops.

TACAN—Tactical Air Navigation System. Ground-based radar and transmitters that send precise navigational information to receivers aboard military aircraft, allowing them to find their targets with high levels of accuracy, even at night or in poor weather.

TOMMY GUN—Thompson-designed .45-caliber submachine gun.

TRIP FLARE—Illuminating device designed to fire a bright white or colored flare, sometimes equipped with a small parachute to retard its fall.

TWO-0H-ONE (201) FILE—A soldier's personnel record, listing dates of service, level of training and awards and decorations. When a soldier was transferred to a new unit, his 201 File was sent with him so that his new commander would have some knowledge of his experience.

VC—Vietcong. The combat arm of the Vietnamese National Liberation Front. Contraction of Vietnam Cong San, meaning Vietnamese Communist. In Laos the Vietcong were known throughout the war by their earlier name—Vietminh.

VIETMINH—Until 1956 the term used by the Vietnamese Communist forces to describe themselves. In Laos the term was used by the Hmong tribesmen to describe both the VC and NVA.

VOQ—Visiting Officers Quarters. A motel-like facility with fairly comfortable private or semiprivate rooms for officers in transit or on temporary duty assignment.

WILLIE PETE—WP, white phosphorus, called smoke rounds. Also used as antipersonnel weapons.

XO—Executive Officer of a military unit.

ZEEP—Soviet ZPU-23 antiaircraft gun.

ZIPPO—Flamethrower.

ZOOMIE—Graduate of the United States Air Force Academy.

Vietnam: Ground Zero is written by men who saw it all, did it all and lived to tell it all

"Some of the most riveting war fiction written . . ."
—Ed Gorman, *Cedar Rapids Gazette*

PHOENIX FORCE

Don't miss the action in two PHOENIX FORCE books you won't find in stores anywhere!

Check out these two high-voltage PHOENIX FORCE adventures:

SALVADOR ASSAULT—Phoenix Force #49 $2.95 ☐
Phoenix Force put their lives on the line as they fight for peace in El Salvador.

EXTREME PREJUDICE—Phoenix Force #50 $2.95 ☐
The streets of Marseilles become a battleground as Phoenix Force uncover a sinister KGB conspiracy.

Total Amount	$ _____
Plus 75¢ Postage	.75
Payment Enclosed	$ _____

Please Print

Name: _____

Address: _____

City: _____

State/Province: _____

Zip/Postal Code: _____

GOLD EAGLE

PFD-1

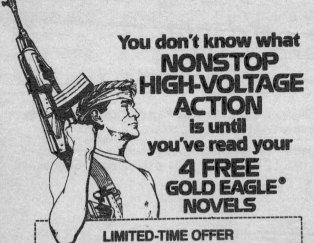

You don't know what
NONSTOP HIGH-VOLTAGE ACTION
is until
you've read your
4 FREE GOLD EAGLE® NOVELS

ABLE TEAM ®
DICK STIVERS

Check out the action in two ABLE TEAM books you won't find in stores anywhere!

Don't miss out on these two riveting adventures of ABLE TEAM, the relentless three-man power squad:

DEATH HUNT—Able Team #50 $2.95   ☐
The lives of 20 million people are at stake as Able Team plays
hide-and-seek with a warped games master.

SKINWALKER—Able Team #51 $2.95   ☐
A legendary Alaskan werewolf has an appetite for local Eskimos
fighting a proposed offshore drilling operation.

Total Amount	$ _____
Plus 75¢ Postage	.75
Payment enclosed	$ _____

GOLD EAGLE ®

ATD-1